She picked up the drawing pad first, which had fallen open as it landed on the carpet. When she saw Beth's drawings she was horrified. Oh, my word. Oh, my word. Dottie went white with shock. She was no psychiatrist but only a fool could not guess at Beth's state of mind. One grotesque drawing was of a soldier with gun raised, and a girl kneeling in front of him, hands held as though praying, head down . . . waiting to be shot? Another was even more horrifying: a lurid black and white picture depicting the girl struggling to undress and just the barrel of the gun pointing straight at her from the edge of the page. Only the girl was in colour. It was obviously a school uniform dress she wore, but dirty and dishevelled. The face could only have been Beth's, with those rounded cheeks, the deep-blue eyes, so like her real mother's, and the ash-blonde hair.

Dottie sat down on the bed to think. What on earth could she do about this?

Educated at a co-educational Quaker boarding school, Rebecca Shaw went on to qualify as a teacher of deaf children. After her marriage, she spent the ensuing years enjoying bringing up her family. The departure of the last of her four children to university has given her the time and opportunity to write. *The Village Green Affair* is the latest in the highly popular Tales from Turnham Malpas series.

Visit her website at www.rebeccashaw.co.uk.

By Rebecca Shaw

A Village Feud

REBECCA SHAW

An Orion paperback

First published in Great Britain in 2006
by Orion
This paperback edition published in 2006
by Orion Books Ltd,
Orion House, 5 Upper St Martin's Lane,
London WC2H 9EA

An Hachette UK company

Copyright © Rebecca Shaw 2006

Reissued 2009

A CIP catalogue record for this book is available
from the British Library.

Printed and bound in Great Britain by
Clays Ltd, St Ives plc

The Orion Publishing Group's policy is to use papers that
are natural, renewable and recyclable products and
made from wood grown in sustainable forests. The logging
and manufacturing processes are expected to conform to
the environmental regulations of the country of origin.

www.orionbooks.co.uk

INHABITANTS OF TURNHAM MALPAS

Willie Biggs Retired verger
Sylvia Biggs His wife and housekeeper at the Rectory
Sir Ronald Bissett Retired Trade Union leader
Lady Sheila Bissett His wife
James (Jimbo) Charter-Plackett Owner of the Village Store
Harriet Charter-Plackett His wife
Fergus, Finlay, Flick and Fran Their children
Katherine Charter-Plackett Jimbo's mother
Alan Crimble Barman at the Royal Oak
Linda Crimble His wife
Lewis Crimble Their son
Maggie Dobbs School caretaker
H. Craddock Fitch Owner of Turnham House
Kate Fitch Village school headteacher
Jimmy Glover Taxi driver
Mrs Jones A village gossip
Vince Jones Her husband
Barry Jones Her son and estate carpenter
Pat Jones Barry's wife
Dean and Michelle Barry and Pat's children
Revd Peter Harris MA (Oxon) Rector of the parish
Dr Caroline Harris His wife
Alex and Beth Their children
Jeremy Mayer Manager at Turnham House
Venetia Mayer His wife
Neville Neal Accountant and church treasurer
Liz Neal His wife
Guy and Hugh Their children
Tom Nicholls Assistant in the Store
Evie Nicholls His wife

Anne Parkin Retired secretary

Jenny Sweetapple Complementary medicine practitioner

Sir Ralph Templeton Retired from the diplomatic service

Lady Muriel Templeton His wife

Andy Moorhouse Social Worker

Dicky & Georgie Tutt Licensees at the Royal Oak

Bel Tutt Assistant in the Village Store

Don Wright Maintenance engineer (now retired)

Vera Wright Cleaner at the nursing home in Penny Fawcett

Rhett Wright Their grandson

A Village Feud

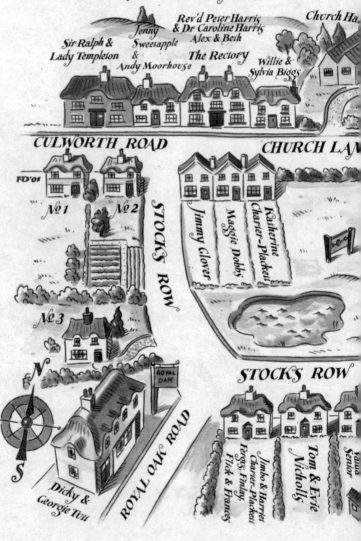

THE VILLAGE OF TURNHAM MALPAS

Jenny Sweetapple & Andy Moorhouse

Sir Ralph & Lady Templeton

Rev'd Peter Harris & Dr Caroline Harris
Alex & Beth

The Rectory

Church Ha...

Willie & Sylvia Biggs

CULWORTH ROAD

CHURCH LA...

FD'01

N° 1

N° 2

STOCKS ROW

Jimmy Glover

Maggie Dobbs

Katherine Charter-Placket

N° 3

ROYAL OAK

ROYAL OAK ROAD

STOCKS ROW

Dicky & Georgie Tutt

Jimbo & Harriet Charter-Placket
Fergus, Finlay, Flick & Francey

Tom & Evie Nicholls

...ma Senior

N
S

Chapter 1

Grandmama Charter-Plackett thumped open the front door, stormed in and dumped her suitcases on the hall floor. Harriet, bed-making upstairs, heard the hullabaloo and went on to the landing to see who'd arrived.

'Mother-in-law! What on earth's the matter?'

'You may well ask! May I have a whisky to revive myself?'

Harriet glanced at her watch. 'Bit early, but obviously you look to have need of one.' She ran down the stairs. 'What's brought this on?'

'Whisky first, please.' She rocked slightly on her feet and Harriet took her elbow, but Grandmama shook her off. 'I'm not in my dotage, Harriet, thank you very much.'

She marched into the sitting room and flung herself down in the best chair in the house, a tan leather winged effort carefully chosen by Jimbo for his personal use. She held out her hand.

Harriet hastily poured her a whisky and gave it to her. 'Water?'

But Grandmama had downed the first whisky and was holding out her glass for a refill.

'I don't want to interfere, but at this time of day . . .'

'Another one and then we'll have a coffee together and I'll tell you all.'

While she made the coffee Harriet could hear her mother-in-law huffing and puffing and muttering to herself. Thoughts raced through Harriet's head. Should she ring Jimbo? By the presence of the suitcases in the hall it looked as though his mother was taking up residence. Should she turn her out this minute without giving her a chance to explain her sudden appearance? Give her no time to get settled? Tell her there was no room at the inn?

Carefully balancing the tray, Harriet went through into the sitting room. Grandmama was sitting bolt upright sipping her second whisky.

'Black, I assume?'

She was answered with a nod.

The two of them were silent until Grandmama had finished her second whisky and was leaning back in the chair with more colour in her face.

'Well?' Harriet asked.

'My dear Harriet, I value you greatly, as you know, and what I am going to ask you is really more than flesh and blood should be asked to tolerate but . . .'

Harriet put down her coffee on the table, just in case, all her senses fine-tuned. In her head she was saying: Jimbo, why aren't you here?

'Can I stay until Anna goes? I'll pay towards the housekeeping, I promise.'

Shocked to the core Harriet repeated, 'Until Anna goes?'

'She'll be leaving in July when Peter gets back. Why on earth he felt the need to go back to Africa after all the trauma the children suffered there I do not know. Do you? Really know, I mean?'

'Peter promised to go for a year to set up the mission, but with all the fighting he wasn't able to do that. But when things so miraculously quietened down he knew he had to go back and complete his work there. He'd got the money we collected for him and there's no one better than Peter to see it spent wisely. They deserve to have someone rooting for them after all they've been through, and Peter knows that if he is there, with God's help, he'll achieve all his objectives. In a kind of way, at the moment those Christians of his need him more than we do, don't they? Otherwise it would look like desertion on his part, right when they need him most.'

'Mmm. I see. He's right, I suppose, but it's put me in a fix. So, if I could just stay here until then?' Grandmama looked pleadingly at Harriet.

'Why?'

'Why? I have put up with just as much as any grown woman should be asked to put up with. The Reverend Anna has taken over my home. Almost every stick and stone of it. I can't take any more.' She got out her handkerchief and dabbed her eyes, avoiding smearing her mascara as best she could. 'I have nothing to call my own.'

'In what way?'

'She has her bedroom, of course, but her computer won't fit in, there being no room for a desk, so it's in my sitting room. She's up at six praying or whatever, and I'm disturbed immediately she starts because she prays out loud. Then she takes a bath, my shower not being powerful enough for her – says it's a trickle not a shower – then she's downstairs making breakfast. So I go down to find my kitchen in uproar and have to clear up before I can begin mine – you know how I like things to be neat and tidy, especially at breakfast before one's senses have fully surfaced – then she's off out, slamming the door as she goes.

'Next news she's back, wanting to talk. I can't be doing with moral dilemmas first thing; I like to wake up gently. Then she wants to do her washing at different times from me—'

'Surely that's helpful. Better than the *same* time.'

Grandmama's brown eyes inspected Harriet's, thinking of the times Harriet had disagreed with her and recognizing that now was not the time for that to happen.

'I suppose it is, but washing all about when you want to make a meal?'

'Come on, Katherine, what is it really about?'

Her mother-in-law hesitated. Appeared to form an answer in her head and then changed her mind.

'Come on, tell me. It won't go outside this room.'

'Nowadays they'd label it a personality clash. Frankly, she's damn difficult to get on with. One has an opinion and it's always completely the opposite from hers. She's the most damn cussed woman I've ever met.'

'You did offer her a home. She didn't ask.'

'I know I did, but how was I to know that Peter was off back to Africa and that I'd be stuck with her – for what is it? – eight months till he gets back.'

'I bet you wouldn't be saying all this if it was Peter you'd offered a home to.'

'No, because he's the loveliest man on God's earth, and that's the truth. Jimbo comes a close second, of course . . . a very close second.' Grandmama's eyes went quite dreamy. 'But I defy anyone to find Peter difficult to live with.'

'Even with all his crystal-clear morals? His closeness to God? His love of sinners? His compassion? His spiritual wisdom?'

Grandmama began to smile. 'Well, perhaps his saintliness might grate occasionally, because I'm a Martha and not a Mary where God is concerned. Organizing the tea cups is much more to my liking than contemplating my navel. After all, one must keep a perspective about God, mustn't one? However, Peter is also a real *man*, and a gorgeous, virile one at that, and I can't quite see how he combines the two. However, we won't go there.' Katherine finished her coffee and sat back to ask again. 'So, having got that off my chest, may I stay? You've got the bed space now with the boys and Flick away from home, and I'd be useful for sitting with Fran if you and Jimbo needed to go out. Time you had some freedom where going out's concerned.'

'Look, Katherine, all this has come as a shock to me, I'd no idea things were so difficult for you . . . oops, that's someone at the door.'

A voice called out, 'Anna from the Rectory, Harriet. May I come in?'

'I'm not here,' Katherine whispered.

'Your cases are in the hall.'

'Damn and blast.'

'Come in, Anna.' Harriet got to her feet and went into the hall to greet her.

'Is Katherine here?'

Harriet agreed she was.

'I hoped she might be. Can I have a word?'

'I don't think so.'

'Ah! As bad as that, is it? Doesn't want to explain?'

Harriet nodded. 'Best to give it a while.'

'I'm so sorry. I'll try harder. But I can't go to live at the Rectory because Caroline and the twins need their space. The twins you see are still having a very bad time. They're worse at night, I'm told. Sometimes Beth screams and screams, and nothing will pacify her. Caroline's at her wits' end. I'll leave Katherine alone, then. Perhaps she might feel better in a day or two. I can't understand what I've done to make her so upset.'

'Let's leave it for now.'

'There's no way I can live in her cottage while she's lodging elsewhere; that simply wouldn't be right. I'll have to find somewhere else. I've an idea one of the weekenders is intending going abroad for a while; that might be an idea, mightn't it? I'll try to work something out with her. Tell Katherine the gas man has been to service the boiler, and it's fine. Tell her I've paid him, so she doesn't need to worry.' Anna opened the front door, made to leave and then turned back to say, 'I'm so sorry about this. I've done nothing deliberately to upset her. I've been so grateful for her kindness in finding me a home, believe me.'

'Don't fret, we'll sort something out,' said Harriet. 'Take your time; you need somewhere where you feel comfortable.'

Harriet drew a deep breath as Anna closed the door. Heavens above. She didn't want her mother-in-law staying; they'd never got on. She peeped round the sitting-room door and saw Grandmama was looking more relaxed, that the double whisky was taking effect. Her eyes closed momentarily and then sprang open but quickly closed again.

She crept into the kitchen and dialled Jimbo's office number.

In a soft whisper she said, 'Jimbo?'

'Who else?'

'It's me.'

'Yes, I thought so. Why are we whispering?'

6

'Are you sitting comfortably?'

'What's happened?'

'Your mother has moved in.'

'She has? Where?'

'Here, in our house.'

'Oh, God! No.'

'Oh, yes.'

'I'm coming home.' Jimbo replaced the receiver and gazed into space. He really didn't want the old battle-axe to live in their house. Absolutely not. In the same village was bad enough but in the same house? *Help*!

He walked into the front of the Store and spoke to Tom who had a queue at his Post Office section, it being pension day. 'I'm going home. Something urgent has cropped up. Won't be long.' Bel was tapping away at the till. 'Bel? OK?'

'Fine, thanks. I can cope.'

'Good.' Usually he took off his straw boater when he was going out of the Store but today his mind was on more important matters.

He strode into his house to be met by Harriet with her finger to her lips. 'Shush! She's asleep. Come into the kitchen.'

Jimbo perched himself on a stool at the breakfast bar and said, 'Well?'

'Well? No, I am not. She wants to live here until Anna returns to Culworth when Peter comes back.'

'Oh, my word, surely not. Have they had a row?'

'It's what your mother calls a personality clash. But the fact is your mother is not getting all her own way and she feels her space is being invaded by Anna. Who appears to me to be a very easy-going person. Anna's been to have a word with your mother but I wouldn't let her. She's very sorry it's happened and isn't sure what it's all about. She's hoping to find somewhere else to live in the village so your mother can have her cottage back, but what are the chances of anyone in the village wanting a rector staying in their house? Zilch. I certainly wouldn't.'

'I see.' Jimbo took a biscuit from Harriet's treasured biscuit tin, snapped the lid shut and put the whole of the biscuit in his mouth. He mumbled, 'Well, Harriet, my dearest, it appears we've been landed. I suppose it won't be too bad. Fran's out at school all day and you're busy out of the house a lot of the time. She has a cousin. I have her address somewhere . . . in my desk. Cousin Audrey, similar kind to Mother, maybe they'd suit for a while.'

'The last time your mother stayed with her she swore it would be the last. Said she'd commit suicide rather than go back.'

Jimbo grinned. 'Oh. Well. That's that, then.'

Between gritted teeth Harriet declared it was all right him laughing but what on earth were they going to do?

'Put up with it? Make life so difficult she'll move back home? On the other hand, we could demonstrate our love for her and say gladly, yes, of course she can stay. We'll make the best of it. Be a test of our charity.'

'On the other hand it could be grounds for divorce.'

'Harriet!'

'If she gets on at Fran like she always does then I really will have something to say, because I'm not putting up with it. Fran's self-esteem is quite low enough without your mother telling her she should do better and where's her Charter-Plackett backbone. If she does it will be Fran and me moving out. Fran may not be the brightest star in the firmament but she is the sweetest and kindest and most thoughtful. Though she does know how to rub your mother up the wrong way and no wonder; Katherine completely undermines her confidence.'

They both heard stirring in the hall and turned to look. It was Grandmama picking up her cases.

Jimbo sprang into action. 'Here, Mother, let me do that. Welcome to the Charter-Plackett residence. It'll be a pleasure having you stay. Which room, Harriet?'

It was on the tip of Harriet's tongue to say, 'How about the shed?' Instead she said, 'Fergus's room. It gets the sun each morning first thing. The left-hand wardrobe is empty.' She sighed, braced herself and went to collect the coffee things from the sitting room.

As Grandmama went up the stairs Harriet heard her say, 'I shall be no trouble, Jimbo, you won't know I'm here.'

We'll wait and see, thought Harriet.

Normally Jimbo would have left her to unpack but the present situation demanded something more. He sat on the bed and said, 'See here, Mother, I'm sorry you can't agree with Anna, though she appears to be a very reasonable person. No, don't start unpacking, just sit down for a moment and listen to me. This is serious.'

Grandmama, eager to fit in, did as she was told.

'I don't agree that three generations living in one house is lovely. It isn't. Fran's just reached the stage when she thinks listening to modern music played as loud as possible is cool. Under no circumstances are you to interfere with that. Harriet tells her when enough is enough and she accepts that. Second. You are not to interfere when the boys and Flick are at home. The whole house echoes with their rushing here and rushing there, and that's how it should be. The kitchen is Harriet's domain and you can help just sometimes. Two women in a kitchen isn't a good

9

idea, as you have found out. Thirdly, and most importantly, you are not to undermine Fran's self-confidence. Compared to the other three she's very fragile in that department. She's missed out on the Charter-Plackett self-confidence that the others all have. Don't ask me why, I've no idea. Never been as strong physically as the others either, really.'

'I did say when Harriet was expecting her that it was ridiculous having a baby at forty-one.'

'You see what I mean? Cutting remarks about something which is none of your business. It's your sharp tongue, Mother. You can stay, but on my terms.'

Grandmama got out her handkerchief. 'You're not very kind to your mother, Jimbo. You should welcome me with open arms. I am your one and only mother. I never thought I'd hear you say what you've said just now. Never. It's hurtful.'

'I mean what I say, hurtful or not. So long as you behave yourself we'll all get along together fine.'

He stood up and kissed her on the top of her head. She clutched his hand and said, 'I promise to behave myself. I shall go out a lot. After all, you won't need me to help around the house, now you've got Dottie Foskett cleaning for you. Though I very much doubt if she is a suitable person to have in your home with two lusty sons and—'

'Mother, there you go again.'

'Sorry! Sorry! Off you go back to the Store. I might pop in later today and see how things are going on. I did have an idea about—'

But Jimbo had escaped. He kissed Harriet, murmured, 'Good luck!' and charged out of the door, relieved to let Harriet cope.

After he'd gone Grandmama sat in the easy chair too

outfaced to begin unpacking. It wasn't easy, this grand-mother business, you weren't quite sure where you fitted in. Nothing felt easy in this life at the moment, especially after her row with her lodger. All Anna had said was, 'I've two more jumpers waiting to go in the airing cupboard. Sorry. Were you wanting to air the sheets? Got to go, or I shall be late and you know what they're like in Little Derehams if you're late.'

Grandmama thought, I should never have flown off the handle. She'd been foolish. Was it really she who said, 'You're a damn nuisance. You've lived on your own far too long. This cottage is small, and though I enjoy the idea of someone coming in and out I do not like the idea of every possible space being taken up with your belongings. The same day every week when I need the airing cupboard to air the sheets before I change the beds, your belongings are spread out over the airing cupboard shelves as though there's no one else living in the house. Well, you'll damn well have cold sheets on your bed and good luck to you.'

She put a hand to her forehead, full of shame. To a rector, too. She wouldn't have said that to Peter had he been lodging with her. Oh, no. She'd have said, 'Leave it with me, I'll see to them, off you go.' What was it about Anna which angered her so much? It was only the little things really, although there was that time when Anna had left a ball point pen on the carpet and it had bled an intense cloud-shaped patch of black ink, which showed up something cruel on her cream carpet. That couldn't be described as little considering how much it cost for that specialist to get it out. Still Anna did offer to pay him herself. Foolishly, she had refused her offer and then, when she found out how much it would cost, regretted her kindness. But that was nothing compared to the row they'd had this morning. All the little niggles had surfaced one after another and by the time she'd finished Katharine was exhausted and Anna on the verge of tears.

Pacing about her tiny kitchen, she had said, 'I wouldn't mind if you kept the kitchen tidy but you don't. I do the meals for the two of us so what it is you do to make such a mess I really can't think. Well,' Grandmama had drawn in a deep breath, 'you stay here and I shall go to Jimbo's. He's got plenty of room now there's only Fran at home, and I'll leave you to live here. It's by far the simplest solution. I'll be gone when you get back. Make sure you have your key.'

Anna was appalled. 'I can't be put in the position of turning you out of your own home. Please, don't go. I'll go.'

'And where exactly will you go, eh? There's not many people I can think of who would feel comfortable living with a rector.'

Now Anna felt like an alien from outer space. 'You're right, there aren't.'

'Therefore *I* will go. There's nothing more to be said.' Grandmama had flung herself up the stairs, steaming with temper and not daring to say another word because she knew she would go clean over the top and she had her reputation to think about. She was so out of breath when she got to the top of the stairs she couldn't have spoken a word to save her life.

Anyway, she'd gone and done it and here she was, bowed but not beaten. She opened the wardrobe door and realized there weren't nearly enough hangers. She called over the banisters, 'Harriet! Have you any coat-hangers, dear, there certainly are not enough in here.'

'I'll get you some more. Just a minute.'

Harriet, clutching a bundle of hangers she'd unearthed in Fin's room, found Katherine sitting on the end of Fergus's bed, looking like a puppet whose puppeteer had let go of her strings.

'Look, here we are. If that isn't enough I'll get some more. I see you've put your trinkets on that shelf. They look nice on there.'

'Hardly trinkets, my dear. They're my collection of very good solid silver snuff boxes I've collected over the years. Couldn't leave them in the house or they might end up in one of the Reverend Anna's jumble sales. See this one? George the Fourth. Look at the inside – as new, silver gilt. Isn't it beautiful? Mint condition. My absolute delight. I'm sure he actually owned this it's so exceptional. They're worth a fortune now. I'm leaving them to the children. There'll be two each and I hope they realize how lucky they are.'

'I'm sure they will, they're certainly very beautiful. Lunch at one? Must get on.'

'Of course, don't let me put you out, Harriet.' She paused for a moment and then burst out with, 'Harriet! I must tell someone. What's finally put the cat amongst the pigeons is that when I wanted to air the sheets I found every shelf in the airing cupboard with a jumper lying flat drying out. I couldn't put a thing in there. It really was infuriating. When I cheerily asked her when the airing cupboard would be free she said sorry but she had two more jumpers waiting to go in and it would probably be tomorrow before I could use it. No thought whatsoever for me and my affairs. Anyway she got chilly sheets for her bed but I couldn't help it. Could I? Very inconsiderate she is. Very. And if that harridan comes again to see me I shall be out. Right!'

The harridan was sitting in Peter's study at the Rectory, head in hands, wondering how to resolve the situation of her absent landlady. She'd tried her best to be accommodating but obviously not accommodating enough for Katherine. She'd been so grateful of an offer of a room when Peter, Caroline and the twins came home so unexpectedly from Africa that she never gave a thought as to how difficult it might be to get along with her. After all, they had both thought it would be a matter of days before she, Anna locum rector, would be back at the Abbey in Culworth, but Peter's decision to return to Africa on his own had turned everyone's world topsy-turvy. She had tried to be a reasonable guest, but Katherine always knew best. Had all the answers. Didn't know how to conduct a reasoned argument. Gave way on nothing at all and left her feeling as though she was scarcely out of nappies. Trouble was, they were both self-opinionated.

She guessed that the next thing would be Caroline suggesting she lived in the Rectory as well as using Peter's study, but that wouldn't be quite right. No, certainly not. The three of them had so many problems to sort, so many hang-ups from their dreadful experience in Africa. They'd heard from Peter only yesterday and it appeared that the uprising had been ended by vicious government intervention under pressure from the United Nations and he was thus more free than he had been to pursue his calling. Praise be. People like him were desperately needed. She dwelt for a moment on the kind of person Peter was and wished, oh, so heartily, that she had his scholarly mind, but above all his compassion.

14

Chapter 2

Usually Fran was home from school in Culworth at around four-thirty and when she got home that afternoon she found her grandmother anxiously awaiting her arrival.

'Hello, Gran, how nice.'

'Hello, dear.' Fran was circled by Grandmama's arms and kissed briskly.

'You and I are going to get on famously. You'll see.'

Fran flung down her school bag and went straight to the kitchen to find her mother. Grandmama followed her closely. 'We always do get on famously, don't we? Where's Mum?'

'She's popped into Culworth to collect some dry-cleaning and get her hair cut. She won't be long. I hope you don't mind, dear, but I've come to stay.'

'Come to stay?' Fran turned from the fridge where she was getting herself a glass of milk. She couldn't mean it, could she? Surely not.

'Yes, dear. I've had a bit of a falling out with Anna, you know, the Reverend Anna, so I decided it was best to leave her to it. Your mother said I could.'

'I see.' By now Fran was starting on a chocolate biscuit, her favourite, Blue Riband, and by the look of Grandmama's face she disapproved.

'I always have one when I get back. In fact, sometimes I have two if I'm really hungry.'

'You know what they say, chocolate before five, spots before nine.'

'I'm sorry, Gran, but you've just made that up.'

Grandmama hesitated. This was the trouble with Fran; she could see through her ruses almost before they left her lips. 'Well, maybe I have, but girls have to be careful. Now you're almost in your teens you won't want to be spotty, will you? You'll want a nice clear skin, like I've had all my life.' Grandmama smoothed her cheek with her fingers. 'See? You can't complain at my skin, can you?'

'No.' The chocolate biscuit eaten, just to annoy, Fran got a second one out of the fridge and took great delight in biting into it and chewing it slowly. 'I'm sorry, Gran, would you like one, too?'

Grandmama had to admit she fancied one. Harriet's lunches were delicious but light and there were gnawing feelings in her insides and two hours to go to the evening meal. 'Very well, dear. Let it be our secret.'

'Milk, too?'

'No, I'll have juice, please. I've got to think of my figure.'

Fran deliberately eyed Grandmama from top to toe and said, 'Of course.'

The friction between them was already evident and they'd only been in each other's company for ten minutes. Grandmama remembered Jimbo's ground rules and groaned silently. Still, she was the adult and Fran the child, she must remember that. 'Homework?'

'Yes. I'll do it straight after this.'

'Is it something I could help you with?'

Fran declared it wasn't. 'I'll have to look on the internet to do some research.'

'In that case I'll leave you to it, and while you do your work I've some reading to catch up on.'

Fran shrugged and, picking up her school bag, went into Jimbo's study.

'Don't you have your own room? To work in, I mean?'

Fran's head appeared round the study door. '*He* wants me to work in here. I have my own desk. *He* enjoys me being with him.'

The emphasis on the word 'He' didn't go unnoticed by Grandmama. The thought occurred to her that maybe the Reverend Anna wasn't all that bad, but then she shuddered and remembered the times she'd lain awake from six o'clock in the morning listening to Anna's prayers and wondered which was worse, that or Fran's sharp tongue. But just maybe the sharp tongue was caused by her grandmother always picking on her. She knew she did, but the child always seemed to catch her on the wrong foot.

Grandmama Charter-Plackett knew she would have to tread very carefully to keep Jimbo on side. Dear Jimbo, her beloved only child. She recollected how furious she'd been when he'd said he was leaving the merchant bank and going to run a village store. '*A village store?*' she'd repeated in her most disapproving voice.

But he'd been so successful, what with the Store and the outside catering and his high-class food mail order company, each enterprise so cleverly supporting the others, so dovetailed. He must be making a fortune. He needed it, though. With both the boys and Flick at Cambridge after years at public school; it must have cost him and Harriet thousands. Such a pity Fran didn't get to

Lady Wortley's like Flick and had to make do with a comprehensive. No hope for her of Oxford or Cambridge. Such a pity.

Fran, almost as though she could read her grandmother's mind, angrily kicked off her shoes and swore that one day, one day, she'd show Grandmama what she was capable of. She longed to go to university like the others and prove her wrong. And she would. She opened her Geography exercise book, determined to prove to Grandmama just how successful she could be.

Harriet came home to a silent house. She dumped her shopping on a chair in the kitchen and went to find her unwelcome guest. She was asleep in Jimbo's chair, her mouth part open and snoring slightly. Harriet had to smile at how vulnerable she appeared, not the feisty lady everyone knew, but an elderly lady in need of care.

She knocked on Jimbo's study door as she always did when Fran was working in there.

'Come in, Mum. I've nearly finished.'

Harriet found Fran in high spirits.

'Just look at that map, Mum. Isn't it good? I'm so pleased with it.'

'It's beautiful, darling. You've drawn a map but not just a map it's . . . artistic, too.' Harriet hugged her.

'It is, isn't it? Mum, is Gran really staying?'

'I'm afraid so, Fran. We'll just have to learn to bite our tongues.'

'I've nearly bitten mine off already.'

'Your dad isn't exactly pleased, but there we are. She is his mother and we have the room.'

'Where's she sleeping, then?'

'Well, I did think of her sharing with you—'

18

Fran shot to her feet. 'You didn't, you haven't—'

Harriet laughed. 'Just testing.'

'Mum!'

'She's in Fergus's room. With him in New York for a year he won't mind.'

'Tea?'

'Won't take long. I'll give you a shout.'

Harriet peeped into the sitting room and saw that Katherine was still asleep.

The delicately flavoured lamb chops served with mint sauce, braised onions, peas and potatoes au gratin revived them all. Jimbo in particular was firing on all cylinders and giving his mother a run for her money. Fran joined in too, in the kindest possible way, and altogether what could have been a disastrous meal, proved enjoyable. Maybe, thought Harriet, things were not going to be as bad as she'd expected.

But then Fran mentioned a school trip she would be going on in the spring.

'Paris? At your age? And still only twelve? Surely, Jimbo, you're not going to let her go.'

'You've got some more news on the French front then have you, Fran?'

'We're staying in a girls' boarding school in the suburbs and having an intense French week. We shall be going out on expeditions, to the shops, to museums, talking to the natives, so to speak, and having every morning, eight until one, learning French in the classroom with native French-speaking teachers. I think it's going to be good.'

'How many days?'

'We travel Saturday, have Sunday to get acclimatized and then leave the next Saturday morning for home.'

Grandmama was horrified. 'Jimbo! I insist you refuse to let her go.'

'Why?'

'She's too young. She's led far too sheltered a life to be allowed to go. What does she know about life? Nothing. Think of the girls she has to mix with, streetwise and far too well informed.' Grandmama drained her wine glass and glared at Jimbo.

'Mother, she'll be almost thirteen when the time comes.'

'She's a mere child.'

'I'm not.'

'You are, my dear, you don't understand what I mean.'

'I do. You mean about boys and reproduction and contraception and that – well, I know.'

Appalled, Grandmama could only say, 'Jimbo!'

Harriet intervened. 'Katherine. Please. Of course she knows what you're talking about, and we trust her completely. We shall have a long talk before she goes and I can't think that it will do anything but good for her to go on this course. I just wish Flick had had the same chance, perhaps then her French might have been a sight lot better than it is now.'

Fran opened her mouth to speak, but Jimbo gave her a meaningful look which silenced her. 'Mother, Fran is going on this trip. I'm pleased she's going and so is Harriet and that is that. I don't want to hear anything more about it.'

'I see. My opinion counts for nothing, then. Girls need even more care than they did in my day. Gallivanting off to that hot bed of sex-obsessed—'

'Mother! I have put an end to the matter.' Jimbo

thumped the table with his fist. 'She is going. I do not want the subject mentioned again.'

Grandmama got to her feet. 'In that case, I shall go to my room, seeing that my opinion counts for nothing in this house.' She left with all her dignity intact. She wasn't going to tell them that *EastEnders* was starting in five minutes on Fergus's TV and she didn't want to miss it. She couldn't think where Jimbo got that masterful streak from, it certainly wasn't from her.

The masterful streak evaporated as soon as his mother had left. 'Don't worry, my darling Fran. I've been told that the girls who are going are considered to be talented at languages and that's good enough for me.'

Fran looked amazed. 'Who told you that?'

'Your French teacher.'

'Did he really?'

'Yes. That's the truth, isn't it, Harriet?'

Harriet nodded.

Fran beamed with pleasure. 'Grandmama just doesn't understand, does she? She's too old, that's the trouble.'

Jimbo smiled grimly. 'Something like that. Now, leave your mother and me to talk, right?'

When the dining-room door had been closed Harriet said, 'You dear chap, thanks for that.'

'Do you think she knows enough to be wise on her own behalf?'

'Yes. Believe me, she knows more than I did when we married.'

'What?' Jimbo began to doubt his decision. 'In that case, maybe—'

'Don't you dare! You've no idea how much she needs this kind of a boost. The others all did so well, and she feels the odd one out. If languages are her forte then so be it. And don't worry about her being streetwise. She said to me the other day, "I don't know why girls make such a fuss about boys. I know all there is to know, and they're really quite ordinary, there's nothing superior or mysterious about them at all." So fret not, OK?'

Jimbo stood up, making ready to leave. 'I'll be in my study for a while. Just a couple of things I need to check.'

'Still worried about the thief, whoever it is?'

'Yes, 'fraid so. They're covering it up so well, somehow making the till balance, but my stock doesn't match up with what's supposedly being sold.'

'You mean that according to the till receipts you've actually got fewer tins of tomato soup or whatever than you should have?'

Jimbo rubbed an anxious hand over his bald head. 'That's right. However, thanks for being so generous about Mother staying. I know she's a trial, but – she is mine and she fought hard to keep my home life secure when I was growing up.'

Harriet pursed her lips ready to kiss him, and he leaned down so she could reach. 'Bless you, darling. I'll do my best. So glad you don't take after your dad.' She grinned at him and he squeezed her shoulder.

'I can assure you I have no intention of straying off the straight and narrow. I've all on keeping up with you, never mind the added complications of the other woman.'

'Jimbo! I warned you what would happen if you did.'

'I have nothing to fear, because I shan't play away. See you.'

Harriet cleared up the table, switched on the dishwasher and went into the sitting room to pick up a novel she was intending to finish that evening. It had got her in its grip and she was eager to get to the end as she hadn't the faintest idea how it would work out. Three pages later her mother-in-law put her head round the door.

'Where is he?'

'In the study.'

'Good. You and I can have a girlie chat while he's busy. I love Jimbo more than anyone else in the world, but he can be confrontational, can't he?'

Harriet reluctantly put down her novel. 'Only when required.'

'Are you sure you want Fran to go to Paris? It's a den of iniquity, you know.'

'It sounds to me as though the girls will be kept very busy. Five hours of nothing but French each day will curb their extramural activities, I think. And she does know about boys, Katherine, and all that, so there's no need to worry.'

'It's appalling to me that children are old before their time nowadays. I knew nothing at her age. Absolutely nothing. It hasn't done me any harm, has it?'

'No, but then our children live in a very different world from the one you lived in.'

Grandmama settled herself more comfortably on the sofa. 'You're right, it most certainly is. I shall have to leave it to your judgement, Harriet. You've stuck with Jimbo through thick and thin. You were so brave to follow him here. That big house, and all that money he earned; you gave up a lot and I admire you for it.'

'Thank you. It was a big step. I can remember once waking up in the middle of the night totally panic-stricken about what we were doing. It took a lot of courage, believe me.'

'I know we don't always see eye to eye, although we're better now than we were, but I will do my best not to interfere while I'm here. I don't suppose there's a drink in the offing? I usually have one in the evening.'

She settled for a gin and orange and slowly mellowed even more as the evening progressed. 'I've never spoken to you about Jimbo's father, have I?'

Harriet shook her head.

'He was the most charming man you could hope to meet. Very good-looking, very handsome and eye-catching, always had the *bon mot*, and charmed men as well as women; they'd be eating out of his hand within five minutes of meeting him. But underneath he was the devil incarnate. An unscrupulous, heartless deceiver, that's what he was, and I found out too late.'

'You never thought to divorce him?'

Grandmama gave Harriet a wry smile. 'I adored him, that was my trouble, and couldn't see why the other woman should be given him on a plate, so to speak. When he came home to me to die I felt as though my love had been rewarded at last.' For the first time since Harriet had known her, Grandmama had tears sparkling in her eyes. 'He was so gracious in death. I wanted to follow him a.s.a.p wherever he was going when he died, but, seeing as he had left all his money to me – much to my amazement – and he was most likely going to hell, I rapidly changed my mind and decided instead to live and spend all the money he'd left me before it all got too late. Just to spite him I've invested wisely and made loads more money than he would ever have intended me to do.'

Suddenly they were both helpless with laughter.

Jimbo had the surprise of his life when he went into their sitting room to find Harriet and his mother with tears of laughter rolling down their cheeks.

'Have you two been at the bottle?'

'Yes,' Harriet spluttered, and she and Grandmama began laughing all over again.

'What's it all about?'

Wiping her eyes, Grandmama replied, 'Never you mind, it's women's talk. Pour me another gin and orange and then I'm off to bed. Give you two some time on your own.'

She stayed another ten minutes, then kissed and hugged Jimbo and left for Fergus's bedroom and a good night's sleep.

When the door was safely closed behind her Jimbo said, 'Thank you so much, darling, for making her feel at home.'

'She really is very astute, you know.'

'I know. Razor-sharp might be a better description, but one can't help but like her.'

'Exactly. She's let me see a softer side of her tonight, but then that razor-sharp brain of hers came into play and we were laughing like I haven't ever seen her.'

'Been all right with Fran, has she?'

'Apart from her objection to the Paris trip, yes, I think so.'

'The new people are in, by the way, finally. It must have taken them a year to move in. The chap came in for bread and milk late this afternoon. He's called Andy Moorhouse and she's Jenny Sweetapple; kept her maiden name when they married. Claims her ancestors came from these parts. I asked him why it had taken so long to move in, but he wasn't forthcoming.'

'What's he like?'

'Wimpish? Smarmy?'

'Oh, well, and there I was thinking there might be some more talent in the village. I'll have to fall back on

Gilbert. He and Louise move into Ron and Sheila's house tomorrow. It'll suit them much better than that minute cottage in Little Derehams, that's for sure. I'm going to bed. I'm starting on the food in the morning for that wedding at the Abbey so it'll be a long day. Night-night, darling.'

'I'll be up shortly.'

'Huh, I bet.' Harriet closed the door behind her, knowing full well he'd be watching *Newsnight* and heaven knew what kind of a film afterwards. Late-night films were an obsession of his and it made her smile, because if she asked him about it in the morning he would remember very little of the plot.

Chapter 3

After Fran had left to catch the school coach the following morning Grandmama decided to rise now there was a chance that the bathroom would be free. She wandered downstairs in her Chinese dressing gown, a present from her Cousin Audrey when she came back from one of her exotic tours, which she never tired of talking about.

Jimbo was just leaving. 'Harriet left some time ago, Mother. Can you manage?'

'Good morning, Jimbo dear. I'll let you know when I become incapable of making my own breakfast.'

'There's some free range organic eggs from Nightingale's farm in the fridge if you want one.'

'I may well indeed. Have a good day, Jimbo. Never forget that your Harriet is a gem. You're a very lucky man, and I hope you realize it.'

'I do. Bye, Mother.'

Grandmama went to stand by the window to watch Jimbo leave. He was a little on the portly side, just like his father, but he strode off with such purpose in his walk. Off to conquer the world, no doubt.

After breakfast she decided to sally forth and call home for a few things she'd forgotten to pack. Her favourite hairbrush, for a start, that moisturiser which she loved, expensive but glorious and her rollers for titivating her hair between appointments. It was a glorious morning. She decided not to cross the Green as it had rained during the night and she hated squelchy grass. So she took a detour and paused to admire Jimbo's Store window display. If she'd been in Oxford Street looking in Selfridge's windows they couldn't have been more tempting, more dazzling, than Jimbo's. He had never been artistic as a child but he certainly was now.

Greta Jones was just coming to work at the Store. They greeted each other like long-lost friends.

'Greta!'

'Katherine!'

'How's things?'

They drew closer together. 'I've moved to Jimbo's for the duration.'

'You have? Whatever for?'

'Far be it from me to criticize a member of the clergy, but we just didn't get on, Reverend Anna and me. Too much alike, I'm afraid.'

Greta nodded. 'It isn't always easy having a lodger.'

'Is Paddy difficult, then?'

'Not at all. He's like a son to Vince and me. Just like a son and so appreciative. Turned over a new leaf, has our Paddy. All he needed was a good home and someone looking forward to him coming in from work.'

'Well, that's nice. She hasn't been like a daughter to me, just plain cussed, that's what. You won't say anything to anyone about what I've just said? But I do need to confide in someone.'

Greta patted her arm. 'You can rely on me. After all, we're comrades-in-arms.'

'Don't remind me. She starts praying at six a.m., you know, out loud.'

'Really?'

'All her washing strewn about the kitchen when I want it clean and tidy. Still, I mustn't say any more. She has tried, and neither of us expected her to be with me for nine months.'

'Sheila and Ron are moving today; the van's just pulling up, look.'

'So it is. I'll get her a welcome-to-your-new-home card. I'll go in with you.'

'She's never been the same since the baby died, has she?'

'Louise?'

'No, Sheila. There's some say . . .' But Jimbo was waiting for her at the door. 'Sorry, Mr Charter-Plackett, I know I'm late. I met your mother and we got talking. See yer, Katherine.'

'And you, Greta.'

'Mother. What can I get for you?'

'A coffee from that miraculous machine of yours and then I want to choose a welcome-to-your-new-home card, please, for Sheila. Oh! And one for Louise, too. Cream no sugar.'

Angie Turner, who'd followed her into the Store, sat down beside her with a coffee in her hand.

'I've been hearing things.'

'You have?' said Grandmama.

Angie nodded her bottle-blonde hair and pursed her lips. 'Things I shouldn't be hearing. About the Reverend Anna.'

'What about her?'

'That you've had the most enormous row with her and you stormed out.'

Grandmama chose her words carefully. 'I did storm out

but we didn't have the most enormous row, I don't know where that came from. We're simply incompatible, that's all. So Harriet very kindly offered me a home for the duration. My cottage isn't large enough for two self-opinionated women.' She gave Angie a smile to soften her words.

'I can believe that. Colin and I get on really well most of the time, it's only when disciplining the boys crops up that we have different opinions. He'd let them do anything, but I'm not having it. I like to be able to take my boys anywhere at all and they behave well and don't show me up.'

'Quite right. You're quite right.'

The door bell jangled furiously and in came Jenny Sweetapple. Well, Grandmama assumed it must be she because she was entirely new and couldn't be missed on a foggy night by a blind man. Her hair was the most alarming peroxide blonde and there was lots of it, which, when they all got to know her better, she swore was natural. It was swirled up into a vast chignon on top of her head and added at least four inches to her height. Dangling earrings filled the space between the chignon and her shoulders. Jenny wore a loosely crocheted sweater in a multitude of purples and acid pinks, black velvet trousers and heavy clumpy shoes more fit for the Himalayas than Turnham Malpas.

'Hi!'

Grandmama hated that word, but she graciously replied with a clipped, 'Good morning.'

Angie returned the 'hi' and smiled.

'Coffee! Where do I pay?' Jenny pressed all the wrong buttons, left a pool of coffee on the machine, dropped the sugar packet on the floor instead of in the waste basket and looked around to pay.

'You don't, it's free. One of the few things in this world that is. You must be Jenny Sweetapple.' Grandmama reached out her hand to shake Jenny's and found her grip warm and strong. Jenny smiled a sweet, all-embracing smile, revealing slightly crooked teeth that gave her a vulnerable look.

'And you're . . . ?'

'Mrs Charter-Plackett.'

Jenny frowned as though the name meant something to her but she couldn't remember why.

Angie Turner introduced herself and welcomed Jenny to the village.

'Thank you. Everyone has been so kind to us. We're really looking forward to living here and getting to know everyone. I've met your holy Joe already; she called yesterday while the van was still here. Nice person, but no thanks.' She tossed her head and smiled brightly, looking as though she thought herself very up to the minute by rejecting Anna's way of life.

'I see,' replied Grandmama 'Well, it's certain you'll find no better Village Store anywhere else in the world than this one. There's everything you need and more. If it isn't here it will be, almost before you leave the Store. That right, Angie?'

'Oh, yes. Do you work, Jenny?'

'I do actually. I'm setting up a massage parlour . . .' She rambled on but Grandmama didn't hear a word, she was too scandalized. A massage parlour? Did she think this was Soho? Whatever next?

She interrupted Jenny's flow and, in her most superior voice, declared, 'I hardly think a massage parlour is suitable here. Have you got council permission to open up a business in a private house?'

'Well, no. But that doesn't matter. It'll only be small. I might have a discreet board outside advertising what I do, and it won't affect the traffic or anything; they won't be queueing out the door.' Jenny giggled.

'I should hope not,' Grandmama snapped.

Angie Turner looked interested. 'My Colin always has tension in his neck and shoulders. Is that the kind of thing you mean?'

'Of course. Any aches and pains, sports injuries, anything like that. Aromatherapy, reflexology. I've done all the courses.'

'I like the idea of aromatherapy,' said Angie, 'all relaxing and that. With my three boys I need to relax more. Are you all set up?'

Jenny sipped her coffee. 'Not yet. I'll let you know. Have you heard of the name Sweetapple before? I'm supposed to have relatives in a village nearby. Dereham Magna, I think it's called. They say my grandparents came from there.'

Wryly Grandmama answered, 'You're a bit late to be looking up relatives. The village disappeared after the Plague, something like six hundred years ago.'

Jenny looked uncomfortable and rapidly changed the subject. 'Oh. Well, I'll just catch the Post Office while there's no queue.' She dropped her empty paper cup in the basket but it missed by a mile.

Grandmama raised her eyebrows at Angie, got up and cleared up the mess Jenny had left behind. Scathingly she commented, 'Some people have been dragged up not brought up.'

Jenny left with a bundle of notes.

'She's on benefit. How are they managing to buy their own house? Lucky them.' Angie went to do her shopping.

Grandmama carefully placed her empty cup in the waste basket, chose her welcome-to-your-new-home cards, paid for them and went home to Harriet, then remembered she wouldn't be in all day and recollected she'd intended to go home to pick up a few things. She tutted at her forgetfulness and sat down to watch morning TV before deciding it was a load of rubbish. Who in their right mind wanted mauve walls and lime green curtains with some dried twigs stuck in a vase and three squares of blue paint pretending to be pictures in their sitting room, or had they called it a lounge? She shuddered, closed her eyes and fell asleep thinking about the odd expression that Jenny had on her face when she'd said her name.

Later in the day she went back into the Store to find Harriet to ask if there was anything she could be doing towards their evening meal. A thin, and to her mind, wimpish man, was standing dithering about, obviously unable to make up his mind what to buy out of the desserts freezer, so she went across to offer him help.

'Good afternoon. Can I help at all? You seem to be at a loss.'

'Oh! Trying to decide what to buy. Jenny usually does this kind of thing, she's so particular, you see.'

'I can imagine. It's a pudding you want?'

'Well, yes. I'll take this.' He hoisted a great party-size cheesecake out and placed it in his basket.

'You must be Jenny's husband, then? How do you do, Mr Sweetapple? I met Jenny earlier. I hope you'll be happy living here. And you? What do you do for a living?'

33

'I'm in social work. My name's Andy Moorhouse.' He offered to shake hands. 'And you're . . .

'Mrs Charter-Plackett.'

His head went back and then dropped right forward. He repeated the name, twice. It appeared to ring bells with him and she waited for him to say something but he didn't.

'Yes, that's right. My son owns this place.' She waved her hand around. 'It's excellent, isn't it, for a Village Store?'

'It is indeed.'

She pointed at his cheesecake. 'Don't you think that's a little large for two? There is a smaller size.'

'Perhaps you're right.' But he didn't change it.

At this moment Jimbo came out from the back carrying a crate of oranges and began stacking them on the green grocery display. While his back was turned to the till, Andy Moorhouse scuttled off to pay for his outsize cheesecake and disappeared on winged feet. The Store bell scarcely stirred as he slipped out.

What a curious man, all kind of slippery and unfathomable. She really didn't care for him at all. He looked as though he needed a good scrub down with a bar of carbolic soap followed by a large plate of dumpling stew. For the second time that day she shuddered. Andy Moorhouse? Then he wasn't married to Jenny, was he? Now that she really didn't agree with. Just one great big con to get his meals made and his socks washed without any obligation of any kind. No doubt they declared their love for each other and agreed they were so special there was no need for a piece of paper to seal their bond. But life had taught her that wasn't always how it worked. She disliked him even more.

★

Andy slipped home with his cheesecake, cutting across the Green without for one moment considering the wet grass and that place where the ground went very soggy with water from a drain which didn't merit any attention from the council. In any case, that patch had been soggy for eighty years that they knew of.

Jenny shrieked, 'We're not made of money, whatever made you buy one as big as that? Here, give it to me.' She snatched it from him, speedily slashed and hacked it in half and then half again, wrapped three-quarters of it in clingfilm and banged it in the freezer. The remaining piece was thrown on a plate to thaw. 'Shan't send you shopping again, mark my words I won't.'

Andy ignored her. He picked up the newspaper and sat down in front of the fire to read it.

'Well, cat got your tongue?'

He gave the paper a shake, a significant kind of shake, and flicked her a mysterious look over the top of it. She snatched it from him and asked, 'You've got news. I can tell. What is it?'

'That's for me to know and you to find out.'

She began tickling him mercilessly, till he was rolling about in the chair incapable of avoiding her slender fingers with their long, square nails.

'All right, all right! Stop it. Stop it!'

Breathless, Jenny flung herself down in the chair opposite him, caught a stray lock which had escaped the chignon and said, 'Well, spill the beans.'

At this moment the doorbell rang and Jenny got up to see who it was, but the door had already opened and a face was looking round the door calling out, 'It's Caroline Harris, come to welcome you.'

'Oh! Please, do come in.'

'I live next door and thought I should pop in to make myself known. I've brought a cake. I didn't make it, Sylvia did; she helps me. I do hope you haven't got allergies or anything and can't eat cake.' Caroline smiled so fetchingly that Jenny was quite bowled over.

'We both love cake. Thank you very much indeed. Andy! We've been given a cake. A sponge, I think, your favourite. I'm not much good at baking cakes, so it will be a nice change for Andy.' That stray lock of hair fell down again and while she attended to it she sat the cake on top of a great pile of books stacked on the hall table. 'Andy!' This time she shrieked his name.

Andy appeared, dishevelled and still breathless from their tickling session. He held out his hand for Caroline to shake. Which she did and then, Jenny noticed, surreptitiously wiped her hand on the side of her skirt. That angered her.

'So what do you do to justify your existence . . . Caroline, is it?'

'Yes, that's right. At the moment nothing except look after my twins. But I am actually a doctor and will be back at work when I'm able.'

'How old are the twins?'

'Beth and Alex are thirteen.'

Jenny noticed Caroline beginning to look defensive. 'They need you at home, do they, at their age?'

'For the moment, yes.' Caroline began to make her exit. 'I hope you enjoy the cake, Sylvia's well known for her baking. I'll see you around, then. Bye-bye Jenny, Bye, Andy.' The smile Caroline gave them both was pleasing, but it made Jenny's resentment mount.

'Lady Bountiful! Didn't even make the cake herself. Who does she think she is?'

36

Andy, rather taken with Caroline's manner, said, 'Hush up. She was only trying to be friendly in the best way she knew. She's a lady, believe it or not, which you won't recognize being as you're not one.'

Jenny playfully lashed out at him with her foot and kicked his ankle. 'Doctor indeed. I bet. Didn't mention her husband, did she? Maybe he's given up on her toffee-nosed attitude and done a bunk.'

'Then again, maybe not. So I still haven't told you about what happened in the Store. Go on, then,' Andy settled himself in his chair and pointed at Jenny. 'Sit down.'

Jenny took a tube of moisturiser from the mantelpiece and began idly spreading it over her arms and hands, rubbing it in with practised sensual fingers, ignoring Andy. Then she began on her legs, smoothing the cream on almost to the tops of her thighs. It was only when he said '. . . got away with it because she withdrew her accusation before it came to court. But I know for a fact she was paid off because she gave me my commission.'

Jenny's ears pricked up. 'Paid off for what?'

'For what she said he'd done.'

Jenny screwed the cap back on the bottle. 'But what had he done?'

'What do you think?'

She hadn't been listening, her mind occupied with her limbs, so she said what appeared appropriate. 'No!'

'But yes. Vowed it wasn't what she said it was and with her withdrawing her accusation he got off scot-free. He won't want that story getting round the village, will he now? Not well-placed Mr Jimbo Charter-Plackett.'

'I met his mother this morning. I thought the name

meant something but I couldn't think what. You must have mentioned him to me before.'

'Quite likely I did.'

'What I don't understand is how you know him.'

'I told you, but you were so busy rubbing that stuff on yourself you weren't listening. When he was at college in Cambridge. I was a college servant.'

'Oh, I see. So you heard it all?'

'Exactly. The servants talked of nothing else for a whole week. All the domestic staff were involved in one way or another, turning a blind eye to what went on, that kind of thing. What a coincidence though, us coming here and meeting up with him after all these years, right out of the blue. Thing is, can we turn this to our advantage?'

'Did he recognize you?'

Andy shook his head. 'Didn't get a good look at me. Anyway, he wouldn't remember a college servant, not he. Oh, no. Far too superior. There must be ways of making him squeal. I'll think about it.'

Andy tapped the side of his nose and gave Jenny a slow conspiratorial smile. He'd make that Jimbo squeal and not half. It might be thirty years since he'd last seen Jimbo but he was as vivid in his mind today as he had been all that time ago. Put on a bit of weight, he had, but he knew him. Oh, yes, he knew him. What was the name of the girl involved? He ought to know because he'd come out of it very well indeed. The money he'd got from her kept him going for a while after he'd been dismissed. Fiona, that was it. Yes. Andy began to plan his approach. There might be more money in this than he could ever have dreamed of.

Chapter 4

Caroline had gone back to the Rectory feeling she hadn't handled Jenny's antagonistic attitude very well at all. Well, she'd more important things to think about right now. This was yet another day when Beth had not managed to go to school. Alex, quiet and self-absorbed as he was, trundled off to school as though he were glad to get away from the house, whereas Beth daren't leave it. What the hell had happened when they were missing in the African bush those six long weeks?

Sylvia came later in the morning now so it was up to Caroline to get some breakfast ready for Beth. She'd no idea if she was still asleep, as she'd allowed Beth to awake in her own time ever since they got back. Disturbing her too early could bring on one of her terrified screaming fits and Caroline, quite frankly, had had enough of those. Alex could calm Beth down but she couldn't.

But she'd decided this morning that she would take her breakfast up to her, wake her gently and see what happened.

Caroline called to her as she climbed the stairs with her tray, 'Beth, darling, breakfast coming up. Are you ready?'

'Yes,' came the reply.

They met on the landing.

'Loo first, won't be a minute.'

Caroline put the tray down on Beth's desk in the window and poured the tea while she waited. Having brought up an extra cup for herself, she sat down on the end of the bed and took a sip. What was it about tea that was so comforting? You didn't even have to wait until it had gone down before you felt the benefit. Beth came back in and sat at her desk, looking at her breakfast.

'This is nice. You and me drinking tea. I missed a cup of tea.'

'Well, you can have as many cups of tea as you like now, for ever and ever.'

Beth looked out over the garden. 'I love this view, your garden, then the Rectory meadow, then the wood and if it's winter you can just see the redbrick of Turnham House.'

'It is lovely. It's your garden as well as mine, you know, you've always worked in it with me.'

'This toast is very tasty. It's just right.'

Beth had developed this annoying habit of never answering anything directly. It was like two conversations going on at the same time.

'Mum?'

'Yes?'

'Alex gone to school?'

'Yes.'

'One day, not yet, I'll go to school.'

'Good, only when you're ready . . . Are you able to tell me yet what makes you wake screaming in the night?'

Beth's knife clattered onto the plate and she shuddered.

'It's all right, darling. If you can't, don't worry.'

'I wish Dad was here.'

'So do I, but he isn't and won't be till next July.'

'I need him here.'

'He can't help it. He has a vocation, a personal vow to God, and we can't go against that. He gave his word to work at the mission for a whole year. He saw us safe home, so now he's gone back. They'll all be so grateful he's returned.'

'Why didn't you ask him to stay?'

'Because it would tear at his heart if I did and I wouldn't want to do that. Don't think he'll have forgotten about us, because he won't. We'll be in his prayers every single day.'

Beth finished her cup of tea and got back into bed. 'I'm going to sleep for a while. It's not the same as having him *here* every day. I could go in his study and tell him everything right now.'

'Can you not tell me?'

Beth replied abruptly, 'No.'

'Look, would you like me to get someone for you to talk to? A doctor or someone? I know people who could help.'

'No!'

'What about Anna? She'll be in the study soon, it's almost nine.'

Beth said no again, but more fiercely.

'OK, I shan't mention it ever again. But you can, that is, if you want to you can.'

'I don't.'

Caroline took the tray downstairs with her and cursed the day Peter had been called to go to the New Hope Mission. She'd gone with him though, gladly and willingly, to get away from the Village because of the one thing which had dominated her life almost from the first week of their arrival: Peter's unfaithfulness. What kind of a life would she be leading right now if the twins hadn't

41

come into it she honestly couldn't imagine. She heard the front door opening and then . . .

'It's only me.'

'Good morning, Sylvia.'

'Good morning.' Sylvia appeared in the kitchen doorway, putting on her apron. 'How's things?' She nodded her head towards the stairs.

'Beth? Not gone to school, I'm afraid. She wants to talk to Peter, I won't do.' Without warning, tears filled Caroline's eyes.

'Well, you know what he's like. Everyone can tell the Rector anything, he just has that way with him. Compassion, you know. Wonderful. He has it in spades. I won't do her room, then?'

'I wonder if she might talk to you?'

Sylvia shook her head. 'I doubt it. It must be something very deep-seated. Alex won't tell either?'

'No. He's always kept things to himself and this time he's even worse. She said last night to me that I mustn't ask Alex, because he mustn't tell. She got quite hysterical about it. So I haven't. But he can't keep it bottled up for ever. I don't think it's just hiding in the bush all that time. I feel sure something happened, that there was an incident of some kind.'

'One day they will get it out and be all the better for it.' Sylvia got out her cleaning things, picked up the vacuum and set off up the stairs, dreading talking to Beth in case she *did* feel like telling her. Whatever must have happened?

But Beth was in the bathroom, taking a shower by the sound of it. Some days she had three or four showers, as though she had to wash something away. It suddenly came to Sylvia's mind about a film her and Willie watched one

Saturday night about a girl who'd been attacked and did just what Beth was doing. Showered and showered time and again. Blamed herself for it happening and trying to wash away her shame.

Sylvia's blood ran cold. If that was it, if it came out Beth had been attacked, she'd go to Africa herself and find and strangle whoever was responsible with her own bare hands. How dare anyone do anything nasty to her dear Beth. She was such a dear, dear girl.

Beth came out of the bathroom, her hair wrapped turban-wise in a hand towel, a bath towel tucked up around her armpits.

'Beth, love, how's things?'

'No different, thanks.'

'Get dried and dressed and come in the kitchen for a chat. I'm baking when I've done the bathroom. You could help me, like you used to do.'

The reply lacked enthusiasm but Beth agreed to help.

They spent a happy hour in the kitchen together making cakes, in particular Farmhouse Delight, which Alex loved, and a lemon curd cake, which was Beth's favourite. Surprisingly, Beth actually stayed long enough to help clear up, even so far as to scrape out the bowl with her finger like she'd always done.

'I'm going to lie down now on the sofa. Thanks for letting me help.'

'The pleasure was all mine. Willie and me think of you as our grandchildren, did you know? We've been so upset about you being missing, imagined all sorts of things, but now we can thank God you're both home and safe. Do you feel grateful?'

Beth, her hand on the kitchen door knob, turned to say, 'Not yet. But perhaps I should be.'

★

It was only some awful old movies and Teletubbies on the TV, so Beth watched the end of it and fell asleep only to wake with one of her nightmares.

The feelings were so powerful, the fear so real, that she could hear herself screaming and screaming but couldn't stop it. Sylvia had popped home for a few minutes and didn't hear. Caroline was in the garden giving it the last of her pre-winter routine and didn't hear. The only one who heard was Anna, using Peter's study as she did every day in his absence.

She rushed into the sitting room and took hold of Beth, trying to comfort her. But Beth fought her off. 'Get off me! Let me go!'

'Steady, Beth, it's only Anna. Please calm down, dear, you're safe at home. There, there, that's better. Gently does it. Nothing to fear. Would you like a glass of water perhaps?'

Beth nodded, dug in her jeans pocket for a tissue, saying, 'Sorry. I didn't know who it was. Sorry.'

'That's OK. Water coming up.' Anna went into the kitchen, ran the tap and carried the glass to Beth. Just as she crossed the hall Sylvia came through the front door.

'Just a minute. What are you doing?'

'Just getting Beth a glass of water.' She held up the glass for Sylvia to see.

'You're not here to look after Beth, you're here to do the Rector's work and that's *all*.'

Anna went through to the sitting room. Beth was still sobbing, though less panicky than she had been. Anna handed her the glass. 'Here we are, Beth dear. Drink it steadily, you don't want to choke.'

Then she turned back to Sylvia in the hall. 'So because

you weren't here I should have left the child to cry? Mmmm?'

'Well, no, but she's best with her mother or me, not a stranger.'

'Her mother is in the garden and didn't hear. You weren't here so what was I to do? There's no need to boil over about it. I'm not interfering, just caring.'

By now they were talking by the study door and neither of them heard Caroline wiping her boots on the mat outside the back door, but she heard their raised voices and couldn't avoid over-hearing their conversation while she struggled to take them off.

Sylvia was hopping with temper and saying belligerently, 'Well, don't bother.'

'You're being unreasonable. I'm not trying to usurp your position with Beth who's known you all her life. Certainly not. I think—'

'Well, don't. This is my domain. Full stop.'

'This is ridiculous.' By now Anna was furious at having found herself in the midst of this petty squabble. 'I have nothing more to say.' She banged the study door shut and left Sylvia fuming.

Caroline had walked into the hall in her stockinged feet so Sylvia had no warning she was listening. 'What on earth is going on?'

Sylvia spun round and immediately felt embarrassed, which brought on a spiteful attack against Anna, concluding with. '. . . So I won't have it, she's here because the Rector isn't and that's all.'

Caroline called out, 'Beth! Are you all right?'

'Yes, thanks, Mum, just woke up frightened. But it's OK now.' The tremble in Beth's voice hurt Caroline to the core.

'Sylvia, in the kitchen, please.'

Caroline closed the door very positively, and asked Sylvia to sit down. 'I will not have rows going on in my house. We have enough problems with Alex and Beth, and we don't want anything else right now. Don't ever speak to Anna in that manner again. She is a member of the clergy doing an excellent job of minding the store, so to speak, while Peter's away. If he'd heard you speak to Anna in that tone you would have been ashamed of yourself, wouldn't you?'

Sylvia began fumbling for a tissue in her apron pocket.

'What on earth had she done?'

Sylvia found the tissue.

'Well?'

'Got a glass of water for Beth because she'd woken up frightened and I'd popped home for a minute and you were in the garden—'

'So you'd rather Beth was left to scream?'

'No, no, of course not, but—' Sylvia wiped her eyes.

'But nothing. I would prefer you to apologize to Anna, it's only right to do so.' Sylvia showed no signs of getting up from her chair. 'Go and apologize to Anna, this minute, please.'

'I will not.'

Exasperated, Caroline suggested she went home and thought about it. 'Come back after lunch, when you've calmed down. You can apologize then.'

'It was like when that Louise was helping the Rector. She tried to take over, remember? She tried to take your place. I won't stand for it again.'

'Only because she thought she fancied Peter and as he isn't here . . .' Caroline stopped herself speaking to prevent worsening the situation.

'I'll go home. Have a think.'

'Good. I can never thank you enough for the care you take of the children, but your love for them must not be allowed to get out of hand, must it? I'm sorry, perhaps I've been a little too forthright, but speaking to Anna like that . . . it's not right, is it?' Caroline put a comforting hand on Sylvia's arm and smiled gently at her.

Sylvia shook her head. Then she tossed her apron on the hall table and fled home to Willie, hurt and upset.

Caroline's discomfort was eased by finding she had an e-mail from Peter.

Darling Caroline,

An auspicious day! We have laid the first bricks of our new church. The local commanding officer in charge of our part of the world has decided that the church and the clinic are urgent and has pulled out all the stops to get things started up for us. He's a charming man, full of goodwill, but Elijah tells me a very different story about him when he was putting down the rebellion. However, one can only speak of people as you find them and he is well disposed towards me. Elijah avoids him as much as he can, and refuses to speak to him if he can avoid it without causing bother. His name is Michael and he comes sometimes to spend the evening talking philosophy! How are my darling wife and my beloved children? Thriving as well as they can without me, I hope. I find it hard and lonely without you all.

Love and more love to the three of you.

Peter

It eased Caroline's distress a little to be able to send an e-mail straight back to Peter, explaining about the upset she'd had with Sylvia and how pleased she was that things were going so well with him.

Lunchtime came and went and still Sylvia hadn't come back, so Caroline, in one of her no-nonsense moods, went next door to see how things stood.

'It's me, Caroline. Can I come in?'

Willie, a devotee of both Caroline and Peter, considered himself above little upsets where they were concerned, and was very angry that Sylvia had behaved as she did.

'Come in, Doctor Harris. Come in.'

'Hope I'm not disturbing you?'

'Never, you're welcome any time. Come about Sylvia? Sit down.'

Caroline sat on the nearest chair.

Willie got straight to the point. 'I've told her she'd no right to say anything at all. The Reverend Anna was only doing what she should have done, helping a child in distress without giving it a second thought. My Sylvia's in bed with a bad head, and it's all her own fault and she knows it.'

'Ah! Right. I see. So is she coming back, do you think?'

Willie looked uncomfortable and finally came out with it. 'I've told her she's not to. Frankly, though she loves coming round to yours, it's getting too much for her, it really is. Mind's willing but the flesh is weak. She's not a spring chicken any more, is she, and I think it's time she gave it up. Maybe we could sit in for you sometime, though I expect both Alex and Beth think they're old enough to manage without us two old fuddy-duddies coming round.'

48

'They think no such thing, as you know only too well. If that's the case, and you're sure that's how Sylvia feels, then so be it. After all, she's been with me for almost fourteen years; she's done her stint. Give her my love when she gets up and tell her not to be embarrassed or anything when she meets me, because we parted amicably, as far as I'm concerned. The children will miss her, though. Are you sure this is what she wants?'

'I'm sure. She won't admit it but I'm sure. And I'm sorry she was rude to the Reverend. Very sorry.'

The cottage was small and Caroline's voice strong, and the sound of their conversation crept right the way up the stairs. Sylvia heard every word without even straining. She was so cold she had to pull the duvet up round her shoulders and she got her handkerchief out from under the pillow and bit on it to stop herself from crying out. Hearing Willie saying as Caroline left, 'See you in church on Sunday, if not before, Doctor Harris, and thanks for being so considerate. It comes to all of us, feeling old does,' was more than she could bear.

She thought she'd die of grief. But Willie was right. All those stairs up to the second floor and the size of that kitchen floor. If it hadn't been for the children and the dear Rector, how she loved him, she'd have given up years ago. Now it had happened. It was the lovely furniture and the ornaments and such she loved, elegant things she would have loved to have the money to buy, but never had and never would.

In her mind's eye she could see the Rector that day when he'd met her outside the cottage in Penny Fawcett she was having to leave. He'd told her how difficult Caroline was finding it looking after the newborn twins and how, when he suggested it, she'd jumped at the chance to housekeep for them and the chance of a bed in that cosy attic room high in the rafters. Those were the days. She turned over and wept.

The very next time she went into the Village Store, Harriet was working in the kitchens at the back. Hearing her voice, she came through to give her a message for Caroline.

'Could you let Caroline know, I've ordered those things she wanted and they'll be in when the van comes on Friday? Tell her—'

'I don't work there any more.'

'Oh! I didn't know. I'm so sorry. Too much, is it?'

'Something like that.'

She'd just finished paying for her shopping when Harriet had come through to see her so she was able to make her escape quickly. But not before just about everyone in the Store had heard what she said.

The whole place buzzed with the news and everyone's reaction to it.

Sheila Bissett thought the world must have come to an end. Sylvia not working at the Rectory? She'd worked there for years and let everyone know she felt a cut above them all because she was privy to snippets of news which she would never divulge, much to everyone's annoyance.

Harriet assumed that Sylvia and Caroline had had words, and could see from Sylvia's face how devastated she was, and felt sad.

Greta Jones guessed it was over the Reverend Anna being there each day in Peter's study and that Sylvia had rowed with her. Greta's guess was the closest, but Sylvia deserved much more sympathy than she, Greta Jones, was willing to give.

Jenny Sweetapple, taking an age to choose a birthday card for her gran, thought: whoever gets the job will be ripe for passing on gossip and not half.

Dottie Foskett was in at the same time and wondered if this was an opportunity for her. She wasn't needed as much at Louise and Gilbert's now that Louise was so much better, so why not have a go? It would be a real step up for Dottie Foskett and no mistake. Cleaning at the Rectory? My word. Oh! Yes! So she paid for her shopping, hesitated for a moment outside by the post box, thinking Dr Harris'ud be certain to say no, seeing it was her asking. No harm in going round there, though.

It was Caroline who came to the door and looked surprised to see Dottie on her doorstep.

'Hello, Dottie! Nice to see you. Are you wanting to see Anna?'

Dottie looked up at Caroline and wondered how she'd plucked up the courage to come to ask for a job. 'Well, actually, the truth is, Doctor Harris, it's like this. I've just heard Sylvia in the Store saying she'd stopped working for you and I wondered if there might be a vacancy?'

Caroline couldn't believe her good luck. People willing to help in the house nowadays were prized above rubies even if their morals were considered doubtful. 'Come in, please. We'll go in the kitchen because Beth's watching TV in the sitting room at the moment.'

Dottie was glad. The kitchen felt more like her, rather than the Rectory sitting room.

Caroline got Dottie seated at the kitchen table. While she put the kettle on Dottie had a look round. My, but this was a lovely kitchen. It spelled welcome in every inch of it. Every single inch. Kind of golden and sunny, it smelled of good food and comfort with its terracotta floor, and the huge Aga so much at home you could have thought it was put in when the house was built. The curtains were so pretty, all kind of old-fashioned and just right in the nicest possible way.

She thought about her own poky place and envy took a stranglehold on her heart. 'Lovely room, this.'

'You should have seen it when we moved in. It was appalling. Milk and sugar, Dottie?'

'Milk, no sugar, thank you very much.'

'There we are, then. Is that too strong? I'm afraid strong tea is a Harris thing, Dottie. Do you mind me calling you Dottie or would you rather Mrs Foskett?'

Dottie began to relax. 'I've been called worse. Most people call me Dottie, if that's all right with you.'

'It is. I must be upfront about this job. I don't need someone to do the light dusting but rather someone to do the harder work like the kitchen floor, the bathrooms, the vacuuming, the door steps, and the top floor bedroom and bathroom. You see, I always have that ready in case we get an unexpected visitor, this being the Rectory.'

'That's right. That night Maggie Dobbs got herself scared out of her wits, she slept there.'

Caroline nodded. 'Well, now, that's just it. If, and I say if, you were to work for me, you must not — and I repeat not — tell anyone at all about what goes on in here. Anything you overhear has to be dismissed from your mind as soon as you leave the house. Do you understand? It is of paramount importance. People have to feel they can tell Peter anything at all and that it won't go further than these four walls.'

'Of course. For years Sylvia knew things we'd all have loved to know but she never split on you, not once. Used to make everyone quite annoyed.' Dottie burst into

52

laughter and then immediately realized Caroline was not laughing. She shut up like a clam. 'Sorry. I do understand and I will be silent on what goes on here. If you give me the job, that is.'

'But do you have time? What with Louise and the old lady you clean for and that retired colonel in Penny Fawcett, you must be kept very busy.'

'Oh, I am, but the old man's gone in a home. His house is up for sale. Pity, he was very nice. Louise isn't needing me every day like she did now she's feeling a bit better. Everyone knows what a good cleaner I am. There won't be no dust left on top of the grandfather clock when Dottie's been round with her duster, believe me. Trained in a convent, you see, and you should try pleasing some embittered old nun, oh my! Holy they might be, but they've eyes all way round their heads. Hard lesson, but I learned it if only to save my skin. You can rely on me.'

'Do you bake?'

Dottie gulped down the mouthful of tea she'd just sipped and laughed. How she laughed. Finally she stopped holding her ribs and said, 'No. I live out of the cheap end of Jimbo's freezer, ask anyone.'

'Right, I see. Well, once I've got Beth back to school I shall be going back to medicine but not yet a while, and Peter will be back in July. I shall want the house in applepie order when I get back each day, any washing and ironing done, lunch for Peter, cleaning done, everything smelling fresh and sweet. And, of course, Peter will need looking after too.'

The whole glorious idea of the situation opening up before her filled Dottie with joy. My God, what a chance! What an eye-opener it was going to be. Looking after the Rector. Bless him, the dear man. Of course she would.

'That sounds right up my street. I'd be honoured to be able to help.'

Caroline got up. 'Come and have a look round the house. The study is only cleaned when Peter is out visiting or whatever. If he's home and in the study, he's not to be disturbed. When you can get in there you may dust his bookshelves, vacuum the carpet, tidy the cushions in the easy chairs and clean the window, but his desk and his computer have to be left completely alone.'

Dottie followed Caroline up the stairs. 'Yes, yes, I'll remember that.'

By the time she'd seen all the bedrooms and the attic and taken a peep in the sitting room and caught Beth's lovely smile when she acknowledged her, and seen the up-to-date washing machines, the stunning iron and the ironing board that came out of a cupboard with no more effort than the use of her little finger, Dottie was enchanted. She should be paying them to clean here. What a pleasure it was going to be.

Caroline laid down a few more ground rules. 'I'm Doctor Harris and my husband is the Rector and we'll keep to that. If you're interested and want to work for me we can discuss terms.'

'I do want. I'd be honoured to work here, believe you me, and thank you for offering me the job.'

'Another thing: if I'm not here and someone comes to the door for the Rector or for Anna, you'll need to knock on the study door, open it and tell them who has come to see them and then show them in. Right! We'll say a month on trial and we'll see how we like each other. It'll take a while for me to get used to someone different because I've been so used to Sylvia, knowing what's where and what not, so you'll have to be patient with me.

Thank you for coming round so promptly. Now, another cup of tea while we discuss terms?'

'Yes, please.'

When Dottie left the house her mind was in a whirl. A kaleidoscope of memories, a rainbow of colours. All the ornaments. The beautiful furniture. The sitting-room fireplace. Absolute bliss. She almost danced along the road on her way home. What luck. And to be paid well, too; it was beyond belief. Start Monday. Yes! She punched the air with her clenched fist. Roll on Monday!

Chapter 5

This was the day when Andy Moorhouse decided to begin his campaign of ruining Jimbo. The secret thing he'd planned, turning it over and over in his mind, and the whys and the wherefores of it, had obsessed him all his waking hours. He'd sort him out for ignoring him like he'd done when he was at college. Very superior he'd been, too full of himself to even learn the names of college servants.

Andy's cunning plan was only half-conceived when he arrived in the Store just as the mothers were coming in for vital bits and pieces before meeting their children coming out from school, that way he'd have the largest audience possible. In his hand he had a piece of Brie, which he intended using as his ammunition.

'Mr Charter-Plackett about?' he asked Tom in the Post Office 'cage'.

'He is. I'll give him a shout.' Tom unlocked himself and discreetly called down to the back office, 'Gentleman to see you, Mr Charter-Plackett.'

They could hear his sturdy stride coming into the front of the Store. He cut an admirable figure this particular day. He wore his vivid red-and-white striped apron with his red-and-white striped bow-tie and the ribbon around his boater that matched it exactly.

He raised his boater in greeting and smiled cheerfully. 'What can I do for you?'

'This Brie. I only bought it yesterday and while I like ripe cheese this is above and beyond. Thought I ought to let you see it.' Andy used a loud voice to make sure that above the hubbub at least some of them would hear. He held up his little parcel of cheese and began to take the wrapping off. 'Here. Look, and I don't need to ask you to smell it. You can't help but smell it.' The offending cheese was held directly under Jimbo's nose. He backed off, took hold of the parcel and examined the wrapping paper. It was his special wrapping paper, he agreed, and the cheese was way beyond being used.

'Very sorry about this. Do you have the receipt?'

Andy pretended to search in his jacket pockets, although he knew exactly where the receipt was, and finally came out with it. 'Here we are. Good thing I didn't throw it away. That's a lesson for you, ladies, keep your receipts.' He smiled almost triumphantly at them. At least they'd heard that bit.

Jimbo immediately did some magic with the till and, with a lot of whirring and clicking, he produced the exact amount Andy had paid for the cheese without causing chaos in his accounts. 'That's your money back and I'll give you another portion of Brie to take home. I can't be fairer than that.'

'Well, I do appreciate this. I was looking forward to some Brie after my dinner. It's most kind but then you need to keep your customers happy, don't you? Thank you very much indeed, Jimbo. May I call you Jimbo?'

He could answer none other than yes. But it tasted bitter in his mouth. What was it about this man that angered him so? The creeping, crawling slug of a man that he was, with his wheedling familiarity and that something about him that made Jimbo feel he'd known him in the far distant past.

Andy knew it would be impossible to break Jimbo by returning damaged goods supposedly bought in his Store because money-wise it would mean little to Jimbo. What he was going to do was ruin his *reputation* to the point where his commercial enterprise would be on the verge of collapse. He decided to prime Jenny about what to say to everyone she met.

She was waxing her legs, however, and was paying an awful lot more attention to them than what Andy was saying. 'Look, Andy, this is a new product for my salon. Feel how smooth that leg is. Try it!'

He dutifully smoothed a hand over her right leg and agreed it was certainly smooth. 'So, wherever you can, bring up the subject of the quality of the produce and how Jimbo is making his living by selling low-grade fodder as top-grade food. Won't be long before the cracks begin to appear and then I shall go in for the kill.'

Jenny looked up and grinned at him. 'Who're you going to kill, then? Let me know and I'll come to watch.'

'Sometimes I wonder about you. I'm not *killing* anybody. I mean, that's when I shall really start crippling his business. It won't take many more visits like the one today to drive a deep dent in his bank balance. You've got to sow seeds of doubt, gently but effectively.'

'Of course you do, but don't forget that everyone to a man thinks Jimbo's business is absolutely excellent. It'll take some heap of denting his bank balance to cripple him. There that's me done, legs like silk. I'm getting the advertising board tomorrow so I shall be able to put it out by the front door and make a start. You'll have to make yourself scarce. Can't have a man about when I've ladies coming for treatments.'

'Not even a spy-hole for me to peep through?'

She flicked a sharp blow to his cheek with the back of her hand, half in fun, half serious.

Andy leapt to his feet in protest. 'One day you'll clobber me once too often. Mark my words. I won't have it.'

Jenny giggled. 'You've already got it, so there.'

They began bickering like children and, before they knew it, everything was as before except Andy intended to remember the blow and use it at some future date, probably giving it back in double measure. He knew he could be like that, did Andy, given sufficient aggravation. The devious schemes of revenge when he felt slighted could bring some frightening ideas into his mind. Savage thoughts fit for no one's mind, let alone his own, thrilled and alarmed him, and his plan to heap agony on Jimbo belonged to those deep thoughts.

Jenny got to her feet, walked across to his chair and stood in front of him, bending over so his face was only inches away. 'Don't ask me to help you with your devilish plans. I'm not at all keen. I want to build up a business here. That beauty shop in Culworth is a load of rubbish, so the money I got for my car when we moved here has been spent on printing a flyer to let everyone in Culworth and beyond know where I am and what I do. You just wait and see, they'll be out of business in no time at all.'

Her eyes were staring and dark, her mouth half cruel, half laughing, and he could smell the wax from the strips she held in her hands. It nauseated him.

'Well, then. We'll see whose scheme comes up trumps, shall we?'

Jenny shrugged. 'Yes, we shall. It'll be mine. I'm determined to succeed this time. I've had two failures from not paying enough attention to the business. Well, it isn't going to happen this time. I'm making it work. No more cancelling appointments because I can't be bothered and that, see?'

She waltzed off into the kitchen to dispose of the waxing strips in the pedal bin and then she had an idea. 'Andy! Let's go to the pub tonight and sit in the bar for a bit, just to celebrate.'

'Celebrate what?'

'Me starting up business again in the front room. Go on. It'll give me a chance to tell everyone about what I'm doing and you to . . . well, whatever it is you intend to do to Jimbo. But stay away from me while you do it. I don't want my business idea tarnished by your daft schemes.'

'In that case, yes, we will. What you calling it, this beauty idea of yours?'

'I decided on *Cottage Cuddles*, but that could be a bit suggestive, so I thought of *Cottage Beauty*. I live in a cottage, it all takes place in a cottage and it's all about beauty.'

'Very good idea. Yes, I like that. I'm calling mine Jimbo's Climbdown Package. J.C.P. Get it? Jimbo Charter-Plackett. Or it could be Jimbo's Crucifixion Package. And it'll be just as painful.' He grinned maliciously.

'You are thinking of going in to work at some stage, are you?'

'Look, I go in, collect a few files, tell them where I'm visiting and then come home, do a bit of phoning around, shuffle the old files, add a couple of new ones with nothing inside them and I get away with it for weeks. They just never notice. Flog in a couple of times at the end of the afternoon looking as if I've been through the mincer and I'm home and dry.'

Jenny sighed. 'How you can dare to do it I don't know, and collecting unemployment benefit, too. One day they'll catch you good and proper and it'll serve you right.'

Full of self-justification he added for good measure. 'I go to court a couple of times a month as well.'

'You shouldn't even be in the job. You forged your qualifications, you showed me. Perhaps I could tell 'em.'

'Don't you dare. I've been drawing money for months and they've never noticed my scam. You'll be doing the same when you start up your beauty business. Running round to the social the minute you put the board out, are you? Tell them you don't want any more money from them? I don't think so.'

'Well, perhaps not straight away. But you've no conscience at all, you haven't.'

'I know and I'm proud of it. Who needs a conscience nowadays?' Andy laughed like drain. 'Come on, then, let's be off.'

'Five minutes.'

Jenny and Andy made as noisy an entrance as was possible so that the people in the pub would have their attention drawn to the newcomers.

Andy had managed to dress properly for once, in a Fairisle pullover with a toning tie and a country checked shirt, and he'd polished his shoes. He was crafty where the psychology of the rank and file was concerned, and guessed that being well dressed in this particular village would carry much more weight than being slovenly.

Jenny had primped herself to the very last inch, just

sufficiently of way-out style to impress. Andy for once had ordered the drinks and they chose a table by the huge open fireplace with its enormous wrought-iron grate and the big box of logs placed beside. The fire wasn't lit tonight as it was a comparatively warm evening, but Jenny rather wished it was lit, being a romantic at heart.

The bar was filling up and she realized that they'd chosen about the best possible table for a full view of everyone. The two of them kept raising their glasses to the punters as they passed, and Jenny began to feel almost one of them, not understanding that it would take much more than weeks for them to be properly accepted. Some of the weekenders in the three cottages behind the Royal Oak had decided it took years, possibly even fifty, to be. But Jenny in her innocence thought they'd already made great strides in settling in.

From where she sat Jenny could watch who went up to the bar. That Jesus woman came in wearing her religious uniform, went to the bar to get herself a drink and found three different people offering to buy one for her. She graciously accepted one of the offers and sat with her benefactor. He was a very handsome elderly man with manners to match, white-haired and tanned and very gentlemanly. His wife looked to come out of the same social strata as him and altogether they made a lovely-looking pair, but she doubted they'd become clients of hers, not the right kind.

That person called Dottie Foskett she'd met in the Store earlier came by with half a pint of bitter shandy in her hand. Ah! Now she just might be interested. 'Hello! Remember me? We met in the Store, earlier.'

Dottie stopped abruptly, almost spilling her drink. 'Hi!

There's hardly any chairs left. Could I sit in this one by you? Do you mind me joining you?'

'We'd be delighted. Wouldn't we, Andy?' Jenny gave him a sharp prod with her elbow to draw his attention.

'Yes, yes, of course I don't mind.' Andy allowed a short pause while Dottie settled herself and took a sip of her drink. 'Do you know Jimbo Charter-Placket?'

'Who doesn't?'

'Does he come in here sometimes?'

'Not often and anyway he's got his mother staying with him at the moment so she'll be keeping him busy.'

'I see. Nice chap. I took some Brie back today which wasn't quite up to snuff. He very kindly gave me my money back and replaced the Brie.'

'Very good that way, very fair.'

'I thought so, too, but he shouldn't be selling cheese that's off in the first place.' Andy managed to look very down in the mouth about the matter.

Dottie agreed Jimbo shouldn't. 'Most unlike him actually. But then there's always the first time, I suppose. You won't have been to one of his catering events, of course, having only just arrived. His food is out of this world. The hazelnut meringues are to die for. And his cold meats, like, they have real taste, not just pink plastic blotting paper. His cricket teas! Well!' Dottie rolled her eyes heavenwards. 'If you're in the team it's free, if you're a spectator then it's five pounds and worth twice that. You don't need no big meal that night you're that full.' Dottie looked into the distance as though still feeling the fullness of a Turnham Malpas cricket tea. 'He does it elegant, like, with dash so to speak and it makes you feel a million dollars. It's like being royalty sitting down to tea at

Windsor. Mind you, the cricket's not much cop but you can't have everything.'

'Obviously there's no tainted food, then?'

Dottie was shocked. 'Here, don't you go round making comments like that. There couldn't be anyone more conscious of food hygiene than Jimbo. My cousin Pat works for him, well, she's his outside catering manager actually . . . ,' Dottie paused for a moment to allow her cousin's elevated position in village life to sink in, 'and they're that strict you wouldn't believe. That cheese of yours must have been a one-off.'

Dottie decided to pretend she'd seen a friend and get herself away. Nasty piece of goods, that Andy.

Jenny stood very hard on his toes with her stiletto heel as Dottie left. Through gritted teeth she said, 'I told you not to say anything when I was with you. You're a toad you are. An absolute toad.'

Andy rubbed his stinging toes. 'You could have broken my toes, you could.'

'You deserved every squeal you made. She'll probably tell her cousin whatsit and it'll make them even more careful. Serve you right.'

The good-looking elderly gentleman came across to speak to them. Andy, unasked, instinctively got to his feet to shake the hand he'd been offered.

'Good evening. My name's Ralph Templeton. Welcome to Turnham Malpas. I understand you're in social work, young man?'

'Indeed I am. A much-maligned profession at the moment but we try our best.'

'I'm sure you do, and you must be Jenny Sweetapple. Very unusual name. Whereabouts are you from?'

'I thought I was from round here and was coming back

to my roots, but I'm told Dereham Magna disappeared as a village yonks ago.'

Ralph smiled. 'Something like six hundred years ago when the Plague devastated the place and killed every one of them. There may have been Sweetapples around then, though I don't think anyone has bothered to find out. Just the same, you're most welcome.' He shook their hands again and went to assist his wife to rise from her chair. 'Muriel, my dear, this is Jenny and Andy, our new neighbours.'

'How do you do? I understand you're starting up a beauty business in the village. That's an exciting new venture for us all. Are you a hairdresser, too?'

'Just working towards my qualifications. Won't be long now.' Jenny smiled and Muriel thought there was something very nice about her, there must be with that lovely smile.

The two of them left with Muriel hanging heavily on Ralph's arm amidst a chorus of heartfelt goodnights.

'That's another two we can forget about. They tried to be gracious, they *were* gracious, but not in our class.' Jenny raised her glass to someone who was leaving and waving goodnight to the two of them.

'You're always on about class. Categorizing people almost immediately. Everyone's equal nowadays.'

'If you think that you're very much mistaken. That Dottie, for instance, is a tart.'

'Honestly, Jenny.'

'She is a tart from top to toe. I *know*.'

'Well, I've just heard someone saying about her starting cleaning at the Rectory on Monday, so she can't be that much of a tart.'

Jenny nearly fell off her chair. 'At the Rectory? My God. Well, maybe I'm wrong.'

Andy went on to the attack when he knew her defences were down with the shock of the news about Dottie. 'What's this about hairdressing? I didn't know you were taking a course.'

'Neither did I, but I knew she liked the idea of me hairdressing so I said it.'

'What will you do if she comes for a perm?'

'Make an appointment for her, then buy a drier and some perming solutions, and I'm in business.'

'But you aren't one.'

'I know but I'm a quick learner. You're not a qualified social worker so that makes two of us.' Jenny patted his leg and giggled.

Although they didn't realize it, Jenny and Andy were being scrutinized by everyone in the bar. None more so than by Sylvia and Willie who were sitting on the old settle at their favourite table, waiting for their drinking friends to put in an appearance.

Sylvia nudged Willie. 'See that, she's too good for him. She's got a heart of gold. Such a sweet face.'

'You're right there. Think they'll make a success of it?'

'The beauty business? Not sure. Might, might not. Tell you what, though, I don't like him. Shifty, that's what.'

'Sylvia! That's not kind. Anyway, how're you feeling now, about the Rectory?'

Sylvia didn't answer until she'd had a long drink of her gin and tonic. A blob of ice floated into her mouth and she crunched it before she spoke. 'I miss it all, the coming and the going, the people I met, everything, but there's one thing for certain – I do not miss that great kitchen door. It seemed to get bigger by the week.'

'We're managing OK without the money . . .' Willie looked up. 'Hello, Jimmy. Sit down. I'll get your drink in.'

Sylvia peered under the settle. 'Not brought Sykes tonight?'

Jimmy's long doleful face grew even more sad. 'No. Just laid in his bed tonight when I said I was coming. I think perhaps he's older than I realized.'

'I'm sorry. He's had a good life, what with you finding him lost and alone and taking him in.'

'I didn't take him in, he chose me. Funny, that was. Can't get over it really. Remember I thought he was a ghost?'

'I do. Gave me a terrible shock he did. Under this 'ere settle and looking so like your old Sykes. Terrible, it was. But he's been a good friend to you.'

Jimmy nodded towards the huge fireplace. 'See that Andy whatsit over there by the fire? Funny chap. Gave him a lift home the other night in me taxi, car broken down he said. But what's he doing wandering about Culworth that time in the morning? There's more to him than meets the eye.'

Sylvia nodded 'She's nice, though. This beauty business might be a step too far perhaps. Might give her a try. I'll hold my opinion on 'em both till I know 'em better.'

'You might be right. Thanks for this, Willie. Now, what's your opinion about the cricket? Do we have a chance?'

Jenny put her brand-new advertising board out by their front door around lunchtime just as Grandmama Charter-

Plackett was approaching the Rectory. Knowing about Jenny's proposal to begin a business, she took her opportunity to make her feelings known.

'Hello, there. What's this you're putting out?'

'Hello. My new board. I'm starting up in business.'

'As a masseuse?'

'Yes. As well as other things. I do,' she began counting her skills off on her fingers, 'reflexology, aromatherapy, massage, sports injury treatments, hairdressing, manicures, pedicures. You name it, if it's beauty or designed to make you feel good about yourself, then I'm qualified to do it.' She smiled triumphantly.

Grandmama was determined to take the wind out of her sails, as she said later to Harriet over their afternoon cup of tea. 'How could anyone genuinely be qualified to do all those things? So I said, "Jack of all trades and master of none." Of course it was lost on her, her having a brain no bigger than a pea. I told her over my dead body was she starting up. Of course it turned out she hasn't got council permission, which I imagine she needs to set up in business in a conservation area such as ours.'

'I expect she does. But does it matter? I'm sure there are more heinous crimes than putting a board out and hoping for the best.'

'If she makes a go of it, and I understand she's doing a leaflet drop in Culworth, we'll have cars nose to tail round the Green. It's simply not on.'

Harriet inquired gently if she'd done anything about it.

'Not yet. I'm planning my strategy at the moment. We'll be having a chiropody clinic and osteopathy and heaven knows what within two years. It's got to stop.'

'What's wrong with extra life and extra money coming into the village? It's progress, that's all.'

'Progress, my eye! What's more, I thoroughly dislike the man.' Grandmama waved an arm vaguely about. 'That whatsit, whatever his name is, he's up to no good.'

Harriet protested, 'You don't know the man. How can you assume he's up to no good?'

'He's shifty and what's more he's taken a dislike to Jimbo.'

'What makes you say that?'

'Instinct,' Grandmama admitted. 'How could anyone dislike Jimbo? He's harmless, isn't he?'

'He can be stroppy. Look how many times he sacked Linda from the Post Office.'

'Look how many times he took her back. Very forgiving, is my son.'

Harriet had to smile. 'You're right there. However, tread carefully. We don't want a massive upset in the village when Peter's not here.'

'Bless that dear man. Not even he could like that Andy. No, not even he.'

She placed her cup and saucer on the low table by her side and showed all the signs of settling down to sleep. So Harriet cleared the tea things, flung them in the dishwasher and began to make a lemon meringue pie as she'd promised Fran she would.

The flap of the letterbox snapped shut so Harriet went to see what had arrived. There was a flyer about *Cottage Beauty* and an envelope addressed to Jimbo. Full name and address but no stamp. Hand-delivered, then. Harriet turned it over and studied it both back and front. There was something odd about it, curious and disturbing, and she hadn't even read the contents. Well, she was a partner in both marriage and business so she'd open the envelope.

It was, well, yes it was, but it couldn't be ... was it

what they called a poison pen letter? Quite definitely it was. The letter wasn't signed but that was neither here nor there because it was the content of it that was horrifying:

Jimbo Charter-Plackett,

The rubbish you serve in your Store, dressed up as gourmet, organic, or home-produced, is nothing more than an absolute sham. Animal fodder tarted up to look like first-class food. You should be prosecuted for offering it for sale. You do not deserve success and I shall make certain you don't achieve it. I shall make sure you are bankrupt before the end of the year. Be warned!

When she'd finished reading it Harriet flung the letter down on the kitchen table, then picked it up and decided to act. It must have been delivered at the same time as the flyer and she guessed who'd delivered that.

She leapt across the Green and straight to Jenny and Andy's door. She'd sort this matter out! Oh, yes. As of now. But there was no one answering. She hammered again and again and still no response. It was damned annoying. What next? Jimbo!

She charged round the Green having realized too late that her shoes were covered with mud by taking the short cut, and straight into the Store shouting, 'Where's Jimbo?' But she was through and in the back before anyone could answer her.

'Jimbo? Jimbo?' He wasn't in his office nor in Greta Jones's mail order office. The kitchens! All was busy in there. They'd begun making the first batch of Christmas puddings and the air was redolent with spices, dried fruit soaked in brandy and joyful busyness which should have cheered her. But not today. Waving the letter in her hand, Harriet said 'Where is Jimbo?'

'In the storeroom, Harriet, getting us more dried fruit out.'

He was there, standing on a ladder and reaching well above his head for a box of Californian raisins. 'Jimbo! There's something you must see.' Harriet waved the letter at him. He glanced down, wobbled a bit, dropped the box as he tried to steady himself – it missed Harriet by a hair's breadth – then the ladder began rocking, and down came Jimbo with an almighty thud, landing awkwardly on the stone floor of the storeroom. The ladder followed him in slow motion and Harriet had to jump out of the way. Jimbo had fallen with his right leg twisted beneath him and was suddenly hit by searing pain.

For a moment Jimbo didn't move or say a word then he let out an epithet which would have done credit to a ship's captain about to take his ship onto the rocks in a Force Eight gale. He writhed with the pain and didn't know how to control himself and behave like a man. All he wanted to do was lash out against the agony of it all.

Harriet looked at his face and saw the grey sweating skin of a man in terrible pain.

Jimbo snarled at her. 'Don't touch me. I think I've broken my right ankle. It's a damn lot more than a sprain. It's hellish painful. Get an ambulance right now. Don't touch me! Whatever you do, don't touch me!'

'Oh, Jimbo! I could drive you. I will. It's all my fault.'

'No, It isn't. There's no way I can get up and you can't lift me, and I can't get to the car. Argh! Just get an ambulance. Argh!' Jimbo shuddered.

So Harriet rang for an ambulance, got Jimbo a glass of water, dispersed the crowd now standing at the storeroom door asking anxiously about Jimbo, dashed about telling everyone what had happened and what were they all going to do, and generally behaved like a woman who'd taken leave of her senses.

Sweat was now running down Jimbo's face, and Harriet rushing about did nothing to alleviate the agony. With a great effort Jimbo said, 'Harriet, Harriet! Please. Calm down.'

'Calm down? How can I with you in such pain?'

'Please, calm down. It's not terminal.' But he didn't know about the letter they'd received.

'OK. OK.' She took a deep breath, and placed the folded letter underneath a box so she wouldn't put it down within his reach. Today was not the day for him to be reading it. 'Don't move. Please don't move an inch.'

Jimbo said rather weakly, 'I've no intention of moving anywhere, it's too bloody painful. What did you want me for anyway?'

'Doesn't matter. It can wait. I'm coming to the hospital with you. I can't let you suffer all by yourself.'

'You're not, you're needed here.'

'Your mother can cope. After all, there's only Fran to cook for, she won't mind, I know.'

'I'm going by myself.'

'Sorry, Jimbo, you're in no position to argue. I'm coming.'

By the time the ambulance arrived Harriet had organized her mother-in-law, sorted out the kitchen staff, who were only too willing to put themselves out when they saw how ghastly Jimbo looked, and talked to Tom about being in charge until tomorrow.

The ankle was a complicated break and Jimbo had to stay

in hospital overnight under heavy sedation. He came home by ambulance the following evening with his ankle intricately pinned, feeling grumpy, exhausted and miserable, to find his mother in residence again.

'Well, Jimbo dear, you know Anna found refuge in those weekenders cottage? Well, as it turned out the husband was taken seriously ill in Australia almost immediately and he got the idea that coming home was all he wanted to do. Didn't like the idea of being buried in Australia, he said. So they've come back, and Anna's back in my cottage again and I'm here to help Harriet and Fran to take care of you till you're mobile again. There now, isn't that lovely? It's all worked out well. Anna and I have had a nice little chat and we're friends again. I'm so glad.'

'I'm pleased my agonizing broken ankle is fitting in with everyone's plans.'

His mother ignored his sarcasm because even she could see he was feeling acutely depressed.

Jimbo was so very rarely ill that he'd had little practice at being a patient and this time was no exception. He snapped at every suggestion made for his greater comfort, refused painkillers, developed a delicate appetite and generally hated the world. The TV came in for a lot of criticism so it became easier to turn it off than have him complaining right through each and every programme. Harriet had to spend more time at the Store, which left Jimbo with his mother virtually all the time, and that became a further irritation for him.

On the fourth day after his fall Harriet suggested he went into the Store, sat on a chair in his office and did some work. 'After all, you've hurt your ankle, not your brain. I'll drive you round there, then you'll only have to walk from the car into the Store. You could even sit on the seat outside for a while.'

Jimbo visibly bristled at the suggestion. 'I'm not an old age pensioner yet, thank you very much.'

He received a sharp retort. 'You're certainly behaving like one.'

Jimbo raised a sceptical eyebrow at her, and suddenly saw the truth of what she said and burst out laughing. Harriet did, too, and it cleared the air. He let her drive him round to the Store and he hobbled out on his crutches and back into his life.

Harriet lingered in the kitchens for a while, leaving him to organize himself. She'd just finished discussing a menu with the kitchen staff when she heard Jimbo roaring her name. 'Harriet! Harriet!'

She dashed into his office and found him clutching the poison pen envelope and reading the letter. Her heart sank.

'When did this come, might I ask? Greta's just found it in the storeroom.' He thrust the letter at her.

'I've read it. It came the day you broke your ankle and I decided it best not to show it to you. It's been worrying me ever since.'

'I should say it has. No signature, I notice. How do they intend ruining me?'

'No signature, that's right.'

'Do you recognize the writing?'

'Of course not.'

'What evil-minded beggar would do such a thing? Did you see who put it through the letterbox?'

'I don't stand at the back of the door waiting for the post to arrive, you know. It came at the same time as a flyer advertising *Cottage Beauty*, or rather I picked it up at the same time. They may have been delivered at different times, I don't know.'

'This is serious. Who the hell could it be.'

'I've no idea. But they mean business, don't they?'

'Oh! Yes.'

They both glared at the letter.

Jimbo looked up at her. 'You should have given it to me sooner. This needs stamping out.'

'These last few days I'd all on not to strangle you, you were behaving so badly. Even your mother couldn't love you. You're right, though, it does need stamping out. But how can we do that when we don't know who sent it.?'

'Get Greta.'

'She's up to her neck with orders.'

'Get Greta.' Jimbo shouted in a tone which brooked no argument.

'Right. Right.'

Greta read the letter but could throw no light on the writer. 'I don't know the handwriting. I mean, who wants to bankrupt you? We were almighty glad for you to take over Mrs Thornton's flyblown, understocked, scruffy shop *and* provide us with a Post Office, what's more.'

'It's a mystery to me. Get Bel.'

Mrs Jones disappeared and in came Bel, anxious that trouble was brewing and unable to think what on earth she'd done to merit an interview in his office.

'You wanted me? I've only a minute; we're very busy this morning.'

'Read this. Any clues. Have we upset anyone that you know of? Disappointed someone? Not dealt fairly with a customer over an order? Can you give us a clue?'

'I'm absolutely horrified. This is evil. Whoever in this village would want to do such a thing?'

75

'So you've no clue?'

Bel shook her head and patted Jimbo's arm comfortingly. 'It must be a crackpot. Don't worry about it. Honestly, just someone with an imaginary grievance, that's what. They couldn't possibly carry it through. I mean, who would?'

'Perhaps you're right. Yes, maybe you are. Nevertheless, we all need to keep our eyes and ears well open the next few days. Listen to gossip, you know.'

Bel grinned. 'Don't we always?' She nudged his shoulder. 'You included. You're the worst.'

Jimbo was particularly lacking in humour that morning and didn't respond in kind to Bel's jocular answer. 'You may be right, but if there's any more of these,' he waved the poison pen letter in the air, 'then we shall have to be rather more serious about it. We'll let this go for now. Thanks, Bel.'

Bel went back to the cash till, but she was less buoyant about the letter than she'd seemed.

Jimbo was weary by three o'clock that afternoon and had to ring Harriet to ask her to collect him. It was when he had relaxed enough to give his mind time to roam that he thought about Andy Moorhouse and his problem with the Brie. Who the devil was he? There was something about him that rang bells. Perhaps if he pushed the fellow to the back of his mind, his name, and why he felt he knew him, might pop into his head unexpectedly.

Chapter 6

Dottie Foskett was having the time of her life working at the Rectory. It was nothing like as hard as working for Louise and Gilbert when they lost the baby. All them kids. My God! The washer never stopped going and neither did the iron with Dottie wielding it. As for the washing up! She felt like Ruby in *Upstairs Downstairs*, always faced with a sink full of pans and dishes. Still, Sir Ron had paid her handsomely and it had all been added to her retirement nest egg.

But working at the Rectory – she couldn't have chosen a better place. The furniture, the bathrooms, the pictures, the ornaments. When she looked at the attic where Sylvia used to sleep before she married Willie Biggs, she wished she'd been there when the twins were babies. She could just see herself sitting the other side of the Aga from Caroline, each with a twin and a feeding bottle, like Sylvia had described. Contentment. That was it. Complete contentment.

As for the twins now. If she'd had children she'd have wanted two exactly like Beth and Alex. Both so well-mannered, never a cheeky answer back and so polite to her. They'd asked if they could call her Dottie and she'd said yes. Made yer belong, like.

Apparently Beth had started coming downstairs to eat

her breakfast so that when she, Dottie, arrived to begin work Beth could have a word with her while she munched her toast and honey and drank her tea.

Inevitably Beth would ask if she would like a cup and of course she always said, 'Yes, please.' And they'd sit and natter for ten minutes, putting the world to rights and Doctor Harris never seemed to mind. Almost appeared to be glad that Beth was able to talk to her. Funny situation really, her not going to school, seeing as Alex went every morning on the school coach that picked up in the village.

The day after Jimbo read his poison pen letter Dottie and Beth got talking about it. Everyone knew that the first day back at work after he'd broken his ankle the letter had been found and half the village had heard him bellow, 'Harriet! Harriet!'

'But Dottie, I can't see why someone would do such a thing. Jimbo's always so kind and considerate.'

'Don't know about that, Beth. Look at that time when Flick was missing. Well, you won't remember. Only about six or seven she was. He was so angry he could have killed someone with his bare hands. He's a powerful temper on him when moved.' Dottie mopped her lips and got up to leave the table and get cracking but Beth delayed her.

'Dottie, is it ever right to kill someone?'

She seemed to have a frog in her throat because her voice was deep and choky as she spoke and that alarmed Dottie.

She sat down again and thought for a moment. 'I can remember when my sister Iris had a baby when she shouldn't have, and it wasn't any too good, up here you know.' Dottie tapped her head. 'You knew it wasn't right because its eyes was so blank kind of, and it was backward everything. I can remember as clear as day my dad saying it should never have been allowed to live, and he cursed modern science. Then there's some people so wicked they deserve to die. It seems so anyway, but it's not in our hands, is it? As I'm sure your dad would say, it's God's decision not ours.'

Beth wouldn't let the matter go, and Dottie wished she would because it was getting too deep for her.

'But what if someone wanted to kill your own sister?'

'Ah! Well, that's different, I suppose. In any case, it's something you've got no need to worry about because, (a) you've no sister and (b) there's not much chance anyone you know would want to kill her if you had, so just let the matter rest. There's no need to be depressing yourself about it, now is there? It's a lovely morning. You should be out in the garden or something. Must go, or your mother will be after me.'

Beth cleared her dishes away while Dottie collected her cleaning things.

'Your mum would love some of them late roses in a vase. Why don't you go cut her some, there's a good girl. There's some nice vases on that shelf in the cupboard under the stairs. Cheer you up.'

Dottie fled upstairs to the attic with the vacuum and her cloths to escape the interrogation. What the dickens was the child worrying herself about killing people for? She'd have to stop having cups of tea with her. She'd come to clean not be a psychiarisk or whatever. Out of the window she saw Beth taking her advice and stayed to watch her.

There was such precision in the way Beth cut the flowers. She'd got the secateurs and was choosing the roses slowly, one by one, so tenderly, admiring each one, lost deep in a world of her own. Dottie was going to open the window and say something but changed her mind, Beth was best left alone to work things out, whatever it was that was worrying her.

She finished dusting the window-sill and turned away to find Caroline also in the attic watching Beth from the other window.

'That's the first time Beth's gone outside the house on her own. Thank you for that.'

'I only suggested—'

'I know you did, don't apologize. And don't feel unable to talk to Beth because you have work to do. She urgently needs someone to talk to and if you're the one that's all right by me. Thanks.'

So their chats over Beth's breakfast continued each of the three mornings in the week that Dottie went to 'housekeep' as she called it. Sounded good, that did. She'd quickly mastered the art of saying casually, 'oh! I'm housekeeper at the Rectory now.' True she got some sceptical sideways looks when she said it but she didn't care. She knew people thought her an ageing trollop. So what? She'd had a great life and comforted more than she could remember.

But now things were on the up. She fervently hoped that Beth would soon be going to school and then the Doctor would go back to doctoring and maybe Dottie Foskett would be at the Rectory to overlook the twins coming home from school and making them a drink or something when they got in. She could fit it in very nicely with cleaning for Harriet Charter-Plackett and the odd morning doing for Louise and Gilbert. She was earning more money than for a long time and feeling her weekly pay from Caroline in her pocket she spotted Jenny Sweetapple's board outside her house and decided to give it a go. What had she to lose? Could be fun. But should she? When she needed a new washing-line and certainly a winter coat of some kind. She'd be an idiot if she . . . why not be an idiot? Treat herself now she was on the up.

She rang the bell full of confidence, only to be brought up short when Andy answered her ring.

'Good morning. Can I help you?'

'Well, I wanted to make an appointment with Jenny. Is she in?'

'She is. Come in. She won't be a moment. Jenny! Client for you.'

There sounded to be a deal of running about and cupboard doors shutting and then down the stairs came Jenny in a short white coat, white trousers and smart white shoes, looking just like an up-to-the-minute American nurse.

What a get-up, thought Dottie.

Jenny smiled beguilingly. 'Yes, how can I help? It's Dottie Foskett, isn't it?'

'Yes. I'd like a massage. That's if you've time. Perhaps I should come back.?'

'I'll just check the appointments book. I think I've a cancellation, . . . yes, here we are. I can fit you in but it'ud have to be right now if that's—'

'Yes, please. Never had a massage before, but now I'm housekeeper at the Rectory I've to keep myself in trim. Can't be doing with a bad back and let Doctor Harris down, now can I?'

Jenny's appointment book was entirely empty of names but she wouldn't let on, it was still early days. She had hoped to attract a much higher class of clientele than Dottie but her money was as good as anyone else's. First she'd give her a cup of herbal tea.

'Drink this before I give you the massage. I like my clients to be relaxed and comfortable before we begin. It's camomile tea, have you tried it before?'

'No. Thank you.' Dottie took a sip of the tea and almost choked. She spluttered, 'It's very different.'

'Yes, but very relaxing. Soothes the nerves, you know. I drink it all the time.'

'Have you got bad nerves, then?'

'Anyone living with Andy would have bad nerves.' Desperately trying to think of something else to say Jenny blurted out, 'Is your husband easy to live with?'

'Never had one, so I don't know.'

'Oh! I beg your pardon, with you being called Mrs . . . I didn't think.'

'That's all right. You don't have to have a husband to live satisfactory, do you?'

'Well, no, you don't.'

Dottie put down her cup. 'There, I've had enough. I'd like to start my massage now. I've to be at the Charter-Placketts in an hour and a half. I can't afford to be late.'

'Righteo. Pop into the cubicle and take off everything except your panties, then wrap yourself sarong-wise in the towel and come and lay face down on the bed.'

This was the embarrassing bit for most people, contemplating nakedness in front of a stranger, but not for Dottie. It had all been part and parcel . . .

'Here I am.'

Jenny began the massage with sweet-smelling oils that were almost intoxicating so beautifully perfumed were they. Her hands were firm but persuasive, strong but comforting, and before she knew it Dottie was completely relaxed.

'That's it! Gently does it. You'll feel a million dollars when I've finished.'

She didn't exactly fall asleep, but dozed, kind of and Jenny began talking to her, asking her about the Rectory and the Charter-Placketts, and especially Jimbo, but didn't seem very interested in Louise and Gilbert. Before she knew it, while luxuriating in the feel of Jenny's hands pressing and manipulating her back, she was telling her about the Rector and his magnetic personality and how everyone adored him without exception and how women fell completely under his charm, though he didn't encourage them, and about Jimbo and how he got his broken ankle and did she know they were having to operate on him because the ankle wasn't setting right, and how he'd had the poison pen letter and how angry it had made him.

Jenny hesitated for a moment, then continued massaging. 'Really? A poison pen letter? Do they know who it's from?'

'No, well, you don't with a poison pen letter, do you? That's part of their game, you see. Apparently they're wanting to ruin his business, they said so in the letter. He's biding his time about this, waiting to see what happens next, which is a surprise because Jimbo can be very hasty and lose his temper in a second. Dreadful, isn't it, how could anyone threaten to finish his business? We all appreciate his shop. Well, he calls it a Store, which sounds more classy. He's given work to dozens of people baking cakes and puddings for the freezers and making jam and chutney and outside catering jobs. My cousin Pat says he's one of the biggest employers in the district. But I wouldn't like to be in the shoes of the poison pen writer when Jimbo finds out. Hell, but he'll be wild. Been to

Cambridge, so he's very clever, you know. Might only own a village shop but he's no fool. A very sharp businessman. Oh, yes.'

'Oh. Right.' Jenny kneaded and pummelled, soothed and pressed.

'But they must be evil, mustn't they, honestly.'

'Indeed.' Jenny finished by firmly massaging each of Dottie's vertebrae. 'There. That's it. Feel better?'

'Feel as if I've been through the wringer, but yes, I think I do feel better. It is for bad backs, then?'

'It can help. Sometimes bad backs are caused by serious tension. Relax the muscles and hey presto! You can get up now.'

Dottie was so relaxed she almost forgot to pay Jenny and had to be asked for the money.

'Sorry. Look at the time. Oh my word! I'd no idea I'd been here all this while. Your next client will be here any minute. I'd better get off. I might come again. It's been very helpful, I'm sure. I'll see what I'm like when tomorrow comes. Just lucky you had a cancellation.'

'Yes, that's right. Tell everyone about coming, will you? Help spread the word.'

'Of course.'

Dottie grabbed a giant sausage roll in the Store, ate it and washed it down with a cup of Jimbo's free coffee, then ambled off to Harriet's, where she regaled Grandmama and Harriet about her experiences in the massage parlour.

'She tells lies, though. Kidded on she'd had a cancellation and could fit me in but she hadn't a single name in the diary. She thought I didn't realize, but you can't catch an old bird with chaff, can you?'

Grandmama agreed. 'What did she talk about?' she said hoping to find out something to assist her campaign to get

Jenny closed down, as well as some ammuntion to rid the village of that creepy-crawly so-called husband of hers.

'Nothing really. I talked about Jimbo's ankle – how is he, by the way? – and about that letter, but she didn't let anything slip. But the massage was divine. I'm walking on air.'

Disappointed, Grandmama lost interest and asked Dottie to start on her bedroom as she needed her afternoon rest.

Back at *Cottage Beauty* Jenny flew into a rage. Andy was seated at the kitchen table, idly going through files from the office. He didn't know what had hit him. Well, he did, but it was the suddeness of it that startled him and caused him to lose his temper.

'That'll do. Stop it! Stop it, will you?'

Jenny kept hitting him with the rolled-up glossy beauty magazine, half angry half laughing, till finally he was so exasperated that he got to his feet and pushed her away quite violently.

'That hurt me! Don't you dare do that again. Dottie's been here saying someone's sent a poison pen letter to Jimbo. Is it you?'

Andy by now had sat down again. 'No.'

'I don't think you realize who you're dealing with. He'll have you, he will, you know.'

'Did Dottie say *I'd* sent it?'

'No, but it was you, I knew straight away. Apparently he's been persuaded to take it calmly but Dottie says he hasn't half a temper when he gets going.'

Andy nodded. 'Not guilty of the poison pen letter, certainly not.' He sat back with a satisfied smile on his face, unperturbed about the lies he was telling. 'One day

I'll have him in the palm of my hand without being anonymous.' He extended his fingers and curled them together tightly as though crushing Jimbo inside his clenched fist. 'That'll teach him for looking down on me at college. Oh! Very superior he was. He doesn't recognize me now because he never really considered college servants worth looking at.'

'Time you knocked that chip off your shoulder. It's pathetic for a grown man.'

'You haven't thrown away that oak smoked ham I bought in Culworth, have you?'

'No, but I shall be soon, it's stinking the fridge out. By the way, don't tell me anything more about what you're doing, then I can truly say I knew nothing about it when you're arrested and thrown into jail.'

The phone rang and it was for Andy. When he put down the receiver he felt uncomfortably close to discovery, as though someone somewhere in the higher echelons at the office had tippled to his ploy and a net was beginning to close around him.

'Who was it?'

'Only the office.' He applied himself slightly more diligently to the files and made a few phone calls to plug a couple of gaps due entirely to his lack of attention to his job. But the panic soon wore off. He wrote out a few cheques for the water and the gas and such, and felt virtuous and on the ball. But he did go into the Store that afternoon and bought some oak smoked ham and stood chatting to Tom, Bel and Dottie for a while to make sure his presence would be remembered.

Dottie went home with her frozen shepherd's pie and as she popped it into the microwave she shuddered. That Andy was a nasty piece of goods and not half. Slimeball, he was. She shuddered again. The massage had been good, though. She'd have another one very soon, it had lifted her spirits so much. Such a pity that someone like Jenny was saddled with that creep.

On the Friday morning Dottie had her routine talk with Beth at the kitchen table. This time she was still in the killing vein but it was about capital punishment, and did Dottie approve of it?

'No, I don't. Neither should you as a good Christian girl.'

'Are you a good Christian girl, Dottie?'

There was a pause before Beth got her reply. 'Well, maybe not. I don't go to church reg'lar as I should, that's certain.'

'Neither do I at the moment. Ever since Africa I can't manage to go out.' Beth said this with her head down and her toast dripping honey on to the table.

'Here, let me do that, you're dripping all over the place.' Dottie skilfully wiped up the mess with a piece of wet kitchen roll. Matter-of-factly she commented, 'You will one day. One thing's for absolute sure: you can't stay in this house forever and a day. What would you do if your dad moved to another parish, eh? Stay on as a lodger? Right fool you'd feel.'

She grinned at Beth in a conspiratorial way and Beth had to laugh. 'I would wouldn't I?' They both giggled about it and somehow Beth's load seemed to have become marginally lighter.

By the time Dottie had finished her Friday chores Beth was waiting for her in the hall. She took a deep breath and asked, 'Dottie, could I walk with you to the church? Not to go in, just to walk there and then I'd come back home?'

There was something so anxious and so intensely sad about Beth that Dottie couldn't have refused her if she'd wanted to. Caroline gave Dottie a discreet nod of encouragement from behind Beth, so Dottie put her wages in her bag and the two of them set off.

The first step Beth took over the threshold, other than going into the garden to choose flowers for her mother, was the most desperately important step she'd ever taken in her life. Her breathing became far too fast, too loud, too rasping, but she forced her feet to move and when she was standing outside on the road she grasped Dottie's hand. Head down, she walked past Willie and Sylvia's, past the gate to the church hall and as far as the lychgate, no distance at all, but to Beth it was a million miles. By the time she arrived there she was trembling from head to toe, her grip on Dottie's hand was fierce and somehow she couldn't let go.

Beth didn't appear to be setting off back, so Dottie asked, 'Shall I walk you back again, love?'

Beth nodded. 'Thank you, thank you very much. I thought I could do it on my own but I can't. On Monday I might go in the church if I feel well enough. Would you come in with me?'

'Well, now, that'll be a turn-up for the book, but yes, I certainly will, only because you want me to, though. Right?'

Beth leapt back over the Rectory threshold, over-whelmed with relief to be safe home again.

God! thought Dottie. What damn well happened to that child in Africa? Something too terrible for her to tell. Yet Alex was going to school as though nothing had happened. Maybe making life normal was his way of dealing with whatever it was.

At home in her old cottage that crouched squat and neglected at the very bottom of Shepherd's Hill, Dottie had to laugh to herself at the idea of her going into church. 'What are things coming to?' she said out loud. 'Dottie Foskett, loose woman extraordinaire, going to church. Oh, my. Oh, my.'

Chapter 7

Andy strolled into the Store two days later carrying a small parcel contained inside a freezer-bag. 'Jimbo in?' he called out cheerfully to Tom.

'In the back with a rep and not to be disturbed, but he won't be long.'

Andy acknowledged the information with a thumbs-up, and began to roam the Store, picking up this and putting down that after a thorough inspection. He bent down to sniff the cold meats as though suspecting they might walk off the counter so full of maggots were they. Tom, beginning to resent this assiduous inspection, unlocked himself from his 'cage' and went to have a word. As an ex-policeman he had a good line in questioning people.

'Excuse me, are you a food inspector or from health and safety? If so I need to see your authorization.' He put his reading spectacles on and held out his hand.

Andy muttered something incomprehensible so Tom asked him, 'I'm waiting. I have a right.'

'No, I'm not. Just whiling away the time until Jimbo comes through.'

'Well, why not have a coffee and sit down in the corner with a magazine. We keep them up to date.'

'I have rights, too. I can look if I want.'

'So you do, but not to give a demonstration of complete

disgust at the products we have for sale. I'll pour you the coffee. Black or white?'

'White, no sugar. Thanks.'

Despite the ham being in a plastic bag Tom could smell it and felt angry. So he was coming in for a further complaint, then? The coffee was stewed and strong but Tom didn't care if it poisoned him. Andy Moorhouse deserved it.

Jimbo came in looking very pleased with himself, and shook hands with the rep, who looked as though he couldn't make up his mind if the deal he'd come to with Jimbo was to his or Jimbo's advantage. When the rep left Jimbo turned and spotted Andy neatly perched on a chair drinking coffee and, judging by his face, not enjoying it very much.

He ignored him for the moment, then gave a demonstration of how clever he had become at manipulating his crutches in confined spaces and eventually arrived in front of Andy, having satisfied himself that all his displays were as immaculate and fresh as it was possible for them to be.

Andy got to his feet, put his half-empty cup in the waste basket and said boldly, 'Just the man I've come to see.' He gave Jimbo the ham and said, 'I kept the receipt. Look, here it is.'

The receipt appeared genuine enough, dated yesterday, and when Jimbo smelled the ham he could do no other but accept it was tainted, worse, actually going bad. He gave Andy a very serious glare, hoping to make him lower his eyes first in which case Jimbo would know he had a fraudster on his hands.

But Andy didn't. He gave stare for stare. Reluctantly Jimbo refunded the money and offered to provide him with a replacement, as he always did.

'Frankly, I don't know if I want it. It's right put me off, has this. Only bought yesterday and intending it for our lunch today and when Jenny unwrapped it . . . well, you can see for yourself. It's off.'

'Please yourself. I can only offer.'

'Well, I need something in return, especially when I know how hard you work to keep your reputation.'

Something in the way he said that last remark got Jimbo's back up, and he retorted, 'I need people like you like a hole in the head. You'll do me a good turn if you never come back in here again.'

'But we'd starve if we couldn't come in here.'

'I doubt it. You've got a car, you can go into Culworth and buy your food there.'

'Well, I'll let everyone know about this. Banned because I've brought back food I bought all in good faith. I wonder if it's legal to ban someone when all they've done is bring back tainted food. I could enquire about that. After all, I haven't been stealing, have I? Well I never. They'll all hear about this. Does this include Jenny, too?'

Jimbo paused before he answered but there was something underhand and slimy about this chap which didn't please him at all and he decided, yes, it included Jenny.

Andy puffed up like an angry turkey cock. 'You've cooked your goose and not half, Mr Jimbo Charter-Plackett. I'll let everyone know about this. Everyone. I'll take the ham in replacement, please, and never darken your door again.'

Jimbo felt quite cheerful at the prospect until he'd calmed down and realized how much harm this weaselly, vindictive little man could inflict, but the realization didn't persuade him to change his mind.

'I mean it, Tom, I don't want him in here again. Ever. He's getting no more free ham or cheese out of me. We're better off without him.'

'Very well. But he's the kind who'll tell everyone he meets about what you've said.'

'I'm not going to fret about that. They all know me better than that scruff and they won't believe a word he says.'

'Let's hope so.'

But Andy had every intention of patronizing the shop, seeing how convenient it was and what good produce was available in there. He'd worked out when neither Bel nor Tom would be working, because now that Jimbo had decided to open until seven he was employing part-time assistants who only worked from five to seven in the evenings and very likely wouldn't know about the ban seeing as they didn't know him.

It worked well for a while until one night when Jimbo was working late redesigning his window display and spotted Andy in the queue at the till.

He backed out of the window and emerged within feet of Andy, balanced on his good leg. 'Thought I told you not to shop in here, that you weren't welcome.'

'Well, desperate, you know, for milk and that, so I thought you wouldn't mind.'

'Well, I do. So please pay for your shopping and leave and don't come back.'

'Jenny's got a client tonight so I'm fending for myself. Thought one little trip to get myself into your good books would be—'

'Well, it isn't all right. I can well do without your patronage. Now, pay and go.'

Andy turned round to speak to the other two people in the queue. 'See what treatment I'm getting. This is all because I brought some ham back that had gone off. And this is how he treats me. Not much of the feelgood factor about that, is there? Him and his reputation. What's he doing selling bad food, eh?'

But he got little satisfaction from his tirade because it was the two Senior sisters waiting and they frequently came at this time to get the best chance of buying bread and milk at reduced prices because Jimbo wouldn't allow it to be on sale after the sell-by date.

'Don't be ridiculous,' one of them said. 'He never sells food that's gone off. Never. Hurry up and pay and let us have our turn.'

There wasn't anyone else to whom he could appeal and Andy saw he was out of luck. Furious because he couldn't make a display of his supposed discontent and spread the word about Jimbo's tarnished reputation he said angrily, 'Here, keep the lot. I don't want any more of your mouldy old food. You can have it.' He emptied his wire basket out onto the counter and didn't bother when the eggs and the bacon landed on the floor and the eggs smashed. He stormed out, livid with temper, only to be greeted by an explosion of temper from Jenny who was waiting for the eggs and bacon to make an omelette for their evening meal.

'And no milk, either. You are a blithering idiot. What are you? A blithering idiot. All because you want to ruin him. I tell you, you've set yourself an impossible task.'

'I'm quite angry enough without you turning on me. The sod. It finished up with me leaving all my shopping

94

behind, including a box of those chocolate brazils you adore.' Andy didn't even have the grace to have his fingers crossed behind his back.

'Oh! You sweetheart, you darling boy. Well, it's a jam butty for the two of us.'

'You mean there's nothing else in?'

'My very words. So you'll have to take me shopping in Culworth tomorrow. I don't like driving when the roads are busy.'

Andy let loose a stream of bad language which infuriated Jenny and in an instant they were fighting like cat and dog. Andy swiped at Jenny and accidentally broke a cut-glass vase that had belonged to her mother and which she genuinely prized. In retaliation she dumped some files of his in the water from the broken vase, which was now spreading across the kitchen table.

Jenny wept real tears over her broken vase and Andy furiously mopped his files with the crocheted mat from the centre of the table.

'Right that's it. I've worked myself to a shred today. Three massages, two reflexology sessions and an aroma-therapy, so just when my business is taking off you can't even get the food in. Well, we'll drive into Culworth and go to that fish and chip restaurant. What on earth that will do to my hips I do not know.'

Knowing when he was beaten, and agreeing she had worked hard today and it really did seem as though the beauty business was on the up, Andy drove her into Culworth to the fish and chip restaurant in Old Street and then on to a fashionable pub they both liked at the top of Kirkgate.

But he wished he'd never gone there because two tables away in the pub were two men from the Social Services offices having an afterwork drink. They were in earnest conversation until one of them glanced up and noticed Andy toasting them with his shandy. He held it high and smiled and nodded as though they were dear friends, but as soon they saw him, the one blushed and looked embarrassed and the other made a rude gesture to him. Honestly, what were the Social Services coming to, making gestures like that? But they were his bosses so there was little he could do. He had to grin and bear it. Then it dawned on him that they actually held his job in the palms of their hands being as they were both his superiors. Oh, hell. Were they discussing him? That flush of embarrassment had looked very genuine. Maybe he'd better turn up to work tomorrow and make a pretence of doing something.

'Can't take you shopping tomorrow,' he muttered to Jenny. 'Got to go into work. Sorry.'

Jenny, on her second gin and tonic, had mellowed a little and took his statement quite calmly for her. 'What's up? Had a scare?'

Andy tried to appear nonchalant and, without looking at them, told Jenny who the two were sitting two tables away. 'Be careful what you say and don't look.'

But she did, she couldn't help it. 'Ask them across. I've enough money to buy them a drink.'

'Absolutely not. No. Don't. It might get too involved.' But of course she did. She got up, approached their table and asked if she could buy them a drink.

Andy saw a big black hole opening up. Don't accept, he kept saying under his breath, but they did and came to join them at their table.

They opened the conversation while Jenny was at the bar ordering their drinks. 'Hi, Andy!' said one. 'Taking the wife out, eh? Nice piece of skirt. Surprised. And how's Andy been enjoying himself today, then?'

This question left a silence, which Andy wasn't quite sure how to fill. But then Jenny came back and handed out the drinks. 'So you're fellow slaves of Andy's, then?'

'We are indeed fellow slaves, aren't we, Andy? Working hard every day in the interests of society. In fact, positively devoting our lives to it, just like he does. Eh, Andy?'

The suits and the manner of their speaking suddenly rang a warning in Jenny's head. Heavens above. They *were* his bosses. What a huge mistake she'd made. The sooner they left the better, before Andy incriminated himself.

But they'd begun a conversation about a big case that was coming up in court and they were asking Andy for his opinion. She knew from his face he hadn't the slightest idea what they were talking about.

'So, you must have some thoughts on it,' said one. 'I know you're not directly involved but it's all they talk about in the office. You must have heard them on about it, Andy?'

Andy framed a sentence which could have fitted almost any case in the courts. 'She should never have declared herself, that was her biggest mistake.'

'Who? The mother or Tessa?'

Andy hesitated. 'The mother.'

They both roared with mocking laughter. 'Typical Andy, always blame the parent never the member of staff. Not all the staff work as hard as you, Andy. How many cases is it you have under your wing now, Andy?'

'Too many to count.' He sniggered, thinking the moment he'd dreaded had passed, and his smart answer would save him from humiliation.

'No, seriously. You're always out on the streets, seeing your cases, Andy. Hardly ever skulking in the office like Tessa, for instance. You put too many hours in, Andy.' He spoke sympathetically and tapped Andy's arm as he spoke. Andy loathed his familiarity.

Jenny, desperate to back him up, put in, 'I'm always telling him he works too hard.'

Both men appeared to take her seriously. 'True. True. I worked out the other day that since he's been with us — eighteen months, isn't it, Andy?'

'That's right.'

'He's never taken a holiday in all that time. Now, that is devotion, isn't it, Andy?'

'Surely the wife,' the one who'd made the rude gesture nodded at Jenny, 'would enjoy a trip abroad or something, wouldn't you, Jenny?'

'Well, you know Andy and his work. Up to his eyebrows most of the time. I can't drag him away.'

'Workers like him are scarce on the ground aren't they Andy? Yes. Very scarce . . . Andy.'

The frequent emphasis on his first name had become insulting. But Andy smirked to indicate he appreciated they were joking, which he blasted knew they weren't. They meant business all right.

Jenny smiled nervously and wished she'd never let the gin take charge of her and make her invite them to have a drink.

As abruptly as they'd come the two of them left, one saying, 'Yes, I agree, very scarce,' and the other saying, 'Perhaps just as well they're scarce. We wouldn't want many more like Andy showing the rest of us up. The game would be up *then*, wouldn't it, Andy?' There was something threatening in both the comments. Jenny groaned and put her head in her hands, and Andy sweated as they left.

He'd been found out. As sure as hell he had. Perhaps not about the qualifications he'd invented but definitely about his poor work record. 'Did I or did I not ask you not to invite them over? I said don't look and I said it might get too involved. But oh, no! Jenny had to do as she wanted without a thought for me.'

'But they were nice chaps and it does you good to show you can hold your own with your bosses, that you're not just a yes man. I thought it went quite well. I tried my best to support you.'

Sarcastically Andy replied, 'Your best? Emphasizing the one thing I don't do, which is work hard. I can't take a holiday because then I'd definitely be found out, once they'd poked about in my files while I was away.'

'I'm sorry.'

'You didn't think.' Andy buried his head in his hands and groaned and groaned. Jenny rearranged her shapely legs and sighed. A long deep silence followed. For ten full minutes not a word was spoken.

Finally Andy finished his shandy and stood up. 'Let's go home, right now. Can you do that, do you think?' He marched out of the bar without a backward glance. Jenny followed but in her own time. Once she started doing exactly what he said there'd be no end to his demands.

Andy was already sitting in the driver's seat with the engine running when she got out there. Silently she slipped into the front passenger seat. He let in the clutch and they lurched off. She opened her mouth to remind him about his seat-belt and closed it swiftly. Serve him right if they had a bump.

But they didn't and, as soon as they got home, he

started on her. Threatening to hit her, shouting, calling her unrepeatable names, moving through the house at a furious pace, as though it wasn't big enough to contain his anger. She'd never seen him so angry. He'd been annoyed many times, but not so deeply bitter, frustrated, furious, disappointed, let down. He was all those by turns. Finally he did hit her. Hard.

Fearful that things might get worse Jenny locked herself in the lavatory. She could hear him going round the house, taking his venom out on the furniture, anything to alleviate his temper. There was one thing, he couldn't get into her consulting room because she always locked it as a deterrent to burglars and the key was safely on a cord round her neck, so the equipment was safe. After an hour of storming and raging everything went silent so Jenny crept out and spent the night on their lumpy sofa.

He slept late the next morning and, as Jenny had an appointment first thing waxing someone's legs, she crept about getting breakfast and doing everything as quietly as possible so as not to disturb him. Fortunately for her he slumbered on and on and on.

Jenny ate her lunch alone watching *Neighbours* and munching on her yoghurt and fresh fruit as meticulously as she could. No good swallowing it down in chunks, she'd read somewhere, did no good at all vitamin-wise.

Best be out when he wakes, she thought, then. Picking up her purse and keys, she set off for a walk. Thirty minutes fast walking was excellent for the muscles and the heart. Why was she such a slave to health? It seemed everyone was nowadays, so why not.

Jenny timed herself by her watch; fifteen minutes out, fifteen minutes back. Should she? Well, should she? Call in at the Store and speak to Jimbo? It was so convenient to pop across to the Store for things. He had such a good stock of everything that a trip to the supermarket on the bypass felt like a waste of time. Besides, his food was so much nicer, so original and his convenience foods . . . well, she bunched her fingers, kissed them and said 'Ooh là là!'

The bell pinged its warning and she was inside. 'Jimbo about?'

'Yes, but we have strict instructions—'

'I know. This is for a talk.'

Jimbo hobbled through, making good use of his crutches, and crooked a beckoning finger. Jenny followed him into his office. Wow! He was cute, was Jimbo, even if a bit stocky.

'Mr Charter-Plackett, I've come to plead.'

'Well, you may but it won't do one bit of good. You're banned.'

Jenny held up her hands, palm forwards and admitted they were banned, but could the ban be rescinded for good behaviour?

Jimbo looked at her face. She was smiling so beautifully his masculine heart almost agreed they could, but then he remembered the ham and the cheese and said, 'No.'

'Not even a teeny-weeny bit of leeway?'

'Not even a teeny-weeny bit.'

Jenny smiled again and Jimbo almost gave in. 'It's not you I take objection to, it's that husband of yours. Neither the ham nor the cheese had been purchased here. He knew it – on reflection I knew it, too – but still he persisted.'

'I know. He's having a bad time at work and—'

'He's a fraudster.'

'No, not a fraudster, more a little cheat.' Again that

smile. What is she doing married to that man when she has such a sweet personality? thought Jimbo.

'Look. OK. You can shop in here but *not*, and I repeat *not*, your husband. Is that all right?'

'Thank you, thank you.' There was such warmth in her voice that Jimbo was glad he'd changed his mind about her. In her own way she was quite a charmer.

'Fair's, fair. Listen, it's my mother's birthday on Friday. Could I book her a massage, do you think?'

'Why, of course.' Jenny's face lit up. 'Eleven o'clock?'

'Excellent. I don't expect a discount. I'm paying full whack so give her a good going over. She'll be thrilled. I hope this misunderstanding won't affect how we get on with each other.' He held out his hand. Jenny shook it, gave him that sweet smile of hers again, and disappeared to get her shopping.

Grandmama almost collapsed with horror when he told her.

'I'm going where, did you say?'

'To *Cottage Beauty* for a massage. It's for your birthday, Mother. Thought it might interest you. New experience, you know. One's never too old to experiment with new things.'

'I most certainly shall not.'

'But I've paid for it.'

'I don't care. I am not giving her the opportunity to benefit from something I wholeheartedly disagree with.'

Fran piped up. 'Go on, Gran. You'll come back a new woman.'

'I don't want to be a new woman, Fran. I'm quite satisfied with the old one, I mean ... I mean, satisfied with how I am.'

102

'Well, if I was saying no so emphatically to a birthday present, you'd say I was a very rude girl and where were my manners and compare me to angelic Flick.' Fran primly folded her arms and waited for Grandmama's reply, which was a long time coming.

Harriet was fit to burst trying to hold back her laughter. Talk about hoist by your own petard, Mother-in-law. Let's see how you get out of that, she thought.

Jimbo's eyes sparkled with amusement while he waited for her reply.

'I do believe, Fran my dear, you have a point.' She patted Fran's arm with approval, 'Thank you, Jimbo, for a wonderful idea. I shall report fully on the experience on my return. Not only that, I shall use it to do my research on how best to put a stop to her antics. Excellent idea, Jimbo, wish I'd thought of it first.'

'Er . . . I have a truce with Jenny at the moment.'

His mother was appalled. 'A truce! How could you? What form does it take?'

Rather sheepishly he admitted to allowing her to shop, but only her, not Andy.

Harriet and Grandmama both registered shock.

'You've what? After all you've said about them.' Harriet couldn't believe his volte-face. 'You turncoat, you.'

'Jimbo! A son of mine should be above such treachery.'

Jimbo held up his hand to silence the pair of them. 'Like I said, only Jenny, not that Andy fellow. I've done it now, so it's too late to protest.'

His mother gave him a lop-sided wry kind of smile. 'She's charmed you, has she? I didn't realize you were still susceptible to a pretty face.'

'It's not just that . . . I . . .'

'Yes?'

'Well, anyway, she smiled sweetly and I couldn't say no. It's all money in the pot. Blame it on my broken ankle. I've been through a lot of late, my judgement must be skewed.'

But Jimbo wasn't nearly so philosophical when he received another poison pen letter, threatening blackmail.

Chapter 8

Soon it was all round the village that he'd got another poison pen letter, and more than one decided on the spur of the moment to go to the pub that night to hear the latest gossip. The contents of the letter weren't known, but that only served to increase the speculation.

'Well, I reckon,' said Willie, wiping the froth from his mouth on the back of his hand, and neatly placing his pint of home-brew on a beer mat, 'it's from someone who thinks they've got a hold on Jimbo.'

'We all know that's what poison pen letters are about, but who the blazes knows something about Jimbo that isn't truthful and above board? He's led a blameless life, he has, ever since he came here. Totally blameless.' Sylvia sat back in the certain knowledge she'd said something which couldn't be questioned.

The rest of them seated round the table nodded in agreement.

'Absolutely, that's very true.'

Vera Wright leaned forward and whispered, '*Since he came here*. Yes, exactly. Maybe it's something that happened *before* he came to Turnham Malpas.' She looked at each of them in turn. But they couldn't believe that. After all, as Sylvia pointed out, he and Harriet were newcomers, so which of them had ever met him before he came to the village?

A silence fell while they studied this matter in depth. Their thoughts were interrupted by Paddy Cleary slapping Don on his back and cheerfully calling out to them all, 'What's the news, then? You're all looking mighty conspiratorial.'

'Oh, hark at him! Going to that college is bringing out the scholar in you, is it?' mocked Willie.

'They're teaching me a lot but I don't think it's turning me into a scholar, more a son of the soil.' He cheerfully grinned at his own wit.

Don, having one of his good days, said, 'Good for you, Paddy, you'll be in charge up at the Big House before long.'

'Naw. Too much responsibility for the likes of me. Quiet life, that's what I'm after. In any case, Michelle's too well entrenched with that sod Fitch for me to have a chance.'

Willie had no time for Mr Fitch but even he could see the injustice of Paddy's remark. 'That's not fair, Paddy, he's had a mind to send you to college where you wouldn't never have got without him and, what's more, you're enjoying it.'

Paddy acknowledged the truth of what Willie said by patting him on his back. 'Hit the nail on the head, you have, Willie. So, what's the topic of conversation tonight at the high table?'

Sylvia laughed. She'd always had a soft spot for Paddy, thief though he'd been. 'Same as everyone else. Jimbo's poison pen letter. What do you think, Paddy?'

He leaned confidentially over the table and asked, 'Anyone taking bets?'

'Bets? We've nothing to bet on.' Sylvia smiled. 'Trust you to think of betting on it.'

Paddy declared emphatically, 'I guess it's Andy Moorhouse.'

'Andy Moorhouse?' they all said in surprise.

'Why, I ask yer?' Willie scoffed. 'We know he's a slimy beggar, but what could he possibly have on Jimbo? He isn't likely to have met him at afternoon tea at his mother's, now is he?' They all hooted with laughter at the prospect of Andy Moorhouse having tea with Grandmama Charter-Plackett.

Paddy tapped the side of his nose and leaned closer. 'You may well laugh. I've no idea why or how, but just you wait and see. You'll find I'm right. There isn't another person living in this village as slimy as him, nor as underhand and shifty, is there?'

'What are the odds, then?' Don asked.

'Don't know yet. I'll let you know nearer the time. Who else, eh? You have to admit he's the likeliest customer. Must move on, it's my turn to buy Vince and Greta a drink. Be seeing you.' Paddy gave a cheery wave and left them to discuss his suggestion.

'Well, he could be right, though why I don't really know.'

'Load of rubbish. Why on earth should it be him?'

Dottie and Beth speculated on the matter during their morning chat the following day.

'You see, Beth, I always thought poison pen letters came about because one had a hold over the other. You know, something that had happened in the past that could be used as a lever to drag money out of someone for keeping quiet, and it goes on and on.'

'You mean the writer knows something bad about Jimbo?'

Dottie paused a moment before she replied. Had she said too much? Hinted at a truth when it was really only speculation? Well, do I mean that? I think I do. 'Yes, otherwise why would they expect Jimbo to pay up?'

Beth leaned forward and whispered, 'You mean, you know what's in the letter?'

'Oh, no. No one does, least of all me. No, I was just thinking aloud.'

'I can't believe that anyone knows anything bad about Jimbo, I've known him all my life. He always seems to be honest and open, and he's so kind.'

Dottie felt herself getting into deep water yet again. 'Anyways, there's nothing you and I can do about it. Well, I must press on.'

Later that morning Dottie was doing the bedrooms and came to Beth's last. There was a spider which needed chasing out because Beth had said she hated spiders. It ran along her bookshelf above the bed as fast as a greyhound, with Dottie standing on the bed in hot pursuit. Then, as she swiped at it with her duster, it ran quickly up a bracket supporting the highest shelf and paraded itself triumphantly along the front edge of it very confidently, looking as if it had no intention of moving house.

Dottie saw this as a definite challenge and lunged at it, but she missed her footing, almost fell off the bed and had to grab the shelf to save herself. All Beth's papers and her drawing pad and box of pastels cascaded down, along with the spider. It escaped across the duvet and Dottie captured it in her duster, rushed to the window to tip it out. 'Nasty thing. Go on, find somewhere else to live.'

She picked up the drawing pad first, which had fallen

open as it landed on the carpet. When she saw Beth's drawings she was horrified. Oh, my word. Oh, my word. Dottie went white with shock. She was no psychiatrisk but only a fool could not guess at Beth's state of mind. One grotesque drawing was of a soldier with gun raised, and a girl kneeling in front of him, hands held as though praying, head down . . . waiting to be shot? Another was even more horrifying: a lurid black and white picture depicting the girl struggling to undress and just the barrel of the gun pointing straight at her from the edge of the page. Only the girl was in colour. It was obviously a school uniform dress she wore, but dirty and dishevelled. The face could only have been Beth's, with those rounded cheeks, the deep-blue eyes, so like her real mother's, and the ash-blonde hair.

Dottie sat down on the bed to think. What on earth could she do about this? When she heard footsteps already halfway up the stairs she shot to her feet and put the drawing pad back. She hadn't time to put it back exactly where it had been or to collect the papers, but she hurriedly switched on the vacuum and hoped no one saw her quick movements.

But it was Beth coming to look for the novel she was currently reading. Dottie switched off the vacuum. It must have been the look of furtiveness and anxiety on Dottie's face at having been caught out, and the papers spread about the floor, that made Beth stare at her. Her eyes flicked up to the top shelf, registering the disturbance to the drawing pad. Neither of them spoke a word but looked for a long moment directly into each other's eyes and each knew the other knew. Beth's eyes were large with remembered horrors, Dottie's tormented and narrowed.

'I – I was trying to catch a spider and I had to climb on the bed and I almost fell and had to grab the shelf and everything came toppling down. I know you don't like them, spiders, you know. Sorry.' She bent to collect the papers.

Beth ignored her apology. 'Did you catch it?' Her voice was throaty and strained.

'Yes, it's out the window now.'

'Good.' Beth glanced up at the shelf again and then looked again at Dottie and silently put a finger to her lips, and walked out without her book.

Dottie shouted, 'It's here! The one you're looking for.'

Beth had gone.

But she was waiting in the hall when Dottie was about to leave. 'Would you come into church with me, Dottie? Please? I've been promising myself I'd do it but I can't, not by myself. I will, if you will.'

'Yes, of course. If you want me to. What about your mum though? Wouldn't she . . .' Dottie's throat was dry as a bone and she dreaded what might happen next.

'I want to go with *you*. Won't be long, Mummy.'

'Very well, darling.'

The church felt damp and cold. Beth thought what a contrast it was to the heat of Africa. The sweat and the flies. The burning sun and the dust and the restless nights.

Dottie remembered the last time she'd been in church was at her mother's funeral, and she felt weak and giddy.

Beth sat down in the back pew and tapped her hand on the pew cushion, inviting Dottie to sit down beside her. 'Not a word to anyone about the drawings, please,' she said. 'No one knows about them not even Alex. I didn't really intend anyone seeing them. You won't tell, will you? Cross your heart and hope to die?'

Dottie nodded and did as Beth had said, crossing herself fervently and damning spiders at the same time. She found her voice. 'But why? What made you draw such ghastly pictures with you in them of all things?'

There was a long silence with the two of them gripping hands, until Beth burst into tears, gut-knotting tears which Dottie could not bear, so she wrapped Beth in her arms like a mother would and hugged her tightly, saying, 'Hush, hush, hush. There, there, there.' They rocked back and forth, but nothing could console her.

'Does your mum know about this, about what happened when they couldn't find you?'

'No! She mustn't know. No one must.'

'Why not? That's what mothers are for. For crying and telling, they're the best.'

Beth lifted her head from Dottie's shoulders and shuffled about, trying to rescue a hankie from her skirt pocket. Dottie got her a tissue from her bag and dabbed her cheeks and dried her eyes. 'Who are you going to tell? You've to tell someone. You mustn't keep it all bottled up. Better out than in.'

Beth grimly shook her head. 'Alex says we mustn't tell anyone. Not anyone.'

'But your mum, she'd want to know. I know I would if you were my girl.'

'I could tell Dad.'

'But he's not here till next July. You can't keep it bottled up till then, you'll never get better at that rate.'

Beth shook her head.

'That soldier with the gun; he's real, isn't he?'

Beth nodded.

'I expect a girl of your age, nowadays, knows all there is

to know about what goes on between men and women, making babies and that.'

Face hidden against Dottie's shoulder, Beth nodded.

'He didn't do it to you, did he? You must tell if he did.'

To Dottie's great relief Beth shook her head. 'No, he didn't.'

'And that picture you've drawn with you . . .' Dottie took a deep breath, fearing to trespass, 'taking your dress off – did you have to undress completely for him? Did he touch you? Anywhere at all?'

Beth jerked violently at the memory. 'Almost.' She rested against the back of the pew and stared at the altar. 'I just wish Daddy was here. He'd understand. I could tell him, because you can tell him anything at all and he isn't angry or embarrassed or judgemental. He always has the right words to say and solves your problems. He sees straight through to the truth of it all, you see. But I'm not saying any more, not now. Thank you for being so understanding. I don't know why, Dottie, but I can talk to you about almost anything. It's such a relief and that's funny because I've never really known you.'

Grateful, Dottie kissed her cheek and said, 'Thank you for that, it feels like a real compliment.'

Beth gave a watery smile and took hold of Dottie's hand again. Dottie stroked Beth's hand while she thought of what to say next.

'I'm not clever, Beth, far from it. Perhaps you know what I've been in the past . . . but . . . anyway, I've seen a lot of life and people and that. Maybe that's why you can talk to me. Talk to me any time. Whenever, if you need someone. I shan't let on to a living soul, right? But I'd feel happier if your mum knew about them drawings.'

Beth stood up, wanting to go.

Dottie stepped out into the aisle to make room for her to leave the pew. 'Show them to her when you can. She needs to know, for she loves you more than life itself.'

'I know. But that's why she must *not* learn about what happened, *because* she loves me and Alex so. It would hurt her so much.'

'Are you sure, you know about, well about . . . sex, you know? I mean, he didn't, did he? You're not just shutting it away? Are you? Because it won't actually make it *go* away if that's what you're doing. You know you'd need tests and things, in case. That is, if he did.' Dottie looked up at Beth, staring directly into her eyes and trying to analyse her state of mind, but Beth's eyes gave away none of her secrets.

Beth began to tremble from head to foot. 'No, I'm not shutting it away. He didn't.'

'Thank God for that, then.'

They walked slowly down the aisle and stepped out onto the path to find the sun shining and everywhere looking its beautiful, almost-winter best, so different from the agony they'd experienced inside the church.

Beth let go of Dottie's hand and said, 'I can manage to get home by myself. Thank you, Dottie, for talking to me. You're full of common sense and so very very honest. You say what needs to be said outright, no messing. You've helped, more than any sermon would.' She gave Dottie a faintly wicked grin and turned to go home. 'Stay there till I get in the house. Please?'

Dottie stood watching her, suddenly afraid she might not be able to keep Beth's secret. It was such a weighty burden. If she didn't have to undress completely, what on God's earth happened next? If only the child would tell her mother, Caroline would have the wisdom to know how to deal with it. That was for definite. Much better than her, that old bottom-of-the-class, good-for-a-laugh, cheap tart called Dottie Foskett, for whom no one had any respect . . . except Elizabeth Harris. Bless her.

But of course they'd been seen. What else could she expect? Nothing, but nothing, could go on in this village without someone peeping through their net curtain, or hearing in the Post Office queue, or overhearing on the bus. So when Dottie went into the Store after waiting for Beth to get back into the Rectory it was already the talk of the village.

'So. Privy to a lot of secrets, are you, Dottie? We saw you talking to Beth. Have you found out why she isn't going to school, then? Because we'd all like to know,' asked Greta Jones, who was just leaving for home.

Dottie put a finger to her lips and said, 'Shush! I'm not telling, I've given my word.'

'Spoilsport. You haven't been at that Rectory more than a few weeks and already you're just like Sylvia. Not a word passed her lips. You know we all want to know why.'

'I dare say you do but I've promised her I won't discuss it. She's one of the very few, if not the only one, in this village who has some respect for me, and that counts for a lot. Anyway, I bet you've got hotter news than me. I understand Jimbo's had another letter and it mentioned blackmail.'

Greta Jones propped herself against the stationery shelves and told all. 'It arrived this morning at the house by hand. Well, I say this morning, certainly some time in the night, because it wasn't there when they went to bed. Threatened to blackmail him over something or other that happened years ago, but I wasn't near enough to hear absolutely everything. Anyway, Harriet and Grandmama have advised him to go to the police. Right to-do there was. I was in the mail order office so I couldn't hear clearly, but that's what he's decided on. Apparently,' she got squeezed up against the packs of pens as someone tried to get past, 'hold on a minute, I'm moving, there's no need to crush me. Honestly, some people they've no time. Where was I? Oh, yes. It's to do with something that happened before Jimbo came here. Something happened that didn't do his reputation any good, I expect, and this poison pen person knows all about it.'

Dottie absorbed all she had to say and drew the conclusion it couldn't be anyone in the village then, could it? For who knew Jimbo all those years ago?

'You wouldn't think so,' Greta agreed. 'It could be any Tom Dick or Harry, couldn't it? Might be a woman, I suppose. It could be, yer know, woman scorned and all that. Anyway, I'll let you know if I hear anything. Must go. I've a casserole to put on for Vince and Paddy. Bit of kidney in it to make it rich. Tasty, that's what.' She bustled out of the door without a minute to spare.

Dottie arrived home with a tailpiece of smoked haddock Jimbo had let her have at half-price. Nice chap, Jimbo. Pity he was having this trouble. But she'd enough trouble of her own without going looking for it. Poor Beth. Could she hint to the doctor about it? No, she couldn't, because Beth had been so stern when she'd said no. She couldn't break faith with her.

It was true the poison pen letter had threatened blackmail. Money was definitely the one thing which would motivate Jimbo to take steps. It was no longer an irritating little joke; it was way past that. The blackmailer was wanting a regular payment of £200 a month in notes, until they decided when it was to stop. As Harriet said, they'd soon get greedy and start upping the amount every year. Their demands would be limitless.

'So, what was it about, darling, this thing they feel sure they can blackmail you over?'

'Some trivial thing I can't even remember. You notice they're too clever to say what my misdemeanour is, or was.'

'I believe you know, but don't want to tell me. And I feel hurt about that. I thought we shared everything.'

'We do. But not this, right? Matter closed.'

'Are you going to the police?'

'I might.'

'You might?'

'That's correct.' He took off his boater and stroked his bald head.

'If you don't go I shall.'

'You won't.'

'I will. If not me, your mother will.'

Jimbo swung round. 'She's not to know.'

'You don't honestly believe that you can keep this a secret? They all know and if they don't by now they will by tonight, so she's bound to find out.'

'You're not to tell her, please.'

'Well, I'm not hanging around when the balloon goes up, believe me. Oh! She's here. I do believe she has more bounce in her step.'

'Is that possible?'

Grandmama entered the house in triumph. 'Jimbo, my dearest boy, thank you so much for the massage. I've never had such an excellent time. I'll have another for Christmas if you think it a good idea.'

'You've changed your tune. What happened to the espionage you were about to carry out?'

Grandmama waved a nonchalant hand. 'Forget it. She's a lovely girl and I'm sorry for her, tied to that oaf.'

'So, Jimbo's not the only one to do a *volte-face*.' Harriet folded her arms. 'What caused this, then?'

Grandmama removed her coat and gloves. 'Here, Jimbo, take these,' she said, disregarding the fact that he was on crutches. 'I was all set for being very critical – in fact, super-critical – but she is very professional, and dressed like an American nurse. She offered me camomile tea, and while I undressed she put on some beautiful whale music so by the time I was laid on the table, which she kindly lowered so I could get on more easily, I was so relaxed you wouldn't believe. Then we got talking and I told her things I've never told anyone but I felt so much better for it. In fact, I've offered to take leaflets round for her in Little Derehams and Penny Fawcett to help push the business on. I said Harriet would give me a lift.'

Jimbo promptly sat down and waited.

'What are you waiting for, dear?'

'For you to tell us, your nearest and dearest, what it was you've never told anyone but you could tell her. Go on, we're waiting.'

'Certainly not.' She smiled at them both. 'I love you both, and that sharp little daughter of yours. Picking me up on being ungrateful for my birthday present. She was quite right, the little monkey. Maybe she's going to grow up like me.'

'In what way?' Jimbo asked.

'Daring to speak her mind when necessary.'

Jimbo groaned. 'Not another one. I can't cope.'

'Don't you like a mother who has something to say for

herself? Or would you prefer me to grumble and complain all the time?'

In the interests of family relationships Jimbo didn't point out that she did grumble and complain a lot. Instead he patted her hand, kissed her cheek and said, 'Did you learn anything?'

'Well, yes. While I was standing at the door saying goodbye to Jenny I spotted that Dottie Foskett talking to Beth Harris right outside the church. Why on earth Caroline has employed her I will never know.'

Harriet put her straight on the matter. 'Because she cleans exceptionally well, and Caroline told me herself she's very pleased with her.'

'But does she know that her and Beth are obviously becoming very close?'

'Caroline will be glad for Beth to be talking, no matter who it is to. She's been too afraid to go outside the house, but Dottie has got her in the garden without even so much as trying and now apparently has got her to go out into the lane, which, as far as Caroline is concerned, is brilliant progress. So I wouldn't go saying anything to Caroline about Dottie because she won't thank you for it.'

'But surely a trained psychologist or psychiatrist would be better. I mean, what on earth has a chump like Dottie got to say that could possibly help Beth?'

'I don't know, but if it works . . . Caroline is worried to death about the twins. Neither of the children will talk about what happened, you see. Alex won't open up at all and he's obviously pushed the whole episode right out of the way, carrying on as though nothing is the matter when clearly it is. At least Beth is behaving oddly, so in some peculiar way she may be getting it out of her system.

Frankly, I daresay Caroline would be grateful for Dottie to have a word with Alex, too.'

'I don't know. In my day, a prostitute counted for less than nothing. Now they're advising the mentally distressed. What are things coming to?' Grandmama got to her feet and declared she was going for a rest. She disappeared upstairs.

'Lunch at one, Katherine,' Harriet called out to her. When she was out of hearing she confided to Jimbo, 'She isn't a prostitute any more.'

'Past it, is she?'

Harriet raised both her eyebrows in disgust at his remark. 'She *told* me she wasn't.'

'God! She hasn't started treating *you*, has she?'

'There are times, Jimbo, when you behave like an out-and-out snob. It's not right and proper, not in Turnham Malpas. Just because she was what she was doesn't mean she's insensitive to people's needs. Maybe she's even more sensitive.'

Horrified at the possibility he might be about to hear further revelations about Dottie's past Jimbo said firmly, 'Please, don't let's go there. Sorry. Sorry. Hand me my crutches, please, I need to work in my office for a while.'

'Shall I make a window this afternoon to take you to the police station?'.

'No, thanks. I'm going to ignore that letter. They can't actually do anything if I won't play ball.'

'Don't be too sure.'

'Of course, I could always ask Dottie for advice.'

'She'll be here tomorrow afternoon; you can ask her then.'

Chapter 9

Jenny's beauty business was coming along apace. She was regularly booked out for the whole of the morning, much to her delight. She was making lots of friendships and learning a great deal more about her clientele than they ever realized. That was the fascinating thing about the beauty business. A beautician became a confidant and best friend if the ambience was right, and Jenny had got it just perfect. The herbal tea, the lighting, the music, and her professional approach did the trick. Of course, all her equipment was of the best, and her outfit smart and almost nurse-like, which inspired confidence, and best of all for Jenny, it bestowed on her clients a willingness to open up.

The things she'd heard while massaging and waxing and whatnot were unbelievable. Of course, not a word of the confessions went out of the four walls of her consulting room – except for the titbits she told Andy of an evening.

Andy. Yes. There'd been a change there. Before he hadn't cared two hoots that he was doing social work when he hadn't the slightest bit of a qualification for it, but now, ever since that night they'd treated two of his bosses to drinks, he'd been edgy. So edgy, in fact, that he'd actually begun going in to work more often, but his bouts of anger had become more numerous. Sometimes he was so boiling with fury he would throw things about, especially ornaments that were dear to her heart. It was true, though, that she had a lot of them, lined along shelves, along the dado rails, on the window-sills, in the bathroom and the kitchen. Now and again she was afraid of him, of his seething anger and his frustrations, but tried her best to be cocky and steely with him. When that didn't work she locked herself in her consultation room and slept on the treatment bed.

The following morning he would appear to remember nothing about his tirade the previous night, for which Jenny was thankful, though it caused her concern. She hadn't noticed if he was drinking more than usual; perhaps that was the problem. Whatever, she'd long since fallen out of love with him. She'd been crazy with love when they first married but somehow all that had fallen away and they were left with companionship, friendship, rubbing along together and sometimes outright fighting, which always cleared the air and for a few days afterwards things improved.

She heard him unlocking the front door now, but didn't rush to greet him as she would have done at one time. He found her tidying up after a client.

'Hello, then. How's things?' Andy flung himself down in one of Jenny's basket chairs. 'I'm knackered.'

Jenny asked with her tongue in her cheek, 'Busy day at the office?'

'I'm not joking. It's harder work making it look as though I'm working than it is working properly. I think I'll give it up and do a hard day's graft instead, it'ud be easier.' He began rolling a cigarette.

'Not in here, if you please.'

'If I want to smoke I shall. I'm gagging for a fag. Now the killjoys have voted for the office to be smoke-free, there's no pleasure going in. Next time you go in the Store, get me some more papers, will you?'

'I won't. It's a disgusting habit.' Jenny stamped her foot when she saw he was ignoring her request. 'I said – not in here.'

But still he continued, fiddling with his little packet of papers and the tobacco, dropping bits and having to rescue them from the immaculate floor. For a man who was incredibly careless with his belongings and cared not one jot about keeping the house tidy, he was intensely precise about his cigarettes.

'Andy, I shan't say it again: not in here, please. I don't want the smell when my clients come. It's not a good recommendation for my aromatherapy and my holistic philosophy, is it? Healthy mind, healthy body and all that jazz.'

But now he was getting his matches out.

Incensed, Jenny dashed the cigarette out of his mouth and the lighted match caught his wrist as it flew through the air. Andy leapt to his feet, his face purple with anger. Jenny, busy stamping on the match to prevent a fire, didn't notice that he was raising his hand to her. Completely out of control he thumped her hard in the middle of her back with his clenched fist, which winded her and made her stagger. She grabbed the table and righted herself only to find Andy hitting her again.

She fled from the room and locked herself in the downstairs loo, which was reserved for her clients. Jenny sat on the toilet lid, very still, very upset. Resorting to hitting her was happening far, far too frequently. So long as it didn't show, that was important. She twisted round, undid the buttons on her white jacket and examined her back in the mirror as best she could. A bruise was coming up in the very middle, right on her spine. By tomorrow that would hurt.

Then she noticed another very red patch on the side of her neck where one of his other blows had landed. That would show; everyone would see it.

Jenny could hear Andy banging about in the kitchen. What was he doing? Surely not trying to make a meal. He never did anything in the kitchen. He'd starve first. Then she heard his voice calling sweetly, 'Jenny! Lunch is ready.'

That was a first. Tentatively she let herself out and went into the kitchen. He'd even bothered to lay the table. Sandwiches, crisps, fruit, coffee.

Jenny was determined not to say anything that might set him off again. She meekly sat down and helped herself to a sandwich. He kindly poured her some coffee and passed the mug across the table to her, smiled and offered her another sandwich. 'Crisps, Jenny? Your favourite, Jenny.'

His thoughtfulness felt very odd. It was strangely frightening, too. She remembered how those two bosses of his had used his name time and again when they spoke to him. What was running through his head? How could kind words be so alarming?

'More coffee, Jenny?'

'Yes, please.'

'There you are, Jenny. More milk? Mmm? Jenny?'

'No, thanks. That's enough. I said that's enough. I don't want any more.'

He kept pouring the milk though, until it reached the rim and began sliding down the side of the mug.

'Stop it, Andy. Stop it. Look at the. mess.'

He grabbed her wrist with one hand, still letting the milk pour out of the jug with the other. 'See *my* wrist? See the burn you made. Shall I burn yours like that?'

'Of course not. No.'

'What do you say, then?'

'I don't know.'

'You say, "Sorry Andy, sorry about your wrist."'

Afraid he might burn her wrist in revenge Jenny repeated his words as he'd asked. She didn't mean them but she knew he meant what he said.

'Easy to do. Right there, look.' He put down the milk jug with a deliberate bang. It was a delicate china one that had been her godmother's. It broke in half, the dear little hand-painted violets on the side falling in two pieces. But Andy pointed at her wrist at the very point where her hand joined her arm and he pressed down hard with his fingernail to show her where he would burn her if he chose. His nail left a thin red line on her flesh.

'You've broken my godmother's jug. I loved that jug.'

'Oh, dear, poor godmother. She didn't think of you when she died, did she? All her money went to the cats' home. Oh, yes. Not a penny for her goddaughter, even though you'd spent hours caring for *her* when you should have been caring for *me*. That money could have made us very comfortable. Don't think I don't know why. It was cos she didn't want *me* to get my hands on it. Never liked me, she didn't.' He lit another cigarette, taking care to make a point of touching Jenny's wrist with his little finger, the lighted match still in his hand.

'I'll clear up.'

'No. no. You do enough. I'll clear up. Any clients this afternoon?'

Jenny shook her head.

'Then we'll go out. Bickerby Rocks, how about it?'

'OK.' Both puzzled and frightened by his rapid changes

of mood, Jenny left the table to find some warmer clothes to wear, knowing it would be windy up on the Rocks.

It was the kind of place Jenny loved. A wonderful view over the surrounding countryside, a pile, literally, of great rocks standing up out of the earth like some primeval worshipping place. She stood at the highest edge of the rocks, the wind blowing her hair, tugging at her skirt, threatening to blow her away any moment. It was magnificent. She turned to see where Andy was and found he was right behind her.

'Isn't this fabulous, Andy? All this space. Look at the sky. Brilliant blue and not a cloud in sight.'

Andy nodded his agreement. He peered over the edge and said, 'Long way down. You'll have to mind the wind doesn't blow you away. It's very strong.'

The wind was so loud they could barely hear each other speak. It whistled and howled, buffeted and swirled around them. Finally Jenny had had enough of it. Her nose was beginning to run, her cheeks felt like ice, and the temptation to allow herself to be whisked away over the edge by the wind was becoming harder to resist. Briefly she pondered on the idea of flying away into that beautiful sky. But she resisted, turning to leave before the temptation overtook her. She found Andy blocking her way, looking at her with the strangest expression on his face.

'Well, let me come past.' She was out on the extreme point of the highest rock with no space to put her feet to get round him. 'Move!'

Andy backed off slowly and deliberately and, for a single blinding second, she felt sure he was thinking of pushing her over.

It passed.

He smiled.

He gripped her elbow so she couldn't fall and they retreated from the edge together.

'I saw a signpost about a museum in Bickerby Village. We'll go and have a look.'

'It won't be open in winter.'

'It might.'

Jenny was shaking with fear. Her mouth dry. Her knees weak. Would he have done it? Would he have really pushed her over? She glanced at him and he caught her eye and smiled, but it didn't quite reach his eyes, and smiles to be real had to reach your eyes. She avoided speaking in case he picked up on the tremor in her voice. Oh, God, had it come to this?

Because of Andy spilling so much milk they'd none for breakfast the next day, so Jenny dashed across to the Store to get some before she began to make the breakfast. It always opened by half past seven and she was turning the corner into Stocks Row by seven thirty-one.

When the front of the Store came into view Jenny stopped, riven to the spot with horror. It appeared as though a bomb had dropped during the night. Both the windows and the glass in the door had been smashed, leaving vast, gaping holes. Someone had viciously bashed the window time after time. Jimbo was there with Harriet, Grandmama and the police, and, as Jenny walked toward them, a window repair company van roared up and parked with a shriek of brakes. More people were rushing out of their houses to find out what had happened.

'Surely to goodness!'

'Has the village gone mad?'

'Who could have done it?'

'But why, that's what I want to know?'

Harriet brought out Jimbo's crutches, as he'd hobbled out without them, and a chair for him to sit on. As she put down the chair she shouted, 'I said sit down. Now. You'll do untold damage otherwise.'

'Harriet! Who's telling us what?'

'I don't know, darling, but take it calmly. It's only bits of glass and no one's been hurt. That's the important thing.'

'I'll kill whoever it is.' Jimbo was beside himself with anger. 'I will. They're evil, that's what. I didn't know someone hated us this much.'

The glass people and the police began to confer, while the crowd of people in various stages of dress and undress grew bigger. The police examined the scene of the crime and found nothing in the way of a weapon. 'It must have been something like a crow bar or a rounders bat they used. Not bricks thrown at the windows because they'd be inside,' they decided.

The police scratched their heads, walked about vaguely looking for clues, asked if anyone had heard the noise. Several voices piped up.

'I heard something about four when I got up for a . . . went to the bathroom, like crashing noises, but I was so tired it never really registered.'

'So did I,' said someone else, 'but I thought it was the dustbin men doing their round extra early. You know what they're like, they come earlier and earlier. No idea it was this.'

There were murmurs of sympathy all round.

'All your wonderful display in ruins, Jimbo. I am so sorry.' This was Linda Crimble, no longer persona non grata as she had been for so long. 'Wish I'd seen 'em.'

'You live nearest, Linda. Didn't you hear anything?'

'No, I didn't. Slept like a log last night, I did. Fancy all that going on and we're all asleep. Didn't hear no alarm go off either.'

'Damn and blast! Damn and blast!' Jimbo could have wept at the destruction. 'The blasted alarm wasn't on. Well, now, if you police have finished and can't find any clues, could this glass company get a chance to put things right? Please?'

The police agreed. Made notes. Questioned anyone and everyone who looked likely to know something and left the glass people to proceed.

Naturally they hadn't the right-sized glass on the van, as the shop window needed thick safety glass, and it would take two hours to get hold of some. Would Mr Charter-Plackett please leave someone to guard the shop while they went away to get it? And he'd need someone to clear the glass before they began.

'Don't you do that?' asked Jimbo, his temper starting to flare again.

'We break out the glass left in the frame but not loose glass lying about.'

Jimbo raised his arms in despair. 'Well, thanks very much. Very thoughtful, I must say. You can see I'm incapacitated, how the hell do you expect me—'

Tom interrupted, 'Don't fret, keep calm, I'll see to it. I'll use my gardening gloves to handle the glass.'

Willie, who'd come to pick up his morning paper as he always did at this time, volunteered to help Tom and so did Jimmy.

'Thanks. Thank you very much. Right. Harriet, you get inside and watch where you walk and serve anyone who's here right now and wanting to shop, as best you can. Linda, get some card out of my office and write a notice saying we're closed.'

Jenny was grateful. She didn't want to incur Andy's wrath by going home without the milk; he always loved his first cup of tea. She'd slept on the sofa last night, fearing to sleep in the same bed as him. He wouldn't have noticed because he usually slept soundly anyway.

Jenny tiptoed into the Store, avoiding the glass, bought the milk and scurried home as fast as she could. He was still asleep, thank goodness. But she'd have to wake him as he'd said he'd be in work early that morning, to have a scout round and see what the others were up to. A clever way to keep ahead of the game, he said.

Of course, thought Jenny, I could always blow the gaffe on him and inform Social Services that his references were forged. That at least was a weapon she possessed. But not much else. No, not much else. What a mess she was in.

Not nearly in as much of a mess as Jimbo felt himself to be. He didn't dare try to get inside into his office for fear he might fall negotiating the debris, so he sat outside on the chair Harriet had found for him and repeated, what felt like hundreds of times, to customers that they couldn't be served until the mess was well and truly cleared up.

He moaned to Harriet, 'Just wish I damn well knew who'd done it. I'd wring their necks.'

'Don't do that, Jimbo, for heaven's sake. What would happen to your empire if you had to go to prison? No. That's not a good idea at all.'

'Suppose not, but it's tempting. If you suspect anyone let me know.'

Harriet finally insisted he went home for lunch. 'I'm

coming with you. We've nearly done inside. We'll open after lunch.' She could see the strain in Jimbo's face. His normally healthy complexion was drained and a frown was etched, forever it seemed, on his forehead.

Grandmama had helped for as long as she could but had had to go home, too exhausted to continue. She greeted them at the front door.

'Good! You've come home and about time. I've made lunch and tidied the kitchen so all you have to do is sit down and relax. Just sorry I couldn't stay longer to help. Jimbo, sit down. As of now. Just do as I say.'

She stood behind his chair and, when he'd seated himself, she said, 'We'll survive this, don't you fret, we will. I've never been so angry. The nasty, evil beggars who've done this to you, I could strangle them with my bare hands.'

Jimbo patted her hand where it lay on his shoulder. 'So could I, Mother, so could I. Thanks for lunch. Wonderful. I'm starving.'

Harriet joined them at the table, deeply grateful for her mother-in-law's common sense. 'I'm so desperate for this.' She took a large bite of her sandwich, chewed for a while and then said, 'Has that creep Andy been in recently with one of his famous "I'm returning this, it's gone off" performances?'

'No. Why? Do you suspect him?'

Harriet shook her head. 'No more than anyone else. Just wondered, that's all.'

Grandmama looked piercingly at Jimbo and asked, 'How many times has he done that?'

'Twice when I happened to be in and once when it was Tom and Bel. They followed company policy and of course offered him his money back and fresh food in exchange. But he's been badmouthing us frequently.'

'How do you know that?'

'Customers tell me.'

Grandmama eyed him speculatively. 'I wonder why.'

'He's intent on ruining me.'

'Did he write that poison pen letter? Is he the one who's thieving, too?'

Jimbo shrugged. 'How do I know? There's been nothing further on that front.'

Grandmama murmured, 'I was in the Store yesterday and saw Jenny. I was sure she'd a mark on her neck as if she'd been punched.'

Harriet, always on the side of women in jeopardy, asked sharply, 'Did you say anything?'

'Absolutely not. Didn't want to interfere. If she's willing to put up with being a battered wife, more fool her. At least that was something I never had to deal with. Thank God. I'd probably have murdered him in his sleep.'

'She may be in need of help.'

Jimbo interrupted. 'And then again . . .'

'What?'

'Discussing their marital relations doesn't help solve the problem of our windows, does it?' Jimbo looked at them both. They both saw how he'd aged since this broken ankle business and what had happened this morning had made him more haggard than ever. 'Let's change the subject. Christmas soon. More work.'

'More money, too.' Harriet smiled cheerfully at him. 'Shall we have our evening party this year as usual?'

'I don't think so. Got a mite jaded about all this jollity for which Jimbo and Harriet fork out a lot of money and for what in return?'

'Darling! Do cheer up. This won't do at all.'

'Does a party really improve our takings? I don't think so. We fulfil all the requirements of a Village Store and they're all grateful for us. They come because we're the only local shop unless they go all the way to the other side of the bypass or right into Culworth. I had thought that supermarket opening right on the bypass would see the end of us. It hasn't. So, why bother?'

Harriet nodded her head. 'Let's do it differently, then. Mulled wine and mince pies in the Store for whoever comes in on the Saturday before Christmas. How about that?'

Jimbo didn't answer so Grandmama filled the silence by saying heartily, 'Good idea, that. Yes. I think that's splendid.'

Jimbo nodded. 'Agreed. I'm going back to the Store to see what's happening, OK?'

'Shall I drive you there?'

'No. I'll walk. The day I can walk without these damned crutches can't come soon enough for me.'

'Are you sure? I don't mind.'

Jimbo growled, 'I'm sure.' And staggered away, much more proficient with his crutches than he had been, but still finding it an exhausting way of getting about.

'I'll be over when I've cleared up.'

Grandmama interrupted. 'Don't worry about that, Harriet, I'll clear up and I'll be in for Fran coming home so do what you have to do, right? Don't worry. If need be I'll cook the evening meal, that's the least I can do. Just let me know what you want.'

'Thank you, Katherine, you're worth your weight in gold.'

★

That afternoon Andy came in with yet another unsatisfactory purchase he claimed Jenny had made from the Store. Andy opened the packet to show him the problem.

'Glass. Just a sliver but that's all that's needed to kill someone.'

Because of pain brought on by fatigue Jimbo had been finally compelled to sit down on one of his customers' chairs reserved especially for coffee drinkers, and so was looking up at Andy. He got to his feet, not in the best of moods.

'How come you're the only customer of ours who finds anything at all wrong with the food I sell? This is the third time it's happened to my knowledge, and I want to know why.'

'There's no need to throw your toys out of your pram. If the food's not right then I want my money back. I mean, glass! How dangerous can it get?'

With a lightning flash of inspiration Jimbo asked belligerently, 'Question is, is it my food?'

'Well, of course it is. I wouldn't come back here if it wasn't, would I?'

'Well, I'm sorry—'

'Look, Jenny bought it in all good faith, and it's dangerous. Quite definitely. I've got the receipt.' He began fumbling in his pocket.

'I don't want to see it. Stop shopping here. I won't even have Jenny in here. I'm not prepared to put up with this ruse of yours any longer. You're a complete fraud. In fact, you're a thief. I don't know why you're doing it but it's got to stop.'

'No replacement, then?'

Jimbo weighed up the matter in his mind and decided to go for it. 'No. And that's my final answer.'

'Right. You've heard him, have you? All of you? Sells dangerous food and then won't recompense me for it. You'll be lucky to have a Store by this time next week. I'll see it closed down. Health and Safety will have a field day with this little lot.'

'I'm damned if I'll have anything more to do with you. You're a pain in the backside. Is it you breaking the windows and sending me poison pen letters? Is it? Eh? Well?'

Andy scornfully eyed him up and down. 'Give me credit for more sense than that. Of course it isn't me.'

'Just get out and don't darken my door again.' Jimbo flung open the shop door and pointed dramatically to the street. 'Go on! Out! Damn you and good riddance!'

'How dare you humiliate me in front of everyone.'

'You can humiliate me in front of my customers but I can't humiliate you, is that it? Believe me, I'm being *restrained*. Fair's fair. Out! Right now!'

'Your humiliation was justified. Mine isn't. I have right on my side, I have. And good morning to you, Mr Too-big-for-his-boots-Charter-Plackett.'

Andy stormed out of the Store in high dudgeon. He'd chosen a good moment for his complaint because the Store was again full of mothers picking up shopping while waiting for the children to come out of school. All the same, because of the pleasure he took in harming Jimbo's business, he'd almost, almost enjoyed the idea of admitting to the poison pen letters and the broken windows, and had stopped himself only just in time.

A deathly hush fell in the Store. The customers were afraid to speak for they'd never seen Jimbo as angry as this. Tom and Bel simply froze.

Harriet had witnessed the whole of the exchange

between Jimbo and Andy and was horrified at what the incident might do to their business. She just knew that Jimbo had really and truly reached the end of his tether. So it was Harriet who broke the silence by saying in her quietest, most considerate voice, 'Jimbo, I insist you go home. Right now. I'll stay on. You go.'

Tom agreed and so did Bel. 'You've done enough today. Just go home, we're all quite capable of holding the fort.'

So Jimbo did. He had a double whisky and then another and sat down in his thinking chair to contemplate just how much damage Andy could do to his business. If he closed the Store down Andy wouldn't have the chance to ruin it. Why not just do the catering side and damn the rest? He would. That would be easier than all this irritation. Yes, he'd close it. While it did well it still needed the other two sides of the business to make it viable. Without the Store he'd have a lot less aggravation and a lot less work, and fewer outgoings on wages and heating and lighting and money tied up in stock. Closing the shop seemed by far the most sensible thing to do. Hang them all. It was as though a great burden had been lifted from his shoulders. It would be easy to cope with the catering and Harriet's Country Cousin mail order. It would also give him a chance to find the time to set up selling the marmalades and such on the internet, which was something he'd wanted to do for a long time.

Yes, he would. And why not? It wasn't written in stone that Jimbo Charter-Plackett had to keep the Store open, was it now? No. If he wanted to close the Store, who could stop him? No one.

Yes, that is exactly what he'd do. Damn them all. He'd close it. Andy was the final straw. He'd close the Store, and let no one try to persuade him otherwise.

Chapter 10

The next morning Dottie rather imagined she'd been let off talking to Beth because she was nowhere to be seen. But just as Dottie had had a word with Caroline and was collecting her cleaning things Beth appeared in the kitchen.

There was something of an improvement in her looks, as though she were finally thinking of digging herself out of that big black hole she'd been in for so long.

'Good morning, Dottie. Hello, Mummy. Have a cup of tea with me, Dottie?'

Caroline switched the kettle on. 'It won't be a moment.'

'Yes, I will.' Dottie dumped her cleaning things in the hall and sat herself down at the kitchen table. 'Nice morning. Good to be out.'

Beth ignored that remark. 'You've heard, Dottie?'

'What about?'

'Jimbo's closing the Store. Isn't it awful?'

Dottie couldn't believe her ears. 'Jimbo's closing the Store? Closing it, as in for ever?'

'Yes, hadn't you heard?'

'First I know about it. I went to visit a friend of mine over the other side of Culworth yesterday and didn't get back till late. I'd no idea. I knew about his broken windows because I saw those when the bus stopped outside. That must have been the last straw.'

'Well, apparently he put a notice on the door yesterday afternoon. He's closing at the end of January.'

'No! But how shall we manage without him?'

'Unless he sells it to someone, everyone'll have to shop in Culworth.'

'That's a bind for people like me what have no car.'

'Exactly. Harriet told Mummy last night on the phone that the first she knew was Jimbo sticking the notice up on the door. She said it was a terrible shock.'

'I should say. His shop makes Turnham Malpas important, you know, because they all come here to shop from Little Derehams and Penny Fawcett and all places between. Well, that's a blow and not half.'

'It is. But we've been lucky all these years having his shop, haven't we? There's not many villages with a shop as good as his.'

'You're right there. But it must be hard work. Keeping it open over Christmas though, the crafty beggar.'

Beth smiled. 'Maybe Harriet will change his mind for him.'

'Maybe, though she's never been involved in the shop very much, has she? More into the cooking and that, is Harriet. Come to think of it, we're lucky to have her, aren't we? Them cakes and puddings she makes for the freezer and that. And those gateaux she cuts into single slices so you can buy just one slice for yer tea. I treat myself sometimes and get a slice. Delicious, they are.'

The two of them discussed which of Harriet's cakes they liked the best, and fell to dreaming about them. Beth was on her second cup of tea when Dottie realized the time and leapt to her feet. 'My God! Oh! sorry! Anna will be here soon and I haven't lifted a finger.'

Beth sat where she was, thinking. A slice of one of Harriet's cakes for tea would be lovely. She had all her spending money saved up so she could easily buy one each for her and Mummy. In fact, it would be nice if she bought a slice for Dottie, too. Could she dare do that? She propped her elbows on the table and rested her chin on her hands and thought about leaving the house, walking round the Green, opening the door and hearing that dear little bell jingling as she walked in. Like old times. Yes, just like old times. Could she, though? Could she really walk all that way by herself, absolutely alone? It would be fun to give Mummy a surprise. It would be lovely to talk to Jimbo.

Better still, it would be nice to give Dottie a surprise. She'd been so kind talking to her like she did. She was so easy to talk to. Dottie was Dottie, full stop. No airs and graces, just, straight-from-the-shoulder talk. No one else had asked her in plain terms what had happened. Plenty of talk about how she felt, would she be able to go out soon? Did she need someone qualified to talk to? Anything and everything but the vital question. Beth shuddered.

Even her mother, who loved her so, couldn't bear, didn't dare, face up to the fact that she might have been raped. But Dottie could and did, and it had helped enormously to say no, she hadn't.

This would be the test of tests, and all she had to do to prove it was to open the door. Beth swallowed hard. Open the door, walk round the Green, a thing she'd done a thousand times before Africa, and walk into the shop. Buy three slices of cake – no, four slices of cake because Alex would be back for tea and she couldn't leave him out. She dwelt for a moment on Alex and the true value of having a brave brother, and decided he deserved a whole cake not just one slice. But that would not be right. Such overt gratitude might open a whole can of worms by making people suspicious and that would never do. Beth didn't even stop to clear the table or clean her teeth. She got her purse out, checked her appearance in the hall mirror and left. If she stopped to tell anyone where she was going she'd never make it.

It felt strange out there in the open air. Each step felt like a mile but she kept concentrating on putting one foot in front of the other, steadily, rhythmically, working hard, controlling every movement.

Grandmama Charter-Plackett was outside her house, supervising the window-cleaner, and asked her how she was. 'No school yet?'

Beth almost turned and ran all the way home. 'No, not yet.'

'Nice to see you out, though.'

Beth hurried along down Stocks Row to the Store. She stood admiring Jimbo's initial Christmas display. He always did two; one on 1 December and the other on the last Saturday before Christmas. The first was entirely commercial and the second was a Nativity scene, which never failed to be more beautiful than any that had gone before. Then Beth read the notice, stuck up on the door the previous day. 'With regret,' it began. Nothing but the longing for a slice of Harriet's gateau could possibly have got her here. Well, now she was here, so she'd better go in.

Beth pushed open the door and headed straight for the desserts freezer, determined to make her purchase and leave as quickly as possible before she met anyone. But not a single cake had been sliced, they were all whole. Now what? Jimbo miraculously appeared beside her.

'Can I help?' he asked softly. He was propped on his crutches, smiling, not asking challenging questions like Grandmama had, just standing there being normal, but extra, extra kind.

'I want four slices of gateau, please. The chocolate fudge one.'

'Right. Your wish is my command.'

Beth froze. She should never have come, her courage had all but drained away. She was about to run when Jimbo laid a hand on her arm and whispered, 'Don't go without your cake. Hold tight to the freezer and *don't let go.*'

So she did. If he offered to give her the slices of cake she wouldn't let him. She had to pay for them herself, or the whole thing would be a waste of time.

Someone, she didn't know who, sliced the cake, wrapped each piece separately, put them in one of Jimbo's fancy boxes and handed it to her. She held it by its fancy ribbon and went to the till. It took all her courage to say, 'Four slices of chocolate fudge gateau', hand out the money, accept the change and get herself out of the Store.

Out on the pavement was Jimbo, waiting for her.

He raised his boater to her and said, 'Good day to you, Beth. You're my best customer of the day.'

'Don't close the Store, Jimbo. Please.' She gave him a small smile and scurried away, scared she might not find her way back home so confused was she in her mind.

She let herself in and stood listening in the hall. She could hear Anna on the computer in her dad's study. Dottie upstairs vacuuming. Mum? Where was she?

Beth put the gateau into the fridge for safekeeping, then

141

went to look for her mother. She was on the phone in the sitting room discussing a locum position at one of the local medical practices. So . . . she was thinking of going back to medicine. Beth's world crashed about her. She fled for her bed and hid under the duvet forever.

When she'd finished on the phone Caroline went to find her.

'Darling? There you are. I thought I heard the front door closing. Have you been out?' But there was no response. Caroline tried cajoling, being forceful, persuasive, understanding, curious. But to no avail. So she decided abandonment might bring a response and left saying, 'Well, when you're ready, come down. I'm not going out.'

There was not a sound in Beth's bedroom for the rest of the day. Caroline crept upstairs twice to see if she was still under the duvet and she was. Out of her mind with anxiety, Caroline spent an absolutely useless day, never quite achieving anything of any value except an e-mail to Peter. Not wanting to worry him, she didn't mention that Beth had apparently resigned from life. If only she could share her anxieties with him. She finished by telling Peter about pieces of news in Turnham Malpas and how much she missed him:

> . . . *Darling, I count the days awaiting your return. It feels so lonely without you, but not nearly so lonely as you must feel for you haven't even got the children to comfort you as I have. They send their love and we remember you daily in our prayers. Don't delay in July. Quite simply, come home where you're wanted so very much.*
>
> *Yours,*
> *Caroline*

No sooner had she sent it than one came from Peter. It arrived so quickly after she'd sent hers, that it obviously wasn't a reply. His read:

To my three dearest people on earth,
I am sitting out in my garden. Well, what passes for a garden; it has been so dry lately the crops will be failing again if we don't get rain soon. The Commander, Michael Amouti, has found the money for the school and it is being built as I speak. I shall use some of the money the village raised to equip it. I can't think of a better use for it, can you? Michael is being his pleasant self, coming to keep me company and helping in any way he can. However, I feel uneasy, quite why I don't know, but I do. Nothing, I expect really, just me missing the advice of my common sense wife.

Elijah has just come in, with devastating news. Michael has been found dead in a local rubbish tip. Elijah declares it is because of what he allowed to happen when the uprising was on. I pray to God there is no revenge for his death.

I do hope the children are recovering well. I think of you all every day, and wish I was with you, but for the moment I am bent on succeeding here. Then I can, with no conscience whatever, come home and stay there. I fancy fishing with Alex, swimming with Beth and a pleasant evening reading and talking with my very dear wife.

Elijah and Winsome send their love. So do I. Much love, in fact, all my love to the three of you.
Peter

Just as she finished reading Caroline heard Alex's key in the door, and quickly erased Peter's e-mail so he wouldn't be able to read it.

'Darling! Good day? The usual?'

'Yes, please.' He sat down at the kitchen table and asked, 'Where's Beth?'

'In bed.'

'I'll go see her.'

'She may not speak.'

Alex looked at Caroline. Caroline looked at Alex and thought, he looked more like his father every day. There was Peter's kind of strength about him, and his compassion, too. He'd become a grown-up in Africa.

'Why not?'

'I don't know.' She went to get the milk out of the fridge and Alex went up the stairs two at a time.

'Beth, what's up?' He jiggled her foot to get her attention.

'Alex?'

'Yes.'

The rising hysteria in her voice alarmed him. 'Alex, I heard Mummy on the phone organizing going back to general practice. I can't bear it. I'll have to go to school. She won't do it, will she?'

'Come out from under the duvet. I can't tell what you're saying.'

Beth slowly emerged, hot and tousled.

'Sit up and shape up. It's me, you can talk to me.'

Beth, as she'd always done, did as he said and told him again.

Alex smiled sympathetically. 'Look, I'm sure Mum wouldn't go back to general practice knowing it would mean you going back to school when you don't want to. I'm going downstairs to ask her, right now.'

Beth shot under the duvet again and Alex went to ask Caroline.

'Mum. Beth's frightened to death she'll have to go back to school. She's got the idea you're returning to general practice. Are you?'

'No, I am not. She must have overheard me on the phone. They rang up to see if I could go back because they've a maternity leave problem but if she'd listened a while longer she'd have found out I refused. Go and tell her.'

'You mustn't, you know, Mum. She must *not* and I mean *not* be left alone. She needs you.'

'Does she? Then why won't she tell me what troubles her? I've tried one way and another and keep hoping, but she won't breathe a word to me. The days go by and she makes no progress at all. Come to think of it, neither of you will tell me what has made you so afraid. Can *you* not tell me?'

Alex didn't reply.

'If your father were here you'd tell him, I bet. Is it because I'm not your natural mother? Is that it? I feel as though I am, and always have done.'

Alex stood in the doorway, unable to find words to express why they couldn't tell Caroline what had happened. 'It's not that. We just can't, that's all.' He turned on his heel and went upstairs.

Alex relayed Caroline's message to Beth and immediately she cheered up. She took in a deep breath and said, 'That's a relief. I need more time. I'm not brave like you.'

'I'm not brave. I just pretend to be, I'm terribly afraid, so I keep plugging away doing normal things, hoping it will all go away, but it doesn't. But we'd no alternative, had we?'

Beth shook her head. 'None. I still shudder when I—'

Alex urgently said, 'Don't. Don't think about it. Push it to the back of your mind. Dad'll be home before we know it, then we can tell *him*. We've just got to make things as normal as we can till he's back.'

Beth put her arms round Alex's neck and hugged him to her. 'He'll have the answers. I might make a target of getting back to school in the New Year. I've been to the Store and bought us some of Harriet's gateau. Tell Mum it's in the fridge. I'll be down in a minute. We can have it now instead of toast.'

Alex was amazed. 'You've been *out*?'

Beth nodded. 'I was frightened to death and nearly didn't make it, but I did.'

'That's good. I'm glad. Once you do it, it's not too bad. I'm all right at school, and going on the school bus is fine. I couldn't go on public transport, though. I still don't do games and I've explained why – all that open space; I just can't cope – and they say, "Fine, when you're ready." You'd be OK if you tried it. On the school bus. We could sit together.'

Beth flung back the duvet and put her feet on the floor. 'I'm coming down. But I'm not going to school. Not yet.'

So the three of them sat round the kitchen table and ate their gateau, got chocolate moustaches and chocolatey fingers, and licked them and laughed. Caroline began to feel hopeful and didn't say a word of praise to Beth for going to the Store all on her own. She thought accepting it as perfectly normal was by far the best thing to do. She felt enormously cheered.

★

Jimbo found that Beth getting as far as the Store was the only thing that lifted his spirits that day. But the regret that everyone expressed about the store closing down almost persuaded him he shouldn't close it. Harriet, of course, and his mother were stupefied by his decision.

'Look, Jimbo, we're having a bad run – your ankle, the windows and the poison pen letters all sent to try us – but we'll get over it like we've done before. Remember when Fran was born and Flick had her accident? We didn't know which way to turn, and our world appeared to fall in on top of us, but we survived. Didn't we?'

'I agree. But nothing you say can change my mind. Health and Safety are coming tomorrow, they rang to say. So that beggar has informed them like he said he would. I could kill him.'

'You're in no fit state to kill anyone so you can pipe down. At least if we're closing it might take the ground from under their feet, whoever it is. Might make them pack it up, eh?' She grabbed him by his shoulders and gave him a shake. 'Love you!'

Jimbo kissed her. 'Thank you for getting on so well with my mother.'

'She's a brick. She's needed, that's why she's easier to get on with. You're to have tomorrow off, right? Your mother and I have planned it. You can do as you like . . . so long as it's nothing.'

'Can't. Health and Safety day.'

'Let's put it this way: if I get an emergency with him I'll send for you. OK?'

Jimbo had to confess to himself that he could manage a day doing nothing very nicely indeed. He'd take the chance while he could. Then an appalling feeling of guilt overwhelmed him. This wasn't the Jimbo of old. What had happened to him? Old age? Surely not.

Jimbo might have thought things couldn't get worse but the following morning Tom was on the phone by a quarter past seven. 'Jimbo, Tom here. Sorry to be ringing so early, but . . . well, I might as well tell you straight off. You've to be told, I have to say it. Someone's thrown bright red paint all over the front of the Store. Both windows and the door, most on the glass, some on the brickwork.'

There was prolonged silence from Jimbo's end of the phone. Then eventually Jimbo said, 'I'll be there. Don't let anyone tread it into the Store, right?' Wryly he added, 'I don't suppose they left an address?'

'No.'

'Thought not.' He put the receiver down and gave Harriet a gentle shake. 'Darling, I've got to go.'

'Where to?'

'To the Store. Don't get upset.'

'There must be something wrong or you wouldn't say that.'

'Tom's rung to say someone's thrown red paint all over the shop front.'

Harriet flung herself back onto her pillows. 'I can't believe this. Right, I'm coming with you.' She flung the duvet off and put her feet on the floor, then paused. 'Oh, God, I feel terrible.'

'You've got up too quickly. I'll have a quick wash and then I'm off. Shan't shave. Bring some old cloths with you, when you come, I'm taking my spare petrol can, there's a couple of gallons in there which should do the trick.' He said all this while hurriedly throwing on the clothes he'd taken off the night before.

Harriet made a move to get up – she felt so desperately sorry for him. 'Don't let anyone light a cigarette. I won't be long.'

When Harriet arrived with a heap of cloths, she was appalled at what she saw. The venom which had initiated this wild attack was too frightening even to contemplate.

Jimbo was pouring petrol into a bucket so he and Tom could soak the cloths in it. 'Good. Lots of cloths. That's the spirit.'

'You need rubber gloves. I'll get some.'

'Mind where you walk!'

She stepped as carefully as she could between the streams of red paint trickling along the pavement and under the seat out at the front. Tears were very close to the surface. She'd promised Jimbo a day doing nothing – what a hope.

Harriet rang the police before Tom and Jimbo started cleaning the front. They promised to come immediately. When they came they went through the usual questioning procedure and finished by saying, 'Mrs Charter-Plackett, is there anyone you can think of who has a grudge against you?'

'The only person we know is someone called Andy Moorhouse. He lives next door to the Rectory. He's been bringing food back he claims he's bought from us and asking for a refund because he says it's gone off. Last time Jimbo refused to refund him the money and told him not to shop here again. He's the only one we know who might have a grudge.'

'It wasn't genuine, then?'

'Absolutely not. We're extremely conscientious about selling fresh food. Ask the Health and Safety – they know how careful we are.'

'Next to the Rectory? Right. We'll go knock him up.'

'Mr Andy Moorhouse?'

Andy was still in his pyjamas, unwashed and unshaven, and therefore did not make much of an impression on a hardened officer of twenty years' experience. He was edgy was Mr Andy Moorhouse. Very edgy.

'That's me.'

'We're making house-to-house inquiries about the paint that's been thrown all over the front of the Village Store. I wondered if you'd heard anything during the night. Sounds of a vehicle pulling up, someone talking, movements or anything at all that will help us with our inquiries.'

'Is that all? I thought at least we must be at war. Coming knocking on our door at this time in the morning. It's not a national emergency. Come back later when I've had time to shower and dress. Honestly. This is harassment.' He slammed the door in his face.

The police officer made a mark in his notebook, and rang the doorbell again.

This time Andy flung open the door and came out fighting. 'What is it this time?'

'Same thing. Look, you can see for yourself.' He pointed across the Green towards the Store and noticed that Andy didn't trouble to look.

'All right, all right. Why you should imagine I have anything at all to do with throwing paint all over the shop I have no idea. I'm a law-abiding social worker.'

'In Culworth?'

'Yes.'

The officer made another note in his little black book. 'Telephone number so I can verify that?'

'In the phonebook, if you must, though why you can't take my word for it, I don't know.' Andy began bristling with temper, although he knew doing so would not give the best of impressions to a police officer who obviously wasn't wet behind the ears. 'Now, have you finished harassing me?'

'No.' He studied his notebook a while longer. 'Do you have a grudge against Mr Charter-Plackett?'

'I've no grudge against anyone. Everyone's very pleasant here, there's never any trouble.'

'A grudge about your claim that his food is not sold in accordance with best practice.'

'Me? No.' Andy caught a determined glint in the police officer's eye. 'Well, I have caught him out a time or two but we settled it like gentlemen should.' Andy gave a happy laugh, but it sounded very hollow to the officer.

'But he refused to recompense you last time. Mr Charter-Plackett was convinced it was all a set-up, and refused to allow you to shop in there any more. In my book I'd have been very angry, especially if my complaints were genuine.'

'They were genuine, but in my job you get used to setbacks, can't let them affect you.' Andy smiled and shrugged. 'What of it? I'm in Culworth every day, no hassle. He's the loser. In any case, with him closing we'll have no alternative soon.'

The black notebook was closed. 'Very true, sir. So, you can't help us at all? There might be something that strikes you, though. Any little thing, no matter how insignificant, let us know.'

'Certainly. I've nothing to hide.' He smiled brightly. 'Only too glad to help.'

The police officer went away unconvinced. He was too

taut, too tense, too shifty was that Andy. The officer had a quick look in Andy's bin, but could find nothing incriminating. He'd be back though. There was a heap more that man didn't want him to know. A whole heap more, he could feel it in his bones.

Andy went back inside, closed the door behind him and stood for a moment resting his back against it. Stupid man! Imagining he would do something as ridiculous as throwing paint. He was a sight more subtle than that. A sly grin spread over his face. Well, that was what he tried to make people think, but the satisfaction he'd got from first breaking the windows, and then, when newly replaced, covering them with that red paint he'd found in the old shed at the bottom of their garden had given him more satisfaction than he would ever have dreamed possible. The letters, though, had satisfied something very deep inside. It was the silence of them but at the same time the wounding, frightening aspect which pleased him. And still no one knew it was him.

All the same he now had two areas of his life to watch out for: the dodgy references for his job and the fact he was hardly ever in the office. Shortly he'd be losing track of what was going on; the longer he stayed at Social Service the more lies he had to remember to keep up the pretence of working hard. In addition to all that, he knew the police officer had left dissatisfied with his explanations. In case they came back while he was out he'd prime Jenny what to say. Out of the blue he'd become disenchanted with her.

To pacify Jenny, Andy'd gone through the marriage ceremony eighteen months ago well aware he was married already to someone else under a different name, about which she knew nothing. So he could leave her at any time, whenever it suited him. He'd paid for the house with his mother's money so Jenny could be turfed out into the street whenever he decided. But at the moment he needed to keep her on side.

Chapter 11

Jimbo was almost beginning to believe it would be easier to keep the Store open than close it, because everyone who came in wanted to spend time giving him a thousand reasons why he couldn't close. His Store was a village tradition, they all loved it, it was a focus for the other two villages and gave Turnham Malpas prestige because of it, and what's more, what would he do not hearing the gossip every day? They all knew he loved it.

Not only that, but when he was at home he had Harriet and his mother giving him a hundred and one reasons why he couldn't close it. But he would do it. He was sick and tired of the crushing burden of keeping up with the stock, checking it, getting it out on the shelves and making sure he wasn't cutting his margins by letting too much disappear off the shelves without being paid for. He'd had to sack two new assistants for stealing in the last two months, let alone the customers sneaking things into their bags. No, he was adamant the Store was closing at the end of January.

The red paint all over the front was the very last straw, and only confirmed his decision. He'd clear out the shop, convert half of it back into a house and sell it, and keep the other half for his catering and the mail order office. Fortunes were made daily on the internet and why shouldn't he with his Harriet's Country Cousin products? On the other hand he might need the whole building if the mail orders took off. He'd think hard about that.

In his softer moments it was Beth's quiet plea each time she managed to force herself to walk into the Store to buy slices of gateau, which weakened his determination.

'Don't close the Store, Jimbo. Please.' Her voice, so gentle and so pleading, broke his heart. He could feel the vast sadness deep inside her and grieved that she had suffered so. Damn Africa. Why the hell had Peter felt the need to go there?

And why had he felt the need to return and leave Caroline with his two children in the Rectory in such a dilemma, because apparently not only Beth was suffering but Alex too, in his own closed-up silent manner. The repercussions of Peter's actions were like ripples on a pond. His own mother had had to vacate her house to make room for the Reverend Anna because neither of them had imagined for one moment that he would go back again and she'd need to stay on till next July. Nothing but nothing appeared to go right in the village ever since he left. They all of them needed him back. Sounded ridiculous to say they needed him, after all, they were all grown men and women. But somehow they did.

And this business with Andy Moorhouse; he was convinced it was him who'd broken the windows, then thrown paint on them immediately after they'd been repaired, and sent the poison pen letters. Why the hell did he keep having this feeling that he knew Andy from years earlier? Something kept nagging at him, but what? And why did Andy seem to think he had a hold over him?

He shot to his feet far too quickly when the answer came to him. His ankle, still in plaster and hurting like the devil sometimes, pained him dreadfully, and he plunged back down on his chair immediately. He knew exactly who Andy was. Of course. A servant at college. One of those who put his hand to anything. He'd pop up serving meals in hall, cleaning public rooms, working in the kitchens and, on occasion, in the porters' lodge. And he'd been the one who'd ... That was it. His evidence had almost finished the Cambridge career of James Charter-Plackett. If anyone should have a grievance it should be himself.

He was overcome with the need to put Harriet in the picture. But should he? Perhaps he shouldn't, though they'd always promised to be truthful to each other. Well, he'd think about it over the next few days. What was that in comparison with almost twenty-five years of marriage?

The need to march about while the whole matter fizzed and bubbled in his mind overcame him and he got carefully to his feet, grabbed his crutches and walked through the house, fingering for some reason things which belonged to Harriet; he found special comfort touching a quilt she was stitching for their bed. It was a mammoth task for her and by far the most ambitious thing she'd attempted since Evie Nicholls had fired her enthusiasm for the craft. She'd chosen warm rusts, soft greens, pale creams, colours which to Jimbo felt to be exactly right for Harriet; they were her colours. Harriet was a star where wives were concerned, a complete and absolute star. If it hadn't been for her he'd never have taken the plunge and left that soul-destroying job in the City. Money by the barrowload, but satisfaction for the soul? No. She'd saved his sanity.

He'd walked about for far too long. So Jimbo sat down

again to contemplate his life a while longer. His mother found him seated in his thinking chair.

'Jimbo, my dear, you're very distressed, aren't you?'

He looked up, briefly puzzled by her sudden appearance. Of course, she was living here.

She laid a comforting hand on his shoulder. 'What is it, my dear? Can I help?'

'I've realized who Andy Moorhouse is. Except that wasn't his name when I knew him.'

'Tell the police! Immediately.'

'No, I've got to think a while longer. Mother, am I doing right by closing the Store?'

'If that's where your instincts take you, then go for it. But maybe ordering stock and filling shelves and window-dressing and the daily grind is something you could get a lesser mortal do for you and then you'd have room for the more important things and time for some leisure, which you are very short of. Harriet deserves far more holiday than she gets, so does Fran and so do you. Think about it.'

She returned minutes later with a double whisky for him. 'Here, drink this. Help the thought processes.'

But within the hour he was ringing the police; his mother had discovered another poison pen letter silently slipped under the back door by someone who was obviously becoming increasingly bold. Closing the Store might be the very best thing to do after all.

The police went immediately to Andy Moorhouse's but he wasn't in. Jenny was, though, and had to face detailed questioning. She knew the answers because Andy had primed her but her heart wasn't in it, so her responses didn't ring absolutely true. She declared he hadn't been up in the night. In reality she didn't know because her fear of him made her sleep in their second bedroom.

'I'm a light sleeper, you see, so I would have known if he had.'

'Why has he chosen to persecute Mr Charter-Plackett?'

'He hasn't. I've said. He's no interest in him. Why should he have?'

'Where did the cheese and the ham come from for that scam of getting your money back? It wasn't bought at his shop, was it?'

'I've no idea. It must have been if he said so.'

'He always speaks the truth, then?'

'Of course.'

'Rare bird then, is Mr Moorhouse, always speaking the truth.'

'Some people are like that.'

'Indeed.' The officer left a long silence and kept on steadily staring at her; she felt as though he were staring into her very soul. Jenny began to sweat. Maybe now was the moment to tell him what she knew. But he destroyed her opportunity by saying, 'Well, then, we'd better come back to see Mr Moorhouse himself. When is he usually back home from his office?'

Jenny's moment passed. 'Six o'clock.'

'Right. Be seeing you then. If there's anything that occurs to you, Mrs Sweetapple, let us know. Here's my number.' He paused as though giving her a second chance. 'Anything at all. Good afternoon, see you later.'

Jenny was so tense the card he'd given her was crushed even before the door closed on him. She rushed for a glass of water the moment he left. Her tongue was sticking to the roof of her mouth. She gulped the water down rapidly and then burped furiously. Oh, God. She couldn't tell the truth unless she knew they'd take him into custody immediately. She couldn't be left with him in the house after she'd spilled the beans. He'd kill her.

Half an hour after the police officer left she heard Andy's key in the door. Immediately she made up her mind she wouldn't tell him the police had called again.

'Jenny! The police are sitting in their car outside the Store. What's happened?'

'Still investigating the red paint, I expect.'

'Oh, yes, I suppose. They haven't been here, have they? Today?'

'I've been in all day.'

'Right.' A grin of satisfaction spread across his face. 'Good.'

He settled himself by the fire, opened the evening paper and asked for a cup of tea.

'Can't, got a client. Here any minute. Get your own, please.'

Andy began to boil with temper. Slowly, insidiously, it overcame him, he rose to his feet and said belligerently, 'Now. Please.'

'Sorry, there's the bell.'

A woman from Penny Fawcett was standing there on the step. Head and shoulders massage to combat stress.

She slid swiftly into her consulting room and shut the door firmly. 'There we are, wrapped in our own little world.'

When Jenny finally emerged from her cocoon, and saw her client out, Andy reached out for the cash she'd been paid. 'Thirty-five pounds, thank you.'

'No! This is my business money. I need to balance the books.'

'Give it to me. From now on I'm in charge of the money. *You* can't bookkeep.'

'Who says?'

'Me.'

'The business money is all mine, that's our agreement. Every single penny. Just let go of my hand, please.'

But he held it tighter and tighter.

'Let go. Please. We agreed.'

'I'm not having you with your own bank account any more. You throw money away like water. Best if I keep it.'

'No. This is mine. I need it for paying for stuff.'

'Stuff? What kind of stuff?'

'Creams and massage stuff, aromatherapy oils, towels, stock to sell, advertising. This is ridiculous. Let go and I'll give you the massage of massages tonight. How about that, eh?' She made her voice tantalizing and wheedling.

Andy gave way. 'I'll keep you to that. Tonight. Right. But after this the money is to be kept by me. I'll pay the bills for you but the bulk of it will be kept in *my* account where *I* can keep an eye on it.' He gave her a glutinous smile, which made her skin crawl. Why did she feel like this? Not long ago she loved him like heck, thought him clever and fun, good to be with – in fact, she was proud to be with him – but slowly his real character had emerged and she wasn't very enamoured by it.

The parts of his life she knew weren't true, like his total lack of qualifications to be a social worker and his disinclination to work honestly in such an important job, weren't pleasant attributes at all. How much more of their life together wasn't entirely true? Was the house his or had he falsified that, too? After all, he hadn't allowed her to be part-owner. All the paperwork was done out of her sight and she'd been presented with a fait accompli.

Now this, wanting to get his hands on money which was rightly hers for her business. Worse still, did she really know the truth about this feud he had with Jimbo Charter-Plackett? She thought not. If it was him who'd done what had been done, where did that leave her? She guessed she was right, that it was him, but this deep-seated fear of him that had developed made her unable to stand tall and tell the police.

The doorbell rang furiously. 'If it's for me, I'm not in. Got to see Caroline about a Beauty Evening for the Women's Institute. I'm out the back door.' She grabbed her bag and left him to answer the clamouring bell.

Fortunately for her Caroline was in and they settled down to an involved talk over the best subjects for the proposed Beauty Evening. Thank heavens, thought Jenny, a glass of wine. They'd arrived at the conclusion that a facial, some Indian head massage, and make-up hints would be the best subjects to build the evening around. But she and Caroline were still debating if they had got the programme sufficiently interesting and had just refilled their glasses to keep the ideas flowing when Beth walked in. She was carrying a glass of apple juice and asked if she could join them.

Jenny patted the sofa cushion next to her. 'Sit here. I say, would you be a model for me?'

'A model? For what?'

'A young teenage daughter going to a party and me using you to teach mother how best to advise her and make her up. You've a lovely clear skin and stunning eyes.

Wouldn't make you look tarty; that wouldn't be right, would it? What do you say?'

'Where would it be?'

'In the small village hall, for the Women's Institute Beauty Evening.'

'When is it?'

'Monday next week, at seven for seven-thirty. The Women's Institute isn't a load of old grandma's, is it Caroline?'

'No, but I don't think it's really Beth's cup of tea, is it, darling? I think perhaps she isn't quite ready for that kind of thing.'

Beth protested. 'No, it isn't my kind of thing, not really, but—'

Desperate to reassure her Caroline said very positively, 'Don't fret, Beth, that's absolutely OK.'

Jenny thought differently. 'Look, ten minutes and it's all over and you go home looking dazzling. Go on, give it a try. Please?' Jenny's beautiful smile, which had captivated Jimbo and Muriel, won the day.

'I will. But on the night I might—'

'Don't you worry about nerves, I'll see you're OK. Believe me.' Jenny leapt to her feet and embraced Beth. 'I'm so glad you'll do it. So glad. You won't need to speak, not a word. Dottie has volunteered very bravely to be the older woman. What fun it's going to be.'

Caroline rather felt things had been taken out of her hands, but at the same time was very grateful for Jenny's positive approach.

'I think we'll do you first, Beth, then the facial, and then move on to the thirty-year-old make-up, then the aromatherapy, then the sixty-year-old make-up, that's Dottie. It's going to be so interesting. Brilliant. The Indian head massage can come last and they can all have a go at that, working on each other.' She clapped her hands together with delight. 'There, I'd better go. I'll have a word at the weekend, Beth, in case you have any questions. Right?'

'Right.' Beth stood up. 'Thanks for the offer.'

'It's a pleasure. Night, Caroline. I'll write out the programme then you'll know what's happening seeing as you're programme secretary.' She left in a swirl of excitement every bit of which left her the moment she exited the Rectory.

She had Andy to face. How angry might he be? The few steps it took her to reach their house gave her no time to settle her nerves. Her heart was fluttering like a butterfly's wings.

Key in door.

Key out.

Close door.

Silence. She slung her key on the hall stand and went to make their evening meal. A glance at the clock told her it was getting late. An omelette, cheese, no ham, green salad and new boiled potatoes would have to do.

She began clattering about in the kitchen and soon had the meal organized. As the new potatoes came up to the boil she heard Andy's footsteps coming down the stairs. Jenny called out brightly, 'Hi! Who was it at the door earlier?'

He came to the kitchen door and Jenny glanced round at him. 'Who was it?'

'You know damn well who it was.'

'How could I?'

'Because they'd been here earlier in the day.'

'Had they?'

Andy moved deliberately to place himself between her and the cooker. 'It was the police, not at all satisfied that I've nothing to do with the poison pen letters nor the damage to the Store. Very, very curious they were. Poking about in all corners of my life and I don't like it. What did you say to them?' His right hand gripped her wrist and twisted her flesh slightly. 'Well?'

'Leave go of my wrist. You're hurting me.'

'That's nothing to what I shall be doing shortly. Tell me! Tell me what you said.'

Jenny began to shake from head to toe. 'Let me go, then I'll tell you.'

'Tell me.' Gripping her wrist as he did made it really hurt when he shook her till her head rattled back and forth. Her hip hit the edge of the cooker and she came close to knocking the pan with the potatoes bubbling and spitting in it because they needed the gas turning lower.

'Let me lower the gas, they'll be boiled to pulp at this rate.'

Momentarily he released his grip while she adjusted the flame. But then Andy gripped both her wrists even tighter. 'Tell me what you said.'

'Honestly. I told them exactly what you told me to say. Word for word.'

'If you did, why were they even more suspicious than before?'

'I don't know what you're so worried about seeing as it isn't you who broke the windows or threw the paint.' A curious expression came over his face and Jenny saw the truth in a flash. 'It *was* you. It was you. And the poison pen letters, too? I can't believe it of you. Whatever did you do it for? And you made me lie to the police. How *could* you. Just let go of me. *Please*.'

Blast. She shouldn't have pleaded. The light in his eyes grew more intense, more hateful. It had only made him more dangerous.

He twisted his grip on her flesh and it made her squeal. 'Let go of me. Let go of me.' But then because of the agonies she was suffering she had to say please again and he almost licked his lips with a kind of deep satisfaction and squeezed her wrist even more cruelly. Now she was beginning to grovel because the pain was so severe. 'Please, Andy. You love me, why are you hurting me like this?'

Somehow the more she pleaded the more he enjoyed hurting her. Her pleading excited him and he enjoyed his power. The stupid bitch. The stupid, stupid bitch. How he hated her long nails the colour of blood, the immaculate make-up, the long, vivid peroxided hair, her waxed legs, her intense concentration on her personal hygiene when he really rather liked a more relaxed earthy approach. He tightened his grip on her wrists, then kicked her shins, both of them, very hard, and enjoyed the shuddering response she gave. This was power and he had her right where he wanted her.

In desperation Jenny began to kick Andy's ankles and twisted and turned as she struggled furiously to escape. Her elbow caught the pan handle and as the pan tipped over, the potatoes and the boiling water shot out and caught Andy's bare arm before they spattered to the floor. The shock of the scald finally threw Andy's escalating emotions clean out of control. He clamped his hands around her throat while she was preoccupied with rubbing life back into her hands. Tighter and tighter. Stronger and stronger. He revelled in the choking sounds she made, the scrabbling of her blood-red nails on the backs of his hands, the desperate gasps then the silence as her body collapsed in his grip and the two of them fell to the floor amongst the scalding water and the still firm potatoes.

He disentangled himself from her body and stood up in the confined space between the cooker and the kitchen table. He examined the redness of the scald on his arm, tested the fingers which had gripped her throat so tightly and then looked down at Jenny. Jenny Wren he used to call her. His Jenny Wren. He bent down and pressed two fingers to the side of her throat. There wasn't even a flicker of a pulse. Not a flicker. So he'd done it. He'd killed her.

Had he meant to? For a brief moment he had, when she'd said, 'Why are you hurting me like this?' What power he'd had at that moment. It had been a pleasure at the end as the life went from her; he'd felt it ebb away like a tide going out, slowly but inevitably.

The new moon was completely obscured by heavy black clouds that night. The Met Office had forecast a clear cloudless night, but in Turnham Malpas the rain came flooding down, accompanied by almost ceaseless rumbles of thunder interspersed with massive flashes of lightning. The chimney stack on number three was struck and the beck on the spare land began overflowing its banks, reaching the back fences of Hipkin Gardens in no time at all. Lightning struck the church steeple and the most enormous crack of thunder anyone had ever heard terrified every single person in Turnham Malpas. No one could sleep. Lights went on while they all made restorative cups of tea and it wasn't until four o'clock that the storm abated and they could snatch some sleep in what was left of the night.

Jimbo, Harriet, Fran and Grandmama were all up keeping an eye on Turnham Beck, which ran past the end of their garden. By the time the rain stopped, the beck had flooded right to the edge of the patio. That had never happened in all the years they'd been living in Turnham Malpas.

Harriet shuddered. 'I don't like this at all. Everything's going wrong. This is a sign.'

Grandmama, tough and determined, pooh-poohed her fears. 'Heavens above. It's only a storm, for goodness' sake. Let's finish our tea and go back to bed. Fran, you're all right, aren't you?'

'I'm for bed. Thank goodness it's stopped. Night-night, everybody.'

But Jimbo, already jittery about life in general, couldn't help but feel that the storm was ominous, and went to bed braced for worse to come.

Chapter 12

Dottie had an appointment for another massage with Jenny the following morning after she'd finished at the Rectory and was really looking forward to it.

Beth asked her, 'Dottie, do you think I would enjoy a massage?'

'Depends how much money you have to spare, it's not cheap.' She put down her cup of tea and rested her elbows on the kitchen table.

'Well, I have lots of spending money because I'm not spending any, am I? And if I haven't enough I know Alex would lend me some. Do you really feel better after it, relaxed kind of?'

'Definitely. Seems to soothe the mind, and after last night that's just what I could do with. It was godawful, wasn't it, all that rain?'

'Yes, but thunder doesn't frighten me. Nor lightning. Does it frighten you?'

'Well, I admit it does. Sounds like the heavens are angry with human beings and they're letting them know. You won't believe it but Penny Fawcett didn't get a drop of rain, and them so close. They could hear it, apparently, cos it was so loud, but they had no rain at all and nothing was struck by lightning. It's funny, isn't it? A storm meant only for us. I wonder what we did to deserve it.' Dottie stood up. 'No good. Got to go or I won't be finished in time for my appointment.'

'OK. I'll clear up.'

But when Dottie went to ring Jenny's bell dead on the dot of twelve there was no reply. That seemed odd because Jenny was going to go through what she was doing to Dottie for the Beauty Evening, just to make her feel relaxed about it then there'd be no nasty surprises. But she rang the bell three times and still no reply. Dottie was certain it was twelve o'clock. She checked her watch, checked her diary. Yes, she was right. No Jenny, then.

She stepped back from the doorstep and glanced up at the windows. Not a sign of life. Then suddenly the front door burst open and there stood Andy. He looked haggard, and, oddly, he was wearing gardening gloves. His shirt-sleeves, usually rolled up to the elbow, were down by his wrists.

'Sorry . . . Dottie, isn't it? Jenny's not at all well. Sorry I couldn't let you know earlier. Got this flu thing that's going about, nasty. Won't be ready to go back to work before next week at the earliest.'

'Oh dear! I am sorry. What does the doctor say?'

Andy paused as though recollecting what had been said. 'Three or four days in bed at least. So . . .' He shrugged and began to close the door.

'Give her my love and say I hope she'll soon be better. I'll ring next week to make another appointment. Bye! Let you get back to your gardening.'

Andy looked puzzled, then looked down at his gloves and said, 'Oh! Yes. Get the weeds out while the ground's wet.'

Dottie stood outside thinking. He could have let her know. She'd so looked forward to it. You'd think he could give her a call. Then she remembered that she wasn't on the phone like everyone else so how could he have rung. How daft can you get? She could have kicked herself.

But for some reason it didn't smell right. He didn't smell right. The whole thing didn't smell right. Dottie wondered why someone as nice as Jenny with her lovely smile had married a man like Andy. Dottie's mother would have called Andy a lying hound. He wouldn't know the truth if he met it in the street.

Then it hit her. What about the Beauty Evening with the Women's Institute? More than likely she wouldn't be fit enough to do it if it was real flu.

Dottie spun round on her heel and went straight back to the Rectory.

'Sorry, Doctor Harris, but it's me again. I've just been to Jenny's for a massage and believe it or not she's in bed with flu. They've had the doctor and he says three or four days in bed before she even thinks of putting a foot to the floor. So it looks as though the Beauty Evening is off, doesn't it? Thought I'd better let you know.'

'Oh, no. We were all looking forward so much to that.'

'So was I. Anyway, I can't think she'll be able to do it. At least you've time to plan something else.'

'Well, yes. Anyway, she can't help it if she's ill, can she? Thanks for letting me know, Dottie. Shall we chance it and hope she'll be better by then? What do you think?'

'Might be better to organize something in readiness. I can't think she'll be well enough to do something like a demonstration. She's a nice girl, very kind, I just wish she hadn't married that dreadful man. He's 'orrible.'

Caroline had to smile at Dottie's description of Andy, which echoed her own thoughts entirely. 'You're right,

170

although I suppose he must have some good points. But I will call tomorrow with something to cheer her up. Thanks again for letting me know, Dottie. See you.'

Caroline closed the door and stood in the hall thinking. It was a surprisingly sudden bout of flu because last night Jenny was full of life, and to already have had the doctor calling? Not a hint of a fever or a bad throat or anything. Oh well, she'd better tell Beth.

As chance would have it, it was Grandmama who called at Jenny and Andy's before Caroline got there. Some of their post had been delivered to the Charter-Placketts' by mistake, and she'd promised Harriet that she'd pop across the road and put it through their letterbox.

But just as she was about to push it through, Andy opened the door to put out an empty milk bottle and wearing gardening gloves.

'Ah! Here's your post. It got mixed up with ours so I've brought it across.'

'Thanks.'

'Is Jenny there? I'd like to make an appointment for my nails.'

Andy shook his head. 'Sorry. She's in bed with flu. She's very poorly. Would you ring next week to make the appointment, please?'

'Oh! Of course. I'd no idea. When did this start?'

'Yesterday. She's very low.'

'Yes, flu can knock you sideways and not half. I hope you've had the doctor.' Andy nodded. 'Give her my best wishes and I hope she'll soon be better.' Grandmama stepped away from the door, waved casually and left calling out, 'Don't forget to tell her I called.'

Andy closed the door and stood thinking he'd have a

problem telling her that when she was wrapped in three black binbags in the cupboard under the stairs. Poor Jenny. He hadn't meant to do it, but when he realized what he'd done he saw it as a very good move on his part. He could sense she was about to blow the whistle at the office in which case he'd be a goner.

In one fell swoop he'd satisfied his need to be rid of her, made certain the house was his with no questions asked, saved his job, prevented her from finding out they weren't really married and stopped all these damn women knock-ing on the door for appointments, as though Jenny was some kind of guru or a female godhead able to solve all their problems.

He sauntered across to the store, intending to beg to be allowed to buy some food for Jenny as he couldn't leave her to get into Culworth with her being so ill and she fancied a hot bacon sandwich and a glass of wine. He made a sorry picture with his drooping shoulders, wan expression and red eyes, well rubbed with juice from an onion to irritate them before he left the house. Jimbo had gone for a hospital checkup so it was Tom who'd been left in charge. Andy stood in the doorway and humbly inquired if in the circumstances he could . . .

Tom called from the Post Office cage, 'All right. Just this once. I'm sorry she's ill.'

Andy collected more than the bacon and the wine but Tom felt inclined to have sympathy with him. He guessed Jenny must be genuinely ill because Andy looked very downcast.

As Bel checked his basket at the till it did occur to her that a hot bacon sandwich and a glass of wine seemed a very odd choice for someone seriously ill with flu. Still, when you were feverish you did get curious fads.

Tom called across, 'Will you tell her we're all sorry she's ill. Hope she'll soon be better.'

'Thanks.'

At home Andy sat down to bacon, a large portion of McCain Oven Chips, four sausages and two shiny fried eggs, thinking as he ate them that it was a relief not to have Jenny telling him how many carbohydrates he was consuming and how bad it was for his cholesterol. Hang his cholesterol, at least he could enjoy his food with her gone. As for that pile of salad in the fridge, that could go in the bin as of this minute; followed by the blasted carrots, fennel, tomatoes, chickpeas, aduki beans and taramasalata. The couscous, yes, that could go, too. Oh, yes! He'd eat whatever he liked from now on. He should have got rid of her last night straight after it happened, but he was so confused with the shock of it all that he didn't think he was sane enough to carry it off – he sniggered at his choice of words – without being found out. In any case the storm would have made any disposal anywhere difficult to achieve. All evening he gloried in his freedom, eating a packet of biscuits and drinking two mugs of hot chocolate with plenty of sugar and no one to say no.

At 2 a.m. that morning after a good day in the office – my, but he'd stayed cool and calculating all day, what a triumph it had been – he went to get her body out of the cupboard under the stairs. His insides heaved with sick as he took the weight of her body in his arms and dragged her out. The back door he'd left standing open and with the tailgate of the car already yawning wide, he heaved her in, covered the binbags with a travelling rug and some carefully placed empty cardboard boxes made to look casually tossed in, and shut the back of the car. Letting off the brake, he slid quietly out down what passed as their garden and glided into Pipe and Nook Lane on his way to Culworth stone quarry, long since abandoned as a working quarry and now used as a tip by all and sundry.

He stood in the pitch-black for five minutes beside his parked car, checking for movements all the way across the quarry. What had been an active quarry for over a hundred years had been a ghost place for the last ten. People had complained to the council about how dangerous the whole site was with its steep sides, ramshackle buildings in the bottom, as well as along the top at one side, gradually falling into ruins and the vast amount of rubbish dumped by an uncaring populace.

Andy reckoned there was absolutely no one about, not even a loving couple in their car. He'd brought a powerful torch with him and plucked up the courage to swing its beam across the quarry in case he picked out someone moving about. It caught the glistening, shifty eyes of rats running about among the rubbish, which made him shudder. He smiled at his caution, then. After all, who would be wandering about the quarry this time of night? But absolute secrecy was essential if his plan was to work.

Satisfied he was safe he opened the tailgate and began sliding her out. His hands caught hold of her feet and he remembered how particular she was about keeping her feet beautiful, how diligent she was about waxing her legs. As he grabbed her hip bones he recollected how determined she was not to ruin her admirable figure by having children. The part of the quarry with the biggest heap of rubbish was about three metres to the left of him, and it was best to drop her there, because she'd be covered over all the sooner. He easily carried her over the necessary three metres – she was light he had to agree, the dieting had been all to the good for Jenny – and he let her roll down there on the least steep side of the quarry.

He followed her down slowly with only the light of his torch to guide him and made sure she was more than covered by the mattresses and the shopping trolleys and the filth of other people's lives besides his own. The climb back up was not so easy but he managed it at last and told himself he'd done a good job.

He drove home, carefully keeping his speed down so as not to attract attention to himself. With the car neatly parked in their back garden and locked up he wandered into the house and felt liberated. Andy punched the air the moment he got inside. 'Hallelujah!' he shouted. He'd got away with it. His master plan had worked. No one had seen him.

He was completely safe.

The perfect murder.

But he couldn't have been more wrong.

Beth had seen him leave and come back.

She was having one of her sleepless nightmare nights sitting at her bedroom window and was looking out at the deep black night with only the lights of the bypass far away across the valley. She had watched him but not realized what she was seeing.

Her mother, determined to keep her company, had unintentionally fallen asleep on Beth's bed so she went to sleep in her mother's bed. Doing so brought her father vividly to mind. And she wished – oh, how she wished – that her father were home and she could sit on his knee with his strong arms around her and tell him why she daren't go to school, and why Alex was too afraid to do sport at school because he feared being out in the open, and what her nightmares were all about. Then at last Alex could tell him what happened in the sticky, steaming heat of an African night when they were in hiding, and both of them could lay their burden of guilt on their father's broad shoulders.

Chapter 13

As he had promised, Jimbo closed the Store on 31 January. He had a week-long sale of all his stock and, on 1 February, set about designing his internet site for selling Harriet's Country Cousin products. He'd already visited all his suppliers, farmers' wives, retired bakers, eager young housewives glad to be making money in their own homes, anyone and everyone who was prepared to work according to his strict rules of hygiene and quality. The result had been an increase in the number of workers and in the lines he could offer. His plaster was now off and hopefully the physiotherapy he was getting would finally put an end to his limping. As his working day no longer anchored him to stock and shelves and display he was beginning to feel at last that life was not the burden it had been previously.

'Best day's work I did closing the shop, you know, Harriet.'

'Is that so?'

'Yes, don't you feel it is?'

'No.' She was quilting and needed to concentrate.

'I thought you would love this new relaxed Jimbo.'

'I do, but it's a grievous blow to everyone else.'

'They'll get used to it. Thousands of villages have lost their Post Offices and convenience stores, they've all had to get used to it.'

'Doesn't mean to say it's for the best, does it? Pension day they can hardly find a seat on the bus it's so busy, all going to Culworth to spend their money instead of in the store.' The corners of her mouth were turned down and she looked grim.

'You really mean it, don't you?'

'Yes. I do. The only one who benefits is J.G. Charter-Plackett.'

'Well, you'll benefit this weekend when we all go to Chichester, Friday evening to Sunday.'

'That's right, but I can't help but think we could have organized ourselves better than we did and kept the Store going.'

'How? How to relieve ourselves of the six-day-a-week grind – well, seven if we really wanted to make a go of it?'

Harriet put down her needle and applied herself instead to Jimbo. 'I am entirely sure that Tom Nicholls, with a bit of instruction, could have taken over a great deal of your burden. Look how he took to doing the Post Office after all the fuss and palaver Linda made of it. Two hours of training and he's hardly put a foot wrong since. Stock maintenance would be a doddle for him because he has an organized mind, and he's very quick off the mark if he spots someone he thinks is stealing. You missed a great opportunity there, Jimbo.'

'Think so?' Jimbo immediately began worrying that she could be right. After all, he had enjoyed the cut and thrust of the daily input of customers, and he had to confess he'd lost his main source of gossip, which had left a yawning gap in his life. 'He'd never manage the window-dressing though, he hasn't an imaginative bone in his body.'

'Ah! But Evie has. I bet with a bit of practice she'd be a

wizard at window-dressing. With her eye for colour and design—'

'All right. All right. Maybe. But all that capital tied up in stock? No, thank you. Chichester here I come.'

Harriet grinned at him. 'Aren't you just a teeny-weeny bit sad that you've no Store to go to? Dozens of people are. All that gossip that used to go on behind the tinned soups? The chats over the coffee machine? Or that frequently asked question: "Is Jimbo in the back?" Or that time Muriel caught you hugging Venetia in your office? Remember?'

Jimbo went to look out of the window while he weighed up how much truth there was in what Harriet had just said. 'I remember. However, I still maintain I've made the right decision. The figures for February already prove that the catering and the mail order are holding up very well now they don't have, in part, to support the Store.' He turned away from the window and, looking Harriet straight in the eye, said firmly, 'No, I've made the right decision.'

Neither of them realized that Fran had been standing in the doorway listening to their conversation. 'Yes, Daddy, but what about me?'

'What about you?'

'I've always wanted to run the Store for you, ever since I was small, and without consulting me, you've left me with no career prospects.'

Jimbo blustered his way through his answer. 'I'd no idea that was how you felt. You should have said.'

'Come on, Daddy, you never even consulted Mummy, never mind me. You just stuck up the notice and that was that.'

'I did. But you're much too clever to be running a Store.'

Fran raised her eyebrows in disbelief. 'And you're not? Come on, Daddy, how many of your year at Cambridge are running a village store. Eh? None, I guess. But you do – well, did – and made a tremendous success of it and loved every minute.'

'Well, that's true.'

'They'll all be worn out by the time they're fifty, working in the City. You got out of the City and you've loved life ever since.'

Jimbo agreed. 'True.'

'A roaring success you've made, in fact.'

Jimbo modestly agreed. 'True.'

'So, what have you thrown away in one mad moment?'

'You tell me, Fran.'

'Your opportunity to be in the hurly-burly of life and my career.' Fran gave both of them a broad grin. 'Never mind, I'll survive. But will you?'

She disappeared as fast as she'd arrived, leaving the two of them stunned.

Harriet picked up her needle and said nothing.

Jimbo turned to the window again and watched Evie Nicholls walking by with her new little dog, Tatty. Of course she'd be excellent at dressing the windows. Which made him think about Tom. He'd be good at organizing the stock, he knew he would because he'd got that kind of mind, that was why he was so good in the Post Office. Everything following a set pattern. Rules to follow. Strict procedures to carry out.

But Jimbo shook his head. No, he'd made the right decision. No one in their right mind ran a village shop. But Fran. Well, at thirteen she'd plenty of time to change

180

her mind about her career. If he strained his neck he could just see the end of the queue of people waiting outside his Store for the morning bus into Culworth. A much longer queue than usual, and he realized that a lot of them would have been shopping in the Store if he hadn't closed, so all their money would have been flowing into his tills. But he shut off his mind and instead dwelt on the freedom closing the Store had given him.

Back to the computer and to checking his new website, which began:

HARRIET'S COUNTRY COUSIN MAIL ORDER

Taste country goodness in your own home. Send today for a free sample jar of fresh raspberry preserve. Our wholesome, country quality preserve has that special tang which only fresh homegrown raspberries, newly picked and in our jam pans that same day, can give . . .

He spent the morning composing other equally tempting slogans for his chutneys, bottled fruits, marmalades, and other jams, and pushed to the back of his mind what Fran had said. But her words had left a thin trail of dissatisfaction in his mind and it niggled him all day.

The irritation that closing the Store had caused was felt all over Turnham Malpas, Little Derehams and Penny Fawcett. The times they'd said to themselves, 'I'll call in the Store and get that . . .' only to realize the Store no longer existed. It was not just irritating, it was maddening. There were few of them on Jimbo's side. And quite a few who felt the pinch of unemployment – Tom, in particular and Bel, as well as the new assistants, who'd been dropped within weeks of having been taken on. Tom had thought about buying the Store from Jimbo, but the amount of capital he would need was beyond both his bank manager and himself. What a mess everything was becoming. Tom did find a job working in the large Post Office in Culworth, but it wasn't a patch on the comfortable chatty job he'd made of working in the Turnham Malpas Store.

But though the lack of the Store was on everyone's lips they did have another piece of gossip to keep them busy: the disappearance of Jenny Sweetapple.

'I swear,' said Dottie to Beth one February morning, 'I swear he's done her in.'

'Done her in?'

'Killed her, you know. Polished her off.'

'What makes you think that?'

'Well, he says she has flu, but within days he's in the Store weeping and wailing and gnashing his teeth because Jenny's left him. He *says* she's gone to stay with her brother in Australia. It doesn't make sense. He told me himself she had the flu, he *said* he'd had the doctor from Culworth to her, but in a week she'd buzzed off to Australia.'

'Perhaps she'd already gone and at first he couldn't bear to tell anyone. Perhaps she hadn't had the flu at all.'

'Mmm. Per'aps. Mind you, I couldn't blame her if she did run off to Australia, or Tasmania – that's even further away – just to escape from him. There's something I don't like about Mr Andy Moorhouse. He's a kind of *nasty* kind of man. Real unpleasant. She was lovely. I really liked her. Very thoughtful, she was. Yer didn't feel at all embarrassed, undressed and that. Lovely smile, too. I don't agree with divorce, but in her case I would. Good at her job, she was.'

'I never met him. But then I haven't been out much. Now I can't even go to the Store for some gateau.'

'You could come down to see me.'

'No, I don't think so.' Beth shook her head. The thought of venturing right the way down Shepherds Hill was too painful to contemplate.

'You could walk down with me after I finish here.'

Beth said no even more emphatically.

'But I would walk you back.'

'No. No. I had thought I'd be back at school after Christmas and I still can't manage it.'

'Have you told your mum yet what's upsetting you?'

'No.'

'Not about what happened with that man with the gun?'

'No.' Beth began clearing the table of her breakfast things to put an end to the questioning.

Dottie started collecting her cleaning things saying, 'The invite's still there, when you want. My house isn't as beautiful as this, I've never had the money, you see. But you're welcome. Humble, but it's home.' Dottie set off to start on the sitting room and then turned back to say, 'Will you promise me one thing? When your dad gets back you'll tell him. Because if you don't, I shall, and I mean that.'

'No. Please don't. Alex and I will.'

Beth thought about telling her father and longed for the moment. She could tell him all about the guns and how terrified Alex and she had been, waiting for Elijah to come, when he dared, with food and water for them, and listening for the sounds of the rebels making their way through the bush to the town. They were always searching, for someone to rob, food to eat, and other insurgents to team up with. Every waking moment had been filled with fear. They heard murder being done on the cart track which led to the nearest little town, and to hear another human being screaming for mercy in the face of death was a sound she never wanted to hear again. At one time they'd contemplated walking along the cart track themselves to get some help, but how could they know whom they could trust? Still worse, being new to the area they had no idea which way to walk to get to the main road where they'd escaped being burnt to death. If they'd known they would have taken the risk and attempted to walk home. Home! If only.

By the time Dottie had finished cleaning Beth was glad to accept her invitation, if only to take her mind off the memories . . .

Caroline, thrilled that Beth felt able to go out, insisted she provided lunch. 'Lunch, Dottie. I can't expect you to provide lunch. Let me put some things in a basket, please, otherwise I shall feel guilty.'

For which Dottie was glad, as there wasn't much in her kitchen for making a lunch for Beth. That blasted Jimbo closing the Store.

'Well, it's very kind of you, Doctor Harris, I didn't expect—'

'Please accept with my thanks. Beth, you'll need your coat.'

She waved them off, sad inside that Beth seemed able to talk to Dottie about things but not to her. It made her extremely disappointed in herself. Where had she failed Beth and Alex that they couldn't talk about their problems to their mother? She loved them as though they were her own and always had done, and she'd tried so hard.

Dottie and Beth talked all the way down Shepherds

Hill. They'd paused for a moment outside the school, listening to the chatter escaping through the windows and watching the dinner van unloading the containers, and for one moment Beth wished she were going into the hall for dinner like she used to.

Dottie said, 'I've often wished I worked in the school just to be with the children. It's lonely having no children of your own. Very lonely.'

Beth said, 'Well, you could always pretend for a while that I'm yours.'

Dottie smiled at her. 'I could, couldn't I? That will be lovely. We'll do that.'

They were so engrossed in their conversation that neither of them noticed Greta Jones going back to the Store after delivering a note to one of Jimbo's mail order workers. She saw them standing outside the school, partially hidden by the dinner van.

What possible contribution could Dottie Foskett make to getting Beth back to normal? she thought. I ask yer. She remembered her from school as that smelly, unkempt girl at the bottom of the class, and look where she ended up, the local girl free with her favours. The times Greta's mother had warned her of the perils Dottie Foskett would be facing in the years to come. But it didn't seem as though it had worked out that way. She'd two or three comfortable cleaning jobs, a skill way above her other attributes, at the Rectory no less, and now she was adviser-in-chief to a distressed Beth. It took some understanding.

But to Beth, Dottie was the most comfortable person to be with. She talked about ordinary things straight from the shoulder, and at the moment that was exactly what Beth needed; she was tired of people tiptoeing around her emotions.

She had a surprise when she saw Dottie's house. It was scrupulously clean, but plain, almost minimal, except her belongings weren't as fashionably modern as they should have been for her house to be described as minimalist. It was lack of money which made her furnishings sparse and Beth could understand why Dottie enjoyed working at the Rectory, because to her it was beautiful.

The kitchen was galley-shaped, with barely enough room for two thin people to pass. But it didn't matter because Dottie insisted on unpacking Caroline's bag all by herself. 'My! Look at this. It'll feed me for a week. This stand pie. Look at that! Delicious. And she's even put in some salad and coleslaw to go with it. Fruit and cheese and biscuits, too. And some crisps! You are lucky to have a mum like yours. So lucky.'

She kept up the commentary as she unwrapped everything, and by the time it was all ready for eating Beth was salivating and couldn't wait to begin.

'Carry it through. I'll light the gas fire, it's a bit nippy today.'

The fire plopped into action as old gas fires do and they sat cosily in front of it with the food on a rickety bamboo table out of someone's conservatory.

Dottie didn't speak while she enjoyed Caroline's lunch. Neither did Beth, mainly because it was the very first meal since coming home from Africa which she could say she truly enjoyed. She cleared her plate, joined Dottie in a second helping of everything and then chose a big fat orange. Having quartered it with a centuries-old knife of Dottie's, she relished pulling the flesh from the skin with her teeth. A messy way to eat it but she didn't care about good manners at the moment.

'Dottie, I loved that. I could eat it all over again.'

Dottie's face fell. 'I'm sorry I've—'

'I didn't mean it really, I couldn't possibly find the room.' She leaned back in her chair, which was small and squat rather like a Victorian nursing chair, beautifully shaped to one's bottom which made it comfortable even without a single cushion to protect one from the hard wood.

She saw the ceiling had a large damp patch on it, that the window wasn't quite square and realized that the floor was sloping down away from the fireplace. Was the house sinking?

Dottie saw exactly what it was Beth had noticed. She cleared her throat and said, 'I pay the rent reg'lar but the landlord won't do a thing. It's hard to keep it nice when it's like this. The bedroom ceiling's even worse, the rain's coming through the thatch. I shouldn't have asked you back. I'm sorry, it was a mistake. Don't come again.'

'I haven't come to see your house, I've come because you're one of the few people I feel safe with, and I know you won't tell anyone what I've told you.'

'I promised I wouldn't. Dottie Foskett might not be up to much but I do keep my word.'

Beth stood up. 'Thank you for lunch. Can I come again sometime? It feels so safe here.' Unexpectedly she leaned over Dottie and kissed her cheek. 'I must go. There's no need to see me all the way home. I can manage. I'm feeling full of confidence today.'

'Are you sure? I'll gladly come.'

'No, I'll go by myself. I'll have to run if I get afraid.' She gave Dottie a smile and a wave. 'Oh! I forgot, I should help to clear the lunch dishes.'

Dottie got to her feet. 'Not in my house you won't. Off you go. See you next week.'

Beth picked up the basket her mother had lent them, got outside the door and wondered if she really could walk all that way home up Shepherds Hill, up Jacks Lane past the school and then Church Lane and home. But the warm, comfy feeling having lunch in Dottie's cottage had given her was still there so she thought she'd be OK.

It was a beautiful winter afternoon, with a glorious blue sky and a splendid sun to take the chill from the wind. She stepped out bravely, one foot in front of the other, methodically, steadily, concentrating. She'd got about a quarter of the way up Shepherds Hill when a car drew up. The man inside offered her a lift. 'I'm going your way. You must be the girl from the Rectory, I've seen you in your garden.'

'No, thank you, I'm enjoying the walk.'

'I'm Andy Moorhouse, you know. My wife's Jenny.'

'I don't know you and I don't want a lift.' Beth left him and strode along the footpath. But he didn't leave her, and slowly followed with his nearside window open, still persuading her to get in his car. 'I'll be delighted to give you a lift to the Rectory. After all, I live next door.'

'I said no thank you. Please stop following me.'

But he did just the same; it seemed as if nothing would put him off.

'I'd enjoy your company. Now Jenny's gone to Australia company is something I'm short of, and people like you are the sort of people this village doesn't have; you know, someone with opinions, with something to say for themselves. Come on, jump in, we could enjoy a chat.'

'I've said it twice now, I do not want a lift in your car.' This time she shouted it good and loud and set off running fast, her heart beating madly, her breath jerking in her throat, and her legs like jelly. She could see the brow of the hill so she knew she wasn't far from the school but it never appeared to get any closer. Then she heard the children playing out in the school yard. His car was still following her but he'd stopped shouting at her now. She raced past the school round the corner into Church Lane and fell against the Rectory door breathless. Her key wouldn't fit in the lock because her hands were trembling so and suddenly he was standing behind her, reaching over her shoulder to help her put the key in the door.

'Get away from me! Get away!' Beth half turned, beating him with her fists. Andy was excited by her spirited response. 'Hey! Hey! Only helping with the key. Calm down.' His hand took the key from her grasp and fitted it in the lock. As the door opened Caroline was the other side of it preparing to open it for Beth, and the three of them met face to face. 'Beth!'

Andy got his side of the story in before Beth, breathless, could speak.

He smiled at Caroline. 'She couldn't get the key in the door, so I came to help. I'm sorry if I've upset her, didn't mean any harm.'

Beth rushed past Caroline and fled into the kitchen, slamming the door.

'Thank you for your help,' Caroline said. 'Heard from Jenny this week?'

'Oh! Yes. An e-mail. She's having a wonderful time. Her brother's taking her on a trip to the Outback next week so she's really looking forward to that.' He made his face resemble an exceptionally weary Bassett Hound and continued, 'We shan't be seeing her again, though. She's divorcing me, you know, staying out there. Made her mind up. Lovely girl, it's making me very upset. I don't believe in divorce, you see – I expect you're the same, being who you are – and I can't understand what grounds she's going to base it on. None of it's my fault.' Out came his handkerchief and he mopped his eyes. 'Still, I'll have to grin and bear it.'

Caroline's instincts told her she should offer counselling to this man and she was on the verge of inviting him in when she recollected the terror in Beth's eyes as she brushed past her and immediately changed her mind.

'Yes, I'm afraid you will. Life can be inexplicably hard sometimes. Thank you for helping Beth. With the key. You know. Good afternoon.'

She closed the door and stood with her back to it thinking. That man had terrified Beth. What's more, that business of the divorce didn't ring true. He was a creep. A fawning, lying creep. Beth! 'Coming, darling.'

Beth was gripping the edge of the sink, shaking from head to foot.

'Darling! Tell me, *please*. Tell me what the matter is.'

Beth shook her head. She was biting her bottom lip and refusing to look at Caroline.

'Beth! How can I help if you don't tell me? Tell me right *now*.' Caroline was shouting, she didn't mean to shout but her anger and frustration couldn't be contained any longer. 'What did he *do*?'

'I was walking home . . . by myself . . . I felt really good after being at Dottie's and I knew I could do it. All the way by myself. Then he pulled up in the car and offered me a lift and I couldn't bear it. He said he knew me.'

'Did you get in the car?'

'No!' She dug in her pocket for a handkerchief and scrubbed at her eyes. 'No, I kept saying no and he kept pestering me. Then I started to run home. I had to get safe. Then I was breathing so fast I couldn't get the key in the door and suddenly he was leaning across me to get the key. He is not a nice man.'

'Darling! He should have taken your word that you didn't need a lift, but for heaven's sakes, Beth, nothing happened, did it?'

Beth stared out of the window still frightened and on the verge of telling her mother about . . . but her mind shut down and that fear flooded through her and she couldn't answer. 'I shall kill him if he comes near me again.'

Caroline was horrified. 'Beth! My God. What a thing to say!'

Beth turned to face her mother and said in a perfectly controlled voice, 'When will Daddy be home?'

'Well, it's February now, so there's March, April, May, June, and he'll be here in July.' Caroline tried pleading with her, something she'd promised herself she would never do. 'Perhaps you'd feel better if you told someone about Africa, and that someone could be *me*.'

Beth's answer was to put her arms around her mother and say, 'I love you Mum. When I met her I knew I wouldn't have wanted that Suzy person for my mother, it has to be you, but you see, Daddy will be able to explain things and free Alex and me from what we've done and I can't say any more than that. Hold me tight. Please.'

The two of them stood hugging, silently saying everything they needed to say to each other, and when tears began to run down Caroline's cheeks Beth brushed them away with her fingers and kissed her cheek, realizing that her mother desperately needed to contribute to her recovery. 'If you promise not to leave me by myself ever at all, I'll go into Culworth with you tomorrow and look at the shops. There. That'll be a start, won't it? You helping me to do that.'

Caroline gave her a great big smile. 'Of course it will. I need some new shoes and we could get you some clothes, couldn't we? It's ages since you had anything new, isn't it? Would you like that?'

'I'll try.'

They heard Anna calling out that she wouldn't be back till tomorrow morning and Caroline answered her. 'Fine, see you then.'

Anna appeared in the kitchen doorway and stood looking at the two of them. She nodded and as she turned to leave she said, 'You two look happy, in fact very happy. That's nice. Bye!'

After the door banged shut Beth said, 'She's not a bad old stick, is she?'

Caroline burst out laughing, the first time she'd laughed wholeheartedly since they'd come back.

Chapter 14

Alex couldn't believe that Beth was going shopping the next morning. He sat on her bed and asked how she would manage. 'I thought you daren't go out.'

'I daren't, but I went down to Dottie's for my lunch. I just felt I needed to go. I loved it; it's nice and safe. That old house is falling down but it's so comfortable, though there's hardly any furniture in it, and I felt really warm for the first time in ages; you'd feel all right in it, too. So I walked home all by myself and everything was going well when that nasty Andy Moorhouse from next door pulled up in his car and offered me a lift and wouldn't accept I didn't want one. I lost my nerve and raced home. But,' Beth looked him full in the face, 'I've decided I'm going to face up to it and *make* myself go out. Like you've done. Be brave for Mummy's sake, she so needs to help us.'

Alex, not given to loving gestures, bent forward and kissed her cheek. 'That's great, I'm glad you went. I expect that chap reminded you of—'

'Don't say it. Just don't.'

'I won't then, but not saying it won't make it go away.'

'When Daddy comes home—'

Alex picked up his school bag. 'I've a load of work to do. Why don't you ask at school for some homework? It would give you something to do.'

'I could, couldn't I? When Daddy comes home—'

'I don't want to think about it. I don't know if I have the same faith in him as I had, not since I fully realized what happened about us, you know, us being born.'

'Well, I have. And I can't wait for him to come home.'

The following morning Caroline went out to their garage in Pipe and Nook Lane, drove the car out and parked at their back gate, thinking it might be a good idea for Beth to feel she wasn't going out under the full glare of the village.

She came out of the house, slammed the back door behind her and ran out down their garden path to the car. She appeared to be in a happy mood for which Caroline was grateful. Beth shut the car door, fastened her seat-belt and smiled at her mother with such delight that Caroline wondered if they were at last on the road to recovery.

As they trundled steadily down Pipe and Nook, narrow and twisting as it was, Caroline spotted in her rear mirror that Andy from next door was leaving at the same time. Some reason she couldn't quite fathom made her decide to pull in and allow him to pass her as soon as she reached the Culworth Road.

Satisfied he'd disappeared into the distance Caroline pulled out and drove on, only to find as she glanced in her rear-view mirror that he must have pulled off and rejoined the road as soon as she went by. She didn't say anything to Beth and could only hope that it was pure coincidence. Maybe he had to leave a letter at some cottage door or other. Whatever his reasons for being behind them again she had to ignore him. Beth, blithely ignorant of her mother's worry, sat silently watching the countryside roll by.

When they reached Culworth Caroline chose to park in the new multi-storey car park, built by the council despite the savage protest of the people of Culworth.

The two of them strolled away from their car, deep in conversation about which shop they should visit first.

'You choose, darling, it's your expedition not mine.' Caroline glanced briefly behind her before she crossed to the stairs only to realize that Andy was creeping along behind them. But to her relief she remembered that the Social Services office was close by, so of course he would be walking this way.

She dismissed him from her mind and engaged herself in shopping. At Beth's insistence they called in the school uniform shop first for a new school skirt, which gave Caroline a tremendous boost. She must be thinking of going back to school. Hallelujah!

After the school shop and a visit to a shoe shop for Caroline to buy her shoes, and a teens shop where Beth could indulge herself, they decided to call in the Abbey Coffee Shop for a rest. It happened to be the busiest part of the morning and they had difficulty finding a table. When they did Caroline asked if she should go to the counter to get the coffee.

'Is it coffee or would you prefer hot chocolate?'

'Hot chocolate with the cream on top, please.'

Caroline had to ask, 'Will you be all right?'

Beth replied happily, 'Yes. I can see you from here.'

'OK.' But she hadn't gone more than a few yards when she spotted Andy cosily ensconced at an empty table. The whole situation became alarming. She looked across to Beth and saw her eyes were focused on her, so she waved her hand and Beth waved back. But while Caroline ordered their drinks and paid for them Andy moved across to their table and engaged Beth in conversation.

'Hello there, Beth. Out shopping I see?'

Beth froze and didn't reply. Instead she fingered her mother's vegetable knife which she'd hidden in her coat pocket. She wanted to get up and move away from him but her legs wouldn't obey her.

'Mind if I join you? Beautiful morning, isn't it? I should be at work but it's too good a morning to spend indoors. Ah! Here comes your mother. Good morning, Doctor Harris.' He got to his feet and took the tray from her.

Caroline felt her anger mounting like a volcano in her chest.

But Andy had his answer ready before she could object. 'I asked Beth if she minded me sitting here, thought perhaps she'd feel unhappy at being by herself. I'll get my coffee now you're here.' He left them to join the queue.

Caroline saw an empty table 'We're moving. Look, over there, that table's vacant. Quick!' She watched the pantomime he performed on arriving to find the table vacant. He looked swiftly round and homed in on their new position.

'Got to the wrong table. How silly can you get?' He seated himself very casually next to Beth and offered her the sugar.

'Mr Moorhouse, Beth and I would like time to ourselves. Would you kindly remove yourself to another table? We don't wish to be unfriendly to a neighbour, but we have personal things to discuss.'

But he smiled. 'Don't mind me. As you see, there isn't another table available.'

'I'm sorry, but please. Go share a table with someone else, not us.'

'Isn't it a lovely village to live in, Turnham Malpas? I don't think you could find a more friendly village anywhere at all. Everyone has been so kind since Jenny left me. So kind. Do you know the other day I—'

Andy carried on making small talk so smoothly and unthreateningly that for a moment Caroline felt she was being very rude to the man. After all, he'd a right to come into Culworth and into a café, too. What could possibly happen in the refined atmosphere of the Abbey Coffee Shop?

Her guard was lowered and they chattered on about this and that, and it wasn't until Beth caught her eye that she remembered how frightened of him Beth was. Maybe her first instincts were right. It was only when he began addressing his conversation to Beth, asking her about school and why she wasn't there on a school morning and he'd seen her in the Rectory garden a few times and was she not well, that Caroline said between gritted teeth, 'If you don't leave us alone I shall call the manager and have you removed.'

'Removed? Whatever for?'

'For pestering us when you've been asked not to sit at our table.'

'Now really, Doctor Harris—'

'You're still here.'

'I've done nothing wrong, but I will go if that's what you want.'

He didn't, however, move.

'Well?'

It was Beth who took action. She picked up his coffee pot, flipped open the lid, and poured the contents down the front of his jacket and trousers. And was it hot! He leapt to his feet and tried to brush the hot coffee from his clothes but it had soaked through in an instant.

He looked at Beth, but instead of the angry response Caroline expected he smiled and said, 'My! What a feisty young lady you are. Very feisty. Wouldn't like to meet you out on a dark night. You'd be a real handful.' His voice and his face were filled with pleasure and not anger as he looked at Beth. But it changed to shock when he saw what Beth had laid on the table, and he slumped into his chair.

To her horror Caroline saw the vegetable knife from her kitchen drawer, somehow cleaner and shinier than normal, lying beside Beth's mug with her fingers gripping the handle.

'I shall use it, if you don't move.' The voice she used wasn't even hers, and the anger in her face wasn't Beth's anger at all. She was a total stranger, with strengths and determination completely alien to her. She snarled, 'Do you hear me? I shall use it, believe me.' She edged the knife closer to him, staring into his eyes as she did so.

'Beth! Get the shopping. We're leaving. Now!' Caroline didn't know if she was moving to prevent Beth using the knife or to get away from this dreadful man. But Beth didn't obey her. She sat stony-faced and deeply angry, staring at Andy. Her grip on the knife tightened a fraction, just enough for him to see she meant business.

Andy merely slurped down the rest of his coffee, smirked at Beth and headed towards the exit.

'Put that knife in my bag this instant.' Beth hesitated for a moment and then dropped it casually into her mother's handbag.

On their way out Caroline and Beth were recognized

by the person in charge at the café that morning. 'Caroline!'

'Beatrice!'

'And Beth! what a lovely surprise. How nice to see you out, Beth. The Dean was asking only yesterday if I knew how you were progressing. I see you're making great strides, he will be pleased when I tell him.' Her sweet, kindly face broke into a huge smile.

Caroline, broken with horror by Beth's appalling behaviour, managed to say, 'Beatrice, you see the man leaving right now in that navy anorak? We've had to leave because he was pestering us. We even moved table and he followed us. You'd best keep your eye on him.'

'Thank you for letting me know. We get all sorts in here. They're all welcome so long as they behave themselves. Sorry about that. Are you both all right?' She laid a kindly hand on Beth's arm.

Caroline replied, 'Don't worry, we're fine, just thought you ought to be aware. Be seeing you.'

She looked at Beth as they left the café and saw her with different eyes. She'd grown up these last months and today, at this moment, looked the young woman she would one day be. Her heart sank. Beth's long ash-blonde hair, fair complexion and lovely bright blue eyes she'd inherited from her mother would shortly be a stunning combination. 'Darling, never, ever do you carry a knife with you. I can't believe you did that.'

Beth's reply was harsh. 'It had the right effect though. He wasn't listening to you at all. He was *enjoying* me pouring the coffee over him.'

Her voice, flat and hard, shocked Caroline as much as her actions did. Where had the real Beth gone?

Beth was filled with revulsion. Home seemed the safest

place to be. 'Mummy, I want to go home. Right now. Come on.'

'Very well. This is the quickest way.'

'We're not in that car park, are we?'

Caroline stopped and thought. 'Oh no, of course we're not. We're in the new one. I must be going mental. But why on earth did you bring that knife with you? What were you thinking of?'

'To defend myself. And you. There's no one going to spoil my life ever again. Not . . . one . . . single . . . person. And if a knife makes me safe a knife I shall use, and I mean it.'

There was that strange voice again that didn't seem to be Beth's. Caroline answered, 'You know full well that's totally against what we stand for. Absolutely. You must never take that knife, or any other for that matter, out of the house again. Do you hear me?'

Beth looked at her and ignored what she'd said. But then they reached their car and Andy was standing beside his with eyes only for Beth. Caroline's skin crawled and she felt sick with fear and disgust.

They drove home in silence until Beth said right out of the blue, 'One night when I couldn't sleep I saw him get in his car and drive away. He came back about an hour later. I couldn't see what he was doing before he set off, but I did think he'd put something in his car boot before he left. Afterwards I thought I'd dreamed it perhaps. But when I think about it now, I'm sure I didn't. It did seem odd. I remember it was the night you'd fallen asleep on my bed and I slept in your bed.'

Caroline scrabbled about in her head to remember when that was. 'Can you remember when?'

'No. All those nights when I couldn't sleep for screaming ran one into the other.'

'They've almost stopped now, haven't they?'

'Thanks to Dottie. I don't know what it is about her but she does help me.'

'How does she do that, when I can't?'

'There's something so comforting and understanding about her, and she calls a spade a spade.'

Hardly able to speak the words, Caroline blurted out, 'Have you told *her* what your worries are?'

Beth placed a gentle hand on Caroline's knee, 'No, but she did ask me if I'd been raped. Which I hadn't.'

The car swerved slightly as she took in what Beth had said. After she'd regained control Caroline said, 'I wanted to ask but emotions got in the way and wouldn't let me. I certainly knew I must, but the words wouldn't come out. I couldn't bear, you know, asking. I suppose I couldn't face what the answer might be, which was utterly stupid of me because it would have been vital for me to know. Tests and such. Don't think that all men are like that, they're not. You only have to look round our village to count up loads of decent men, loving and kind like your dad. He's a great man to be married to.'

'I know he is. But that Andy Moorhouse wants locking up. Here we are. Shall we put the car away?'

'Yes, you open the door.'

Andy saw them opening up the garage doors as he arrived home. Not having the privilege of his own garage he only had to manoeuvre his onto his now flattened garden and lock it up. He got inside his house before Caroline and Beth, and stood in his kitchen thinking about Beth.

Ever since Jenny he'd relished the idea of women

cowering because of him. Women longing for him to dominate them, women submitting to his anger, grovelling just like Jenny did. It gave him such power, the kind he'd never had over anyone, man, woman nor child, in all his life. He wiped the sweat from his top lip and the ecstasy from his mind. Fancy that little bitch carrying a knife. God! She was a handful and not half. His pulse raced at the prospect.

The mother was no fool though. She wouldn't tolerate someone like him thinking about her precious daughter in that way. Huh! But what did she know about life, the real, hardbitten knife-edge kind of life he'd led? She'd have spent her whole life being cosseted and cared for, protected and loved by everyone who met her, and that was something he had never had; real, deep, lasting love. Not that he was desiring deep lasting love from Beth. No, it was about domination, sexual satisfaction and submission. Andy's mind roved over Beth's good looks. She was a beauty with her flawless complexion, startling blue eyes and slender young figure, almost a woman but not quite yet. The sweat broke out again; face it, she was gorgeous. He recollected the look on her face when she'd poured the coffee over him, the passion surging within her, the disgust and the barely veiled hatred, too, which thrilled him. And then the knife! He was right, she was feisty and not half.

Across the kitchen he saw the chocolates he'd bought for Jenny before . . . before he'd throttled her. He could give them to Beth as an apology, and why not? Give him a chance to see her, perhaps make another move forward in gaining her confidence. He dwelt on the idea for a few minutes, dwelt on the thought of touching her, stroking that blonde hair . . . The phone interrupted his thoughts.

'Andy Moorhouse speaking.'

He listened and found to his horror that it was the head of his department speaking.

Nine o'clock sharp tomorrow morning with his case files for a department audit. See you.

He put the phone down and felt his world fall apart. This was the summons he'd been dreading would happen one day, perhaps next month, or the next, or the next. But not right here and now. The fake references, the hours spent away from the office, the colleagues who shunned him. His carefully constructed empire was toppling down on his head, remorselessly.

Should he run before the final showdown?

Might be a good idea after Jenny.

He'd miss his chance with Beth.

Leave the house he owned?

He glanced at the chocolates again. He didn't *have* to face the music in the office. If he did a disappearing act, they couldn't get at him if they didn't know where he was. The chocolates. Just a glimpse of her before he left.

That damned telephone call had ruined his pursuit of her. Another day, a few weeks, and all that lovely promise of beauty could have been his to control. He washed his face, combed his hair, threw some aftershave on, and opened the front door to find Inspector Gould and his sergeant – triggered by Caroline's call about his night-time escapade and the episode in the Abbey Coffee Shop – each holding out their identification, just about to ring the bell.

'Fortunate that, Mr Moorhouse. Very fortunate. Need a word. We'll come in.'

Gould and his burly sergeant were in the hall in an instant, staring at the box of chocolates in his hand.

'Going somewhere, Mr Moorhouse?'

The sergeant asked, 'Nice chocolates those. Taking them to a friend, are we, Mr Moorhouse?'

Andy couldn't speak. Thoughts raced through his head. He couldn't speak for thinking. Why were they here? They'd finished with him, he thought. Why were they ringing his doorbell? More clues? Had they found Jenny?

Trouble was they didn't speak. Just stood there like vast lumps of dumb, unmoving stone, staring at the box of chocolates.

Eventually he broke the silence. 'Well, officers, what can I do for you? I was just going out. Hope it's not important.'

'We want you at the station. Questions to ask that's all.'

'What about? I've helped you all I can with the store vandalism. I've got to take these.' His mind became obsessed with his mission to see Beth.

'On foot? Then we'll accompany you, and *then* we'll go to the station. You're willing to come?'

'Of course. I'll help in any way I can. Must deliver these.'

They edged him out of the door after checking he had his key. If it hadn't been for his obsession about delivering the chocolates to Beth he'd have realized he was confirming their suspicions.

He strode purposefully to the Rectory door, and rattled the knocker.

It was Alex who came to the door. 'Good afternoon. How may I help?'

'Is Beth in?'

'Yes, but she's busy and can't come to the door.'

He thrust the box at Alex. 'Give her these. From Andy, with my apologies.' He stepped away from the door and the police officers hustled him away.

As they stuffed him into their car, carefully parked out of sight at the top of Shepherds Hill, the sergeant said, 'So we were right. You were stalking Beth Harris.'

The rapid walk to the car had woken Andy up. 'That is absolutely ridiculous. Of course I haven't been stalking her. They live next door and we happened to go into the Abbey Coffee Shop today at the same time and shared a table. What's wrong with that?'

But they didn't answer and left him to sweat all the way to Culworth.

Now there was no Store for meet people in, it was slowly becoming common practice to gather by the bus stop even when there wasn't a bus due. They would sit on the seat to wait, in the hope that someone they knew would miraculously appear. That day there were three people waiting: Greta Jones, just finished work for the day; Sheila Bissett, waiting for the bus to Little Derehams and wishing she was still living in Turnham Malpas; and one of the weekenders, Joyce, who was spending extra time in her weekend home.

They all three watched the police hurrying someone into their car and when it drove past, heading to Culworth, Sheila was able to see who was in the car.

Sue gasped with horror. 'My God! See that? That was Andy Moorhouse.'

'It wasn't!'

'It was. Believe me.'

Greta Jones tapped the side of her nose. 'Always knew he was a wrong 'un.'

Joyce the weekender wanted to know who they were talking about. So they had an in-depth discussion about

Andy and his Jenny and how she'd dumped him and gone to Australia.

'Left us right in the lurch with the Beauty Evening at the Women's Institute meeting, she did. Not like her to do something like that. Always kept her appointments did Jenny. A very nice girl with a lovely smile.'

Greta nodded approvingly. 'I've always had my suspicions about that Australia business. She never said nothing did she, about a brother in Australia before she went. Then she's supposed to have flu, then she's supposed to have set off to Australia in the middle of it. I ask yer, it just doesn't add up. I reckon he did her in.'

Joyce made a mental note to tell the staff where she worked this whole new tale from the idyllic place she called her country retreat. They always loved her tales about the village.

Sheila gasped, eyes wide with amazement as she looked at Greta, 'You don't really think so, do you?'

'Oh, yes, I do. He's always struck me as being a nasty beggar. Look at that trouble with the tainted food he claims he's bought from the Store. Working there, I know full well that Jimbo wouldn't allow such a thing to happen. He's mustard on food hygiene, believe me, I know.'

A thought occurred to Sheila. 'I wonder where she is now?'

Greta rolled her eyes. 'A sight lot nearer Turnham Malpas than Australia, I should imagine.' She drew closer to the two of them and whispered, 'I know for a fact that house has a cellar.'

'You don't think she's bur . . . That is disgusting, and him tucking into his supper with her laid . . . How could he?' said Joyce.

'If I'd done someone in,' said Sheila, 'I'd take the body

to the old quarry. They'd be lost for ever amongst all the stuff that gets dumped there. The council never clear it up.'

'Or throw 'em over Bickerby Rocks, make it look as though they'd fallen over.' Greta nodded knowingly.

Sheila and Joyce shuddered. Joyce said, 'But how would he get her up to the top, carrying her?'

'No, you're right there, though she is very slight.' Greta, having further weighed up the possibilities of Jenny's whereabouts, declared finally, 'My money's on the quarry.'

'Bus coming.' Sheila picked up her bag. 'Keep me informed of further developments.' She leapt on the bus with greater ease than in the past, having lost so much weight.

Chapter 15

The weeks rolled by. Andy had been released by the police because there was insufficient evidence to convict him of having murdered Jenny and he was plausible about the visit to the Abbey Coffee Shop. But he had been dismissed from the Social Services with decisions about his future still pending and was now living on benefit. His car was sold, and he lived the life of a hermit apart from going once a week into Culworth for his food shopping, and no one volunteered to sit next to *him* on the bus. His name was on everybody's lips week after week and he got short shrift from everyone. They all guessed he was guilty and, so far as they were concerned, it would stay that way until proved different.

Over their morning cup of tea Dottie and Beth discussed it yet again. Dottie said for the umpteenth time, 'I can't understand why they haven't accused him of murdering her. After all, it didn't seem right, her being the kind of person she was, that she promised your mum about the Beauty Evening and then wham! She disappears overnight to Australia and hasn't been seen since.'

'Neither can I.'

'Can't find no evidence, I expect. But you have to admit her disappearance was a mystery; here today, gone tomorrow.'

'I still think, Dottie, that she never had flu at all. I think she'd already gone when he told you about the flu. She was fully alive the previous night, and not ill at all, because I spoke to her here in the sitting room about the Beauty Evening.'

'Exactly. That's my point. Coming for lunch today? I'd like it if you did.'

Beth nodded. 'I've got a load of homework to do this morning. I swear they give me more to do than when I was at school. Still, keeps me busy. But, lunch at yours is definitely on. After Easter I'm going back to school.'

Dottie beamed. 'I'm pleased, so very pleased. That is good news. You'll be all right on the school bus 'cos it'll take you right into the school, won't it?'

'And I'll have Alex, too, and the girls get off first and then it goes on to the boys' school. Coming home it's in reverse so I'll be absolutely fine. Thanks for being a good friend.'

'That's all right. Going back to school will make life a lot more normal and you'll be safe.' Dottie got to her feet, patted Beth's hand and smiled at her.

It could have been coincidence but when Beth, feeling much more confident about walking out in the open, had started to walk home after lunch at Dottie's that day, Andy appeared at the entrance to Syke's Wood as though on cue. Beth's head had been full of the talk she and Dottie had had after lunch and suddenly, without the slightest warning, there he was, smiling his most ingratiating smile.

Keep calm, keep calm, Beth said inside herself.

He waved to her and crossed the road to join her. 'Can't let you walk all that way up Shepherds Hill by yourself, now can I?'

He was wearing a kind of Sherlock Holmes hat and a

heavy overcoat that gave him an air of respectability, a complete change from his navy anorak; it was like a new identity. He adjusted his stride to hers and began asking her if she'd started back at school yet.

Beth stopped and, not looking at him, said, 'I wish . . . to walk home . . . by myself. Would you please walk ahead of me?'

'But I feel you need company – you never know these days, walking alone – and I shall be proud to walk with someone as charming as you. Because you are charming. You might not realize it, but you are.'

Beth stood rooted to the spot and didn't answer. Nothing could happen so long as she didn't move. That was the secret; ignoring him and keeping quite still.

Andy, baffled by her lack of response, tried taking a grip on her elbow to push her into walking along with him.

But he couldn't move her. 'Do you hear me? Walk with me. You'll come to no harm. Not with me.'

Then he tried wheedling and cajoling and persuading in the lightest, brightest of tones but Beth ignored him.

'Did you know there's some baby foxes just out of the den in the wood? They're magic to watch. Would you like to see them?'

By now she was rigid with fear and didn't know how much longer she could remain motionless. The desire to run was paramount in her head.

The stile leading to Sykes Wood was a matter of a few feet away and she pondered on bolting for the wood, but squashed that idea immediately. She had to stay in the open where someone, anyone might see her.

Then he was breathing heavily, his face close to her ear and she smelled garlic and drink on his breath. Her nose wrinkled in disgust.

'Do you hear me? How much longer will you stand here? Answer me, you little bitch, answer me.'

His language and his attitude to her grew more alarming by the minute, and he tried again to pull her towards the wood. Her mobile phone was worse than useless to her because he'd never let her use it. Just when her desperation had reached uncharted waters, Mrs Jones, on her way home from the Store, hove into view round the bend.

She was yards away but picked up on Beth's panic immediately. She saw the grip he had on her arm, smelled his animal energy, and knew this was her moment, her drama.

She ran towards the pair of them, shouting and swinging her shopping bag, arriving just at the moment when Beth couldn't physically resist his pulling any longer. So intense and focused was Andy that he was unaware of Mrs Jones's voice until the shopping bag hit him across the back of his head. Momentarily he lost his balance and relaxed his grip. He called Mrs Jones some foul names, but she didn't care. Released, Beth began running, short of breath through fear, but away she went, heading for the school.

Mrs Jones continued hitting Andy about his head and shoulders with her bag until she'd driven him into escaping her by running up the hill towards the village. Mrs Jones followed him as best she could but neither he nor she could see where Beth had disappeared to when they finally arrived in Jacks Lane. All appeared normal; the geese were demonstrating their authority to one of the Charter-Plackett cats, the children were playing in the schoolyard for their afternoon break, Kate Fitch was supervising and Beth – well, she'd disappeared completely.

Andy, knowing he couldn't inquire from Mrs Fitch if she'd seen Beth as that would look suspicious, had to retire to his house, bowed but not beaten, to watch from his window.

Beth was hiding in the school kitchen with Maggie Dobbs. 'I want my mummy,' she said, just like she'd done when she was small at school and wanted to go home.

'See here, Beth love, you're safe with Maggie Dobbs. No harm'ull come to you. Why, you're quite out of puff. Now, come on. Stop the tears, you're safe now. Maggie's in charge and nothing nor nobody will get at you while I'm here. Sit on this chair, and I'll get you a glass of water. There you are, that's it. Now, here's the water, cold as ice out of this tap, do you a power of good, it will.'

Beth sipped clumsily out of the glass, water dripping on her chin which Maggie wiped off with a clean tea towel, feeling Beth shivering right inside herself as she did so. She repeated her request. 'I want my mummy. Please. Beth's going to be sick.'

Maggie nodded. She took her brand-new mobile phone from her bag and gave it to Beth. 'You dial the number. I'll speak.'

So Maggie spoke and Caroline was there in minutes. 'Darling!' She said, and they were clutched in each other's arms.

'I want to go home.'

'Of course. Thank you, Maggie, for taking care of her. Thank you very much. I'll explain later. Sorry.'

Caroline, with an arm around Beth's shoulders, hurried her home. 'It's all right, Beth, we're nearly there.' She didn't realize that Mrs Jones was rushing to catch up with them.

'Doctor Harris! Doctor Harris!'

Caroline turned to see who was speaking to her. 'Come in, come in.'

Mrs Jones followed her into the Rectory, breathless but determined to have her say. 'You all right now, Beth? I saw it all, that's why I've come.'

Caroline led the way into the kitchen. 'Sit there, Beth, till you catch your breath. Now, Mrs Jones, what is it? What did you see?'

'I saw it all happen. Has she told you?'

'No.'

'Well, that Andy Moorhouse must have been waiting for her coming home from Dottie's because when I got round the bend by Angie Turner's there was that sod holding Beth's arm and trying to pull her into Sykes Wood, dragging at her arm, he was. I raced up and swung my shopping bag at him. Feel, it's heavy, two jars of marmalade in it I've bought for a neighbour, and it shocked him and he let go, and your Beth ran like hell, and he and me followed her, but we couldn't see her when we got into the village. He went home and I stood and waited to see where she'd gone. If you need a witness you've got me. I saw him doing it.'

Caroline laid a grateful hand on Greta Jones's arm. 'Thank you, thank you. I'm almost out of my mind with worry. I shall ring the police immediately and if they want to talk to you about it, will that be all right?'

At this moment Anna walked in to the Rectory, intending sitting down in Peter's study and putting in some spadework on her Sunday sermon.

'Oh, hello. Has something happened? Shall I make myself scarce?'

Caroline, almost beside herself, said, 'It's Beth. Andy Moorhouse has assaulted her. Greta witnessed it.'

'Oh! Beth, my dear, I'm so sorry. What can I do to help?'

Greta piled in with, 'I saw it. He tried to drag her into Sykes Wood, and these two jars of marmalade . . .'

Anna looked pointedly at Caroline and then went round the kitchen table and put her arm around Beth's shoulders. 'My dear. What a shock. Shall you and I sit in your dad's study for a while till your mum's sorted out what to do? Mmm?'

Beth nodded. Anything that would bring her dad close would be a help. So she and Anna sat quietly side by side on the sofa in his study, and Beth looked round the familiar room and immediately felt cherished.

'Why is he doing this to me, Anna?'

'It's because his mind has got very bent.'

'What does he mean to do?'

'Probably all he wants to do is look at you and admire you. You're a very beautiful girl, you see. Don't feel it's your fault that you're beautiful, it isn't, not at all. With a Dad who's so good-looking you're bound to be beautiful. Just look on it as his mind not functioning properly; his is like a jigsaw all in pieces in a box and needing to be sorted. If your mum rings the police then it'll mean the police questioning you, though. Do you feel up to that?'

Beth was silent, then she said, 'I've faced worse.'

'Oh, my dear, I'm so sorry you're having this dreadful time. I'm always ready to listen, you know, should you ever—'

'No. No. Thank you. You're very kind. There's only Daddy who—'

Anna dabbed Beth's tears away with a tissue. 'Absolutely. Yes, I understand. Absolutely.'

In the kitchen Greta Jones was saying the same word just as emphatically.

'Absolutely. It's got to be the police, there's no avoiding it. I haven't imagined it; it's just as I say. I'll be in all afternoon if they want to question me and I shall tell the whole truth. I shan't mince my words, so don't you fret. The nasty devil. He must have been waiting for her just by the stile. Bought a new overcoat and a winter hat, Russian like, fur and them earflaps it has, instead of that old anorak. Changed his appearance completely, which is suspicious in itself. With Greta Jones on Beth's side, as well as everyone else in the village, you won't go far wrong, Doctor Harris. Don't you fret, we'll get him. I'll see myself out.'

Caroline wondered how many more appalling incidents Beth was going to have to take on board. She'd never get better. The police. Right now.

Inspector Gould was at the Rectory within twenty minutes accompanied by a woman police constable. After half an hour they were seen by Grandmama – who happened to be bored to tears and was looking out of the sitting-room window in the hope of someone passing by – knocking at Andy Moorhouse's door. She had to crane her neck a little as the door wasn't easy to see from where she stood. She waited, eyes glued to Andy's vivid purple door. It took ten minutes of concentrated watching before there was any movement. But she was rewarded. Out of the front door of his cottage came Andy, handcuffed to the constable and accompanied by the inspector. He was whisked away towards Culworth at speed.

Later that afternoon Mrs Jones was rewarded for her enterprise by two women police officers pulling up outside her cottage. They went inside and her neighbours counted the minutes until they emerged. But they didn't take her with them because five minutes after the car left, she was shaking her new yellow duster out of her front window. So what did she know that they didn't?

The police, with the help of Beth telling how she saw Andy leaving in the middle of the night in his car, finally dragged the truth about Jenny's disappearance from Andy. Jenny Sweetapple's remains were found in the quarry after a thorough clean-up and removal of ten years of accumulated rubbish. It was a mammoth task with the police on duty whenever the digger was working and when it wasn't. But there she was under a mattress, beneath a shopping trolley, under a pile of cardboard boxes and grass cuttings and wrapped in three torn binbags ... anyway, she had been found at last. To think they'd been harbouring a murderer all this time. Mind you, they'd never liked *him*, had they?

Everything went very flat after Jenny Sweetapple was found. It was such a long time to the trial but they were all agreed on one thing: they'd sit in the public gallery and see him sentenced.

Weeks rolled by, sometimes slow, sometimes fast, till it was time for the Annual Village Show. Only a month to go and Peter would be home. No one wished for his return as much as Caroline, for she longed to be held in his arms and feel again the comfort of his presence. Beth's avowed intent to go back to school after Easter never happened. What with the attempted attack on her by Andy Moorhouse and the subsequent questioning by the police, she was back almost at the beginning of her troubles. Alex had three weeks away from school due to stress, he said, but in reality it was his heart breaking for his twin.

Putting on the Show was its usual frantic hard work but somehow the joy had gone out of it and it felt like slavery rather than the happy occasion it had used to be. The rivalry was there when it came to the prize-giving, though, but even that had lost its sharp edge. Jimbo closing the Store became an even worse trial than it had been when he first closed, and he was on the receiving end of a few acid comments from people who in normal circumstances thoroughly approved of everything he did. He didn't even offer to supply food for the tea tent as he had always done, and that caused Pat Jones some heartache when she volunteered to run it, forgetting Jimbo's ready supply of food wouldn't be available.

Stocks Day, with Anna Sanderson in the guise of the Grim Reaper, somehow didn't have quite the same meaning, because the outfit she wore was the one Muriel had lengthened for Peter the first year he was in Turnham Malpas, and it was so long on her the hem lay on the grass and when she walked she had to hold it up for fear of tripping over it. They couldn't ask Muriel to alter it as Muriel, well, she wasn't quite herself of late and that was another thing which upset everyone. Despite the trials of making sure she didn't trip up over her long skirts, Anna made a really good fist of being the Grim Reaper. Willie had fitted her with a special microphone because practising a week before the big day proved that Anna's voice wouldn't reach the huge crowds, especially if it was windy. Willie's forethought saved the day for Anna; they could hear every word. Some of them felt quite tearful about her leaving when Peter came back, especially those who had received her sympathy and valuable advice at times of trouble. All in all they supposed they were glad it was Anna who'd been shepherding them through what had proved difficult times.

Though they all remembered how they valued Peter and longed for him to be back. Come back, Peter, was the cry on everyone's lips.

And come back he did. Caroline went to the airport to meet him, eager to see him but almost afraid of how to behave when they'd been separated for so long.

She was standing at the arrivals exit, amongst what appeared to be a vast crowd of other eager greeters. Living in a village for so long she'd almost forgotten how many people there were crammed into the metropolis and began to feel like an ant, unknown and insignificant. There was no missing Peter, though; at six feet five he towered above most of the exiting passengers. His hair was lightened by the sun and his eyes were bright with anticipation, but he was thin, oh, how thin. She raised her hand to attract his attention and his eyes fixed on hers. He hurried towards her, thrusting his way through the crowd until he was within touching distance. For a brief second they simply drank in the sight of each other, too emotional to smile, and then, what joy, they were in each other's arms.

There weren't words adequate enough to express how they felt. They hugged and kissed till all reason had vanished. Finally Peter said, 'Let's get to the hotel, then we can really talk.'

'Am I glad you're home, my darling. I've been counting the days, it's been so long.'

Caroline had booked an airport hotel room so after a brief taxi ride they were in their room, free to talk at last. At first they made general conversation, chattering about this and that, none of it of any consequence except they were putting out feelers, trying to reach the closeness they'd always enjoyed.

Peter finally asked the question he'd been wanting to ask from the moment they met. 'Well now, what about the children? Will you tell me truthfully what the problem is? How are they really getting on?'

Caroline said they were fine, not wishing to spoil his first few hours with problems.

Peter looked at her and said, 'Caroline! Please, my darling, stop shielding me, I know things are *not* fine.'

Startled, Caroline asked, 'How? Has someone e-mailed you?'

'No one but you. But I do know from yours they're not flourishing. It's what you left out, you see.'

Caroline sat down on the bed and invited Peter to join her. He put an arm around her shoulders, saying, 'Go on, then. Tell me, please. Have they not improved at all?'

So Caroline had to tell him the whole of the story, of their dread of wide open spaces, of Beth's fear of leaving the house, of Andy Moorhouse and about Beth taking a knife out with her, which made Peter gasp, and Jenny's murder, of Beth's screaming nightmares and Alex's ability to calm her down.

He listened silently, almost withdrawn, while he assimilated what had happened.

'You see, Peter, they won't confide in me. They both say they'll tell you when you get home. I feel I've let them down very badly. Perhaps if I'd been their *real* mother they'd have been able to tell me, but I'm not and they can't. I just hope they can tell you, because they'll never get cured if they don't tell someone.'

Peter released his hold on her and went to stand at the

window and look down at the crowds thronging the street on their way to an evening out at the clubs.

'Elijah told me something of what had gone on. About the massacre, the wholesale destruction of the villages, the burning of our church and your clinic, which we've now rebuilt and improved on with some of the money the village sent to us, and the raping . . . she . . .'

'No, not Beth, she did tell me that.'

'Thank God.'

'But something happened which has frightened the life out of them and they need you desperately.'

'All I have to do is to deliver papers and reports to the mission headquarters here in London tomorrow morning and then we can go straight home.' He turned from the window and said, 'Never as long as I live am I going out there again. Never. I'm being entirely selfish when I say this but there were some days when I could barely function for pining for you, Caroline. Occasionally I thought I heard your voice and turned to see you but of course you were never there. I suffered utter devastation in my heart. *Actual* pain. Just to see you would have been enough. I love you so very much and I shall never be parted from you again.' He opened his arms wide and she rushed into them.

Chapter 16

In the event it was almost eleven o'clock and the bright summer evening already gone before they reached Turnham Malpas. Peter drove most of the way home, glad to be at the wheel again and eager to get home where he belonged. Caroline could feel her burden lifting the nearer they got, and she could sense contentment filling her very bones. She rested her hand on his thigh as he drove and he turned to smile at her. 'Happy?'

'Never been happier. I just want to hear you singing in the shower when you come back from your run, then I'll know you're definitely home.'

'Running! It'll be a while before I get back in my stride. Three miles seems like a marathon. I've done no running at all for almost a year.'

'You've lost a lot of weight, far too much, so I wouldn't worry about three miles each morning, that can wait.' She smiled at him but he didn't return it.

They reached the bend in the Culworth Road and were almost home.

'I'll drive up Pipe and Nook, shall I? Give ourselves a bit of privacy for a while longer?'

Caroline nodded. She imagined that the children would be in bed but she hadn't taken Beth's sleeplessness into consideration. She was watching from her bedroom window and was down the stairs and opening the back door almost before Peter had got his luggage out.

'Daddy! Daddy!'

She ran down the path in her bare feet and flung her arms about him, clinging to him like a limpet.

'Darling, Beth. How I've missed you.'

'I'll go get Alex, he mustn't miss this.' She raced away with Caroline calling after her, 'Your slippers, Beth!' But she didn't heed the warning and went straight to wake Alex by shaking him vigorously and shouting, 'He's here! He's here. Come on.' Then she raced downstairs again to put the kettle on.

Alex's greeting was more subdued than Beth's but then he had been woken rather abruptly and was taking time to wake up properly. The handshake he offered Peter was ignored and he was clasped in his father's arms like it or not. 'You've grown since I saw you last. But that's only to be expected. You need to put some weight on, Alex.'

'So do you, Dad.'

'Yes, but I've been where there's not much food about. Maybe you're thin because you're growing so quickly. That'll be it.' But Peter felt this unexpected estrangement from his son very badly. Beth was hanging on his arm as though she would never let him go, but Alex almost made him feel there was no place left for him in the Rectory any more. He looked at Caroline and she gave a faint shake of her head so he pretended he hadn't noticed Alex's lack of enthusiasm. 'Come on, Alex, get the mugs out, and mine's the blue one, don't forget.'

Alex did so then filled the teapot to the top and got out the biscuit tin, and they sat round the kitchen table and tried to draw closer together.

'So what's been happening in the village while I've been away?'

Beth got in first. 'Jimmy Glover's Sykes has died of old age and he isn't getting a new dog, says he can't be bothered with the walking. Evie Nicholls has bought a puppy and she's called it Tatty, and it is! Jimbo has closed the Store, and—'

'Jimbo's closed the Store? Really?'

The three of them nodded and said yes.

'What does he do all day?'

'Works on his new website where he sells his mail order stuff and apparently Mrs Jones is working so hard she's going to have to work full-time or get an assistant.'

'How does everyone manage without the Store?'

Caroline told him how difficult it was but that now they had two mobile shops that came round instead, although it wasn't the same at all. She recognized then that Peter was looking exhausted, and decided it was time he went to bed.

'Children, it's time Daddy went to bed, he needs to sleep. Can we tell him the rest of our news tomorrow? Would you mind?'

Beth protested indignantly. 'But you've had Daddy ever since yesterday. We want to talk to him, too. You're not tired, are you, Daddy?' But then she looked at Peter and saw the fatigue in his face, and agreed he did need to sleep. 'All right, then. We'll go to bed. Night-night, Daddy. So glad you're home. We'll talk tomorrow.' She reached up to kiss his cheek, patted his hand and disappeared upstairs. Alex gave him a curt nod, managed a small smile and followed her.

Peter said, 'I'm going to sit in my study for ten minutes then I'll be upstairs.' He trailed a finger along Caroline's jaw then bent his head to kiss her mouth so tenderly it was almost like the kiss of a butterfly, then his face lit up with a beautifully generous smile, glowing with love. *This* was the Peter Alexander Harris she'd married, the man she adored.

In his study Peter found his files, neatly arranged, just as they always were, except now they were sorted differently. The papers on his desk were spread about too casually for his liking, the computer at a different angle, the keyboard too close, the chair too high, the sofa facing the wrong way, and the matching easy chair loaded with a collection of odd cushions, none of them his own.

So how had she got on? He leafed through the parish diary and had a wry smile for some of her comments. Nothing appeared to have occurred that couldn't be rectified; same place, same study, same church, but different. He'd imagined everything would be the same but it wasn't, not quite. Did it matter?

Beth with a knife she was apparently quite prepared to use. Alex almost sullen in his attitude towards him. Thank God for Caroline, she was still the same. Without her . . . where would he be? He really needed to hold her in his arms, to explore her closeness, touch her skin, smell her hair, her perfume, everything and anything that was her. He roared up the stairs two at a time, went into their bedroom to find Beth in a sleeping bag on the floor his side of the bed snoring gently, and Alex in his sleeping bag on the rug his mother's side of the bed, also apparently fast asleep. Caroline looked up at him and put a finger to her lips, then gestured towards Alex. Obviously he wasn't asleep.

This could be overlooked for one night but after that . . . When he finally got into bed he drew Caroline close to him and they lay together, talking softly. 'The best thing about tonight is that glorious shower I've just had. I'd forgotten how good it was.'

'Just think, you can have a good shower every single night from now on, and morning come to that.'

'It's worth coming home just for the shower.'

Caroline half sat up in bed to say, 'Cheek!'

'What about us, Dad? Is it worth coming home for us?' said a voice from the floor on Caroline's side of the bed with more than a hint of pleading in it.

'Alex! I was only teasing your mum. Of course you and Mum and Beth are why I'm here. And am I glad to be home. Believe me. God bless you, Alex. Goodnight.'

There was a silence filled with Beth's gentle snoring and then very quietly, but sincerely, Alex said, 'And God bless you, too, Dad.'

Chapter 17

Caroline woke the next morning to find Peter no longer in bed beside her. She listened for him moving about downstairs, but it was quiet. He must be in his study. It seemed a long time since she had woken feeling as peaceful as she did this morning. She was so glad he was home again and that she could speak to him whenever she wanted and not have to wait for e-mails or phone calls he made when he could.

It was six-thirty in the morning, but Peter wasn't in the Rectory. He was in the church saying his prayers. He'd found the huge key for the main door of the church exactly where he'd left it and had smoothed his fingers over it, enjoying its age, its shape, its familiarity. Then he pushed open the door and walked in onto the stone flagged floor, and it was then that he knew, finally, he was home. He gazed up at the rafters and rejoiced.

For some reason prayer did not come easily to him this morning. He knelt in the memorial chapel as always, but the throb of excitement he'd felt when he walked in didn't help him to concentrate. Maybe it was because he couldn't settle to sleep last night as he had hoped, for he'd been dog tired. Thoughts had raced through his head, tumbling over each other, one after another, till he became even more exhausted. At last his mind had unwound and, slowly but surely, deep sleep had caught up with him.

When he rose to his feet half an hour later he was a man refreshed in mind and spirit. He locked the church door. Took off his track suit, tucked it under the porch seat and set off for his run. But the legs weren't working like they had and his energy levels were low, so his three-mile run was shortened to one mile and he arrived back at the Rectory sweating and out of breath.

Caroline was in the kitchen getting breakfast. 'Good morning, darling. Three miles as usual?'

'No. I couldn't do it, I'm so out of condition. One mile, that's all. Going for a shower.'

'Well, that's what you came home for, remember? A good shower.'

Peter grinned. 'OK. OK. Children awake?'

'I thought I heard them about.'

'Won't be long.'

They had a joyful breakfast together, laughing and joking as though he'd never been away. Alex in particular had lifted his mood and enjoyed pulling his dad's leg. They were just finishing their breakfast when Dottie Foskett let herself in at the front door.

'Don't panic, it's Dottie.'

Peter looked surprised.

'Good morning, Dottie. The Rector's home at last,' Caroline called out.

Dottie stood in the kitchen doorway putting on her cleaning apron. 'Well, this is lovely, Rector, having you here at last. Welcome home.' She gave him a big nervous smile.

Peter thanked her for her welcome, and hid his surprise

very well. This was something Caroline had forgotten to tell him.

Caroline began clearing the table. 'Sylvia tells me she's full of admiration for your cleaning abilities. She enjoyed staying with the children while I went to meet Peter.'

'She's very nice, is Sylvia. I had the idea she might be a bit annoyed with me taking her job, but she wasn't at all. She's just like a grandma to the twins and they played snakes and ladders with Willie as though their lives depended on it. The poor chap was worn out!'

'They've always liked playing that game with him. He takes it so seriously.'

'Right. I'll press on, then. The usual?'

'Yes, please.'

After Dottie disappeared Peter asked, 'Sylvia's all right, is she?'

'Yes. Long story, I'll tell you another time.'

The twins chattered away to Peter, helping him to catch up on the news, and before they knew where they were it was Anna's key they heard, brisk and businesslike as usual.

'That's Anna, darling, you'd better go.'

'Clean my teeth first.'

Alex got up from his chair and set off to race his dad to the bathroom. He won but graciously gave Peter first turn at the basin. 'I'll take my brush up to the other bathroom. Put me some toothpaste on, please. I might start sleeping up there, what do you think? I've always liked that bedroom.'

'Ask Mum.'

Anna was waiting for him to appear. She felt rather out of place in his study, it so very much belonged to him. She'd kept it tidy, tried to keep his files orderly, but somehow she had the feeling she would be at a disadvantage the moment he walked in. She recognized that he was one of those men who have no idea that they are very attractive to women. His sex appeal was renowned at the Abbey and it was that which worried her.

It was nothing that he did, because he came in quietly, having knocked first, and he'd stood, hand outstretched, smiling and saying, 'Good morning, Anna.' And as she expected, she was immediately overwhelmed by the vitality of the man.

'Hello, Peter, nice to have you back.'

He went to sit on the sofa and she offered him the desk chair, which he refused. They both spoke at once and Peter said, 'No, you first.'

'I can't remember what I was going to say.'

'Well, I'll start. I had a quick flip through the parish diary last night and I found some of your comments absolutely spot on. Have you enjoyed being here? I hope so, because I love it here and from now on I have no intention of offering my services anywhere else at all.' He smiled as he spoke and she smiled back.

'You say that now but wait another few years and something else will come to tempt you.'

'It won't. Tell me, how did you find the children? Caroline's very concerned about them. How have you found them?'

'I've not really had much to do with them, but Beth is very disturbed, and she's kind of keeping it bottled up, except at night when she has screaming nightmares, or so I understand. Alex is disturbed, too, but he's tried to carry on as though nothing has happened, which it obviously has. I just hope his dad will be able to help him, because he won't allow Caroline to know what troubles them both.'

'I shall tackle that problem at an appropriate moment. Is there anyone in the parish who is in dire trouble at the moment?'

'Not dire trouble, just the usual worries, but—'

'Yes?'

'There is one who is deeply worried.'

'Who's that?'

'Sheila Bissett.'

'That's not like her.'

'Oh! Well, she is. We've had a few talks but she is adept at steering the conversation away from her problem. Maybe you could get somewhere with her, I'd be glad if you could.'

'Any clues?'

'Well, her daughter Louise had a premature baby who was badly deformed, and they thought blind too, and he died rather suddenly when he was in an incubator fastened up to tubes and wires without which he couldn't exist. Sheila's never been the same since. I daren't think what I'm thinking. She wouldn't, would she?'

'I'd be surprised but one never knows what people will do when faced with that kind of tragedy.'

'Apart from that, we've had a murder – newcomers . . . Jimbo's had a bad fall from a ladder and seriously broken his ankle, he's been the subject of some poison pen letters and damage to the shop so he's closed it. Otherwise everything has gone according to plan . . . and . . .'

'Well, that's enough to be going on with, heavens above. A possible murderer in our midst and everything's going to plan?'

Anna had to smile. 'But my word, Peter, I've found it hard to fill your shoes. So far as your flock is concerned, no one, but no one, can take your place. If you think about going away again I honestly believe they'll lock you up in that old prison in Little Derehams that Mr Fitch restored, and never let you go, and you'll be taken by armed guard to take the Services. I've been told to stay on here and give you a chance to take a holiday and help the changeover, so there's no loose ends, you know. You're not going back again, are you?'

'Definitely not.'

'Well, I'm living at Grandmama's and have been since last September, so it'll take a while to pack I've collected so many things. My microscopic flat at the Abbey is empty now so I can go back when I want. Do you feel ready to pick up the threads?'

'Absolutely, well, almost. I wouldn't be averse to you staying a while longer to bridge the gap, so to speak.'

'I could keep well away from your study. I've got things I could do out and about. Would that be OK?'

'God bless you for standing in for me so well. I'm sure they all appreciate what you've done. A couple of extra weeks would help me to orientate myself.'

With a rueful smile Anna began picking up her own bits and pieces from the desk. 'I don't think they feel *that* enthusiastic about me. However, a few more months and perhaps I might be more acceptable to them, though I doubt it. One very big plus, though, has been the chance to use your books. You've a marvellous library of theological books. I'm envious, Peter. They've been very helpful.'

The phone began to ring, then. Peter pointed to her, suggesting she answered it, but she refused. So he picked up the phone. It was Jimbo, and the mad mess that had been his life for so many months began falling into place.

He spent the whole of the next week catching up with everything, seeing people, preaching, praying, attending to administration, telling everyone he met how much the money they had raised had helped the little mission church he'd grown to love. Saturday soon came round again and he had not yet spoken to his children about their problems, but then neither of them had suggested he did. But that night Beth had one of her screaming nightmares. Caroline immediately began to get up, but Peter said, 'No. Let me go.'

The moment Beth saw her father standing in the doorway she continued screaming but from under her duvet.

Alex came down from the attic, pulled the duvet off Beth and grabbed hold of her, saying, 'Hush, hush, you're home now, safe at home. Gently, gently. Mum's here and Dad. Hush, hush. Remember we came home. We're OK. Right?'

The sobbing began to subside and although she clung to Alex she did become calmer.

Caroline appeared in the doorway with a glass of water and gave it to Peter. He held it out to Beth and she took it from him. 'Thank you.' She gulped a few more times and then drank the water down greedily. When she'd finished it right to the bottom she gave the glass back to Peter and said, 'Daddy?'

'Yes, darling, what is it?'

'Are you staying here for ever?'

'Of course. I told Mummy only the other night that I was never going away from the three of you ever again, because I can't bear to be parted from you.' He knelt beside the bed so he could hold her hand to reassure her.

She rubbed her eyes, pulled the duvet around herself

and grabbed hold of his hand, gripping it tight. 'I wonder . . . is there time to talk, right now? I need to tell you something that happened and Alex does, too. We've been longing for you to come home and we can't tell anyone else. We're so scared, Daddy, just so scared.'

'Yes, there is time, nothing like the present actually.' Alex stayed but Caroline melted quietly away.

Alex perched on the end of her bed and left it to her to begin. Beth cleared her throat once or twice and then whispered, 'You see, we can't tell Mummy, she loves us so much it would break her heart. You love us lots but you're strong and you'll manage, you see, and you'll understand and tell us what to do.'

'Tell me, then. Close the door first, Alex.'

The moment he sat down again Alex plunged straight into the story.

'You know they set the car on fire when those rebels stopped us that night? Well, we ran like hell from that car and only just in time because it was roaring with flames in seconds. It was dark and we couldn't see and we kept falling and picking ourselves up and then we lay down to get our breath back and we saw . . . in the light of the flames . . . we saw them shoot the missionary. He was such a nice man and trying so hard to help them grow better crops on their land, but they killed him just the same. How can they, Dad, kill the ones who are helping them to make better lives for themselves?'

'If we knew the answer to that a lot of the world's problems could be solved. So?'

Beth answered him. 'We lay all night waiting for the dawn so we could see where we were. Daddy, it was terrible and we were so hungry, and all we wanted was to be home with you and Mummy. So we thought when it was light we'd be able to find the road and walk along it to home. But we were silly to think that because there were soldiers and rebels going by all the time, spreading out into the bush and searching for anyone they could and if they didn't approve of them we could hear them begging and screaming as they were being killed. The soldiers and the rebels had machetes and guns and coshes, and you didn't know which was which, a government soldier or a rebel.'

Peter shuddered.

'We walked to where we thought the road was but we realized we couldn't walk along it as it was too dangerous. Well, Alex said it was and we had an argument. Anyway, we made a hideout for ourselves, Alex found a stream and he tested the water first and said it was all right but during the night we got stomach ache from it and we daren't drink any more – well, we did when we got desperate. Then two nights later we heard Elijah softly singing "The Lord's My Shepherd", you know how he loved that hymn? So we crept out to find him. We were so glad to see each other.'

Peter commented, 'He is a very brave man, is Elijah.'

'He is. He hadn't much to give us because he was short of food, too, but Winsome had made some vegetable broth and he brought us some, so we ate half and saved the other half for the next day. Alex asked him to take us home but he daren't. He said we'd be the first target being white. So he left us water and some bread and said he'd try to get back and not to move from where we were. Then we panicked because we thought maybe you and Mummy had been . . . killed, you know, if they were killing white people. And we cried.

'Alex had a stick and made a mark on it each morning with a sharp stone so we knew exactly how many days, were going by. It was only two before Elijah was back with another vegetable broth, but it seemed an age. Before he came the next time . . . we . . . you tell, Alex.' Beth gripped Peter's hand and couldn't look at him.

'It was the soldiers and the rebels passing by, you never knew when, so we were always on the lookout. Sometimes there were only one or two, sometimes ten or twelve. Believe me, Dad, we learned how to keep absolutely still. But then this soldier on his own stopped to have a . . . pee . . . not far from us and whether he could smell us or his hearing was so acute he could hear us breathing I don't know, but he came on closer and closer.'

It was Beth's turn to shudder.

Alex had beads of sweat on his forehead and he was fidgeting continuously with his hands. 'He was carrying a gun and had a machete in his belt and a kind of truncheon. I can see him so clearly, even now. There's a camouflage cap on his head and he's slinking along as though in fear of his life, just like us. He stops and listens, looks around and must have caught sight of something or seen a slight movement, and he walks straight towards us. We lay there, not speaking, not looking, for an age. I hope he thinks we're dead but he prods me with his gun and tries to roll me over so then he knows we're a-a-live.'

His voice broke and Alex had to stop. Peter hadn't been looking at him while he'd been speaking, hoping he would feel able to speak more freely, but now he turned towards Alex and said, 'When you're ready, Alex, take your time.'

Beth was still holding his hand and not looking, but when Alex couldn't carry on she looked up and said, 'He asked us for food. You know, pointed to his mouth, but we shook our heads and he was angry so he kicked Alex and then me. Then he kicked me again and I shuffled out of his way, and he shouted but we didn't know what he said and we didn't know what to do to pacify him. I just wished we had something to give him, something he could sell, and I thought about my watch, and perhaps it would make him go away, so I took it off and he snatched it and put in his pocket.'

'But I've seen you wearing it.'

'Yes, I know, Dad,' said Alex. 'Then he gestures with his rifle butt telling us to stand up. So we do. He takes one look at Beth and leers, and kind of sneers, really disgusting it was, then he demonstrates he wants her to take her dress off. I shout no, cos she's got nothing left to wear underneath. I guess what's coming but there wasn't anything I could do to stop him, he was pointing his gun at her.' Alex could feel hysteria mounting inside him.

Peter dwelt on his own daughter facing this; it was more than he could bear. His voice thick with emotion, he comforted Alex. 'He'd have shot you if you'd tried to stop him, and then where would Beth have been? Left all alone. You did right.'

'I know. I know.' For the first time since they'd come home Alex wept.

Beth let go her father's hand and stood up on the bed to reach the highest shelf. She pulled her sketch pad out from the very bottom of the pile of books. 'Look. It's all here. I drew it.' She watched him as he turned the pages and saw such a shocking expression of horror on her father's compassionate face. It was too terrifying for a child of his to see. Beth closed her eyes.

Peter needed all his intellect, all his strength, to overcome his suffering and take control of the situation. Between Beth and Alex, who to comfort first? His initial reaction was a need to vomit copiously, right where he was, but he swallowed hard and managed to control the urge.

'Now . . . now we've got so far you'd better tell me the rest. You're both here, so you survived. How did you do it?' Whether he wanted to hear the answer to that question he didn't know, but he had to hear it, for their sakes if nothing else. It was Alex who answered him.

'She's kneeling down, like in her picture, struggling to get her dress off, he puts his gun down so he can . . . so he can . . . expose himself, he's lots of stuff round his waist, you see, so I grab the gun in a flash and swing it like a cricket bat and hit him on the back of his head with all my strength and he falls down half on the ground and half on Beth,' Alex had to stop then, saying almost apologetically, 'It all happens so much quicker than I can tell. She screams, I hit him again so he's definitely unconscious. I push him off Beth, she's covered in blood, and we wait to see if he moves, but he doesn't but I keep the gun pointing at him just the same.'

Beth interrupts, 'He didn't know what to do to fire it but it felt reassuring. We waited an age and he didn't move at all so Alex pushed at him with the gun and rolled him over and we realised . . . ' Tears tippled down her cheeks.

'We realized we'd *killed* him.' Alex began crying again, not like a child, but like a man.

Peter drew in a loud throttling kind of breath, unable to believe that his beloved children had been forced to murder to save their lives. Beth still couldn't bear to see her father's face. 'We're so sorry, Daddy. So sorry. And so afraid. We didn't mean to do it, honestly we didn't. You do believe us, don't you? Alex only hit him to save me.

Shall we get taken back there to go to prison? That's what we're so frightened of, and I can't bear to go back to Africa, just in case they—'

Peter asked, 'But what then, Alex, what happened to him? Were you sure he was dead? Did you run away?'

'We couldn't run. Only Elijah knew where we were.'

'Ah. Yes. So?'

Alex had to reply because Beth was still choked with her tears.

'We moved away from our hiding place and found some soft ground. We dug a big hole with some pointy stones and our hands and the end of his gun, then we dragged him by his feet and put him in it and c-c-covered him over.' Alex shuddered with disgust at himself.

'What about his gun?'

'We had that with us and buried it with him. We did think of keeping it, Dad, but then we worked out that if we were caught with it they'd ask where we got it from, and we decided we couldn't tell how we came by it, because that would have been the worst thing to do.'

'And Beth's watch?'

'We plucked up courage, well, we *forced* ourselves, to search his pockets for his name and we were going to put it on his grave, and Beth said, "He's not having my watch" and took it back. But he'd no money, nothing of any value except about five rounds of ammunition, so we buried those as well.'

Peter closed the sketch book laid it aside and put an arm around each of them. 'Is there anything else you need to tell me before I speak? Any little thing. Or a big thing? Anything?'

'Nothing. It was a whole week before Elijah felt it safe enough to take us to his village so we lived with the body all that time. When Elijah came at dead of night we thought it was another soldier and we'd buried the only weapon we had to defend ourselves, and we were so frightened. Then we heard him whistling his hymn.'

'Beth. Alex. We're not going back to sleep until we've resolved this. Now listen carefully to what I say. Both of you. Right? You must understand you are not in any way to blame for what has happened. In defence of your sister, Alex, you had absolutely no alternative. Just think how you would have felt if you'd not hit him with the rifle and you'd had to watch . . .' Peter had to pause because he was shaking with emotion. 'That . . . that would have been ten thousand times worse. But you were brave and put a stop to it just in time. I am eternally grateful for your courage. You will always be a brave man in my eyes.

'The guilt is all mine, not yours. I am the one who chose to go to Africa. I am the one who wanted us all to go. I am the one who allowed the missionary to bring you home that Friday night. I am the one, the only one, who carries guilt, and if anyone should go back to Africa to do a prison sentence it's me. You see, you've been brought up in a home with the highest of Christian principles and I took you to a country where sometimes those kind of principles are challenged *every day* by the kind of evil we can only imagine. Here in Turnham Malpas high principles are safe to have; in Africa you met a situation which demanded an entirely different set of rules and for which you were totally, totally unprepared. I exposed you to that, and so I have to beg your forgiveness. I am so grateful that you came through it all.'

He held them both close and kissed each in turn. 'I am so *proud* to have such brave children. This doesn't mean I'm saying you can go round killing people, you understand that, don't you? You can't, and I never ever want to hear that my beloved, darling Beth is going about carrying a knife. That is forbidden, you understand that, too, don't you?'

Using that harsh, venomous voice which had so upset Caroline, Beth said, 'I just wish I'd had Mummy's vegetable knife with me when we were there. I could have stuck it in his ribs, *straight* into his heart. That would have been him sorted.'

Appalled, Peter almost shouted, 'Beth! Have you not heard a word of what I've said?'

Beth looked him straight in the eye, frank and unafraid. 'Yes, of course I have, but it wasn't you about to be . . . you know . . . it was me. I know I mustn't carry a knife and I won't, and I do know what you've said, and I love you for being so understanding, and if you're sure I shan't be struck dead or something for what we've done, then I shall be brave and go to school and out and about, but I'll never forget what's happened to Alex and me. I owe my life to him. He was so brave and so clever. It was him kept us alive, not me.'

Alex spoke up. 'Shut up Beth. You were brave, too.'

'But it's true.'

'I'm only too sorry for what you had to go through, Alex. It was above and beyond what a boy of your age should have to face.'

Alex looked at Peter with eyes like deep pools of anguish. 'Dad. We don't want Mum to know we . . . *murdered* somebody.'

'I can understand what you mean, but you couldn't have a better person as your mother and she's cared for you all these months I've been away and I know she feels hurt you weren't able to tell her.'

Alex felt he needed to explain. 'But we didn't mean to *hurt* Mum, that was what we were trying to avoid, trying *not* to cause her pain, but perhaps now we've told you . . . we thought perhaps it might make her not love us any more and we couldn't bear that, you see . . . You've taken responsibility, though none of it was because of you . . . But are we free? We can't be, can we? Free for ever?'

Peter had to admit they couldn't be free from the memories for ever, but that on the other hand they didn't intend it, they had very good reasons for what happened and surely that made them innocent, didn't it? 'Your bravery isn't in question, nor your integrity, and you've not to allow it to influence the rest of your lives. You, Beth, must promise me faithfully you'll never carry a knife again. Please.'

She looked him straight in the eye and gave her solemn promise, then promptly asked, 'Are you going to tell Mummy?'

'I haven't decided. If I do, I know she'll feel, as I do, that you have nothing to fear, that it was done totally in self-defence. We'll talk again whenever you need to, anytime you want to. Anytime, and I mean that.'

Before Beth got back into bed she put her arms around Peter and clung to him as though she would never let him go. 'I just knew things would be better when we told you. I love you so much, Daddy. And Mummy, too. I wouldn't change her for the world. Never, ever. Good-night, Daddy. Thank you for listening to us. We've been waiting for you to get back. Waiting and waiting.' She tightened her arms round his neck and kissed his cheek. 'I love you. Now we've told you I feel so much better.'

Peter held her close to him, deeply, deeply grateful she

was there with him, and he could shield her from at least some of life's trials. 'Goodnight, my darling, sleep tight.'

'I shall, Daddy, now you're home. No more screaming.'

Alex said, 'Come and say goodnight to me, will you, Dad?'

'I most certainly will.'

Peter looked round the attic bedroom and saw how Alex had made the room his own. 'It is nice up here. You're quite right, it is a very nice room.'

'Dad, I'm so worried about Beth. I've never been so frightened in my life. Most of the time I tried to convince her I wasn't frightened, but I was, all the time. It was terrible and I'm not going to go anywhere in the world where that might happen again. I can't face it.'

'Being strong when you're feeling scared, that's true bravery.'

'I tried to think what you would do, and I did it as best I could, but Beth, poor Beth . . . she cried and shrieked that night after we'd buried him. I couldn't stop her. We were awake all night. She was so frightened he wasn't really dead and he'd come round and get out of the grave, because it wasn't all that deep, and he'd come back in the night for her. We'll have to be so careful for her, Dad, always. This Andy person has brought it all back.'

'I know, Alex, I know. And we will be careful of her.'

'Dad . . . I'm sorry I haven't been very nice to you. I'm all right now. After what happened in Africa it almost seems a small thing that you did because, as it turned out, it gave Mum us, so good came from bad, didn't it?'

Peter hesitated for a moment and then agreed with him. 'Well, there you are, yes, it did. I'll say goodnight or is it good morning? We'll sleep in tomorrow, OK?'

'Goodnight, Dad.'

'Goodnight, Alex. You're a brave chap.'

Peter leaned over his son's bed and planted a kiss on his forehead, 'Friends again, then?'

Alex nodded.

Caroline, half asleep and waiting for Peter to come back to bed, became conscious that he was kneeling at his side of their bed praying. She opened her eyes to look at him, and saw tears rolling down his face, flooding onto his hands, which were clasped beneath his chin, fingers tightly clenched. Oh, God, what had he learned to make him weep like this? She never interrupted him when she found him praying but tonight her rule had to be ignored. She shuffled across the bed to bring herself closer and gently laid a hand on his.

Softly she whispered, 'My darling!' But she got no reply. It was as if she didn't exist. After a while the tears began to slow, but all he could say was, '*Mea culpa, mea culpa.*' He took hold of her hand and kissed it and his tears fell upon her hand.

Chapter 18

'Hello, Jimbo? Anyone at home? It's Peter from the Rectory.' Peter closed the front door behind him and listened to the silence in the house, thinking how his life had changed since he'd last stood in this hall.

It was Grandmama who appeared first. 'Peter, my dear boy!' She reached up to hug him and then dared to kiss his cheek. 'The others are all out, so come and talk to me for a while. If you've any messages for Jimbo or Harriet I'll pass them on.' She ushered him into the sitting room and gestured for him to sit in Jimbo's big leather chair, which he fitted into beautifully.

'Well, now, Peter, you don't look your usual self, not got that peace which is normally very evident in your face. This Africa business . . . the children. Are they all right now you're home?'

'No, but I'm confident they will be. Eventually.'

'They've been very disturbed, you know. But I expect you know that from Caroline. She's been worried sick.'

'I know. The children have finally told me all about what happened and they are beginning to feel better about it.'

'So what did happen when they were missing?'

Peter shut down immediately and it passed through Grandmama's mind that he'd aged quite dreadfully. 'I have their confidence and I'm afraid I can't tell anyone anything at all. I really came to see Jimbo and ask about the Store closing.'

'Well, all I can say is he decided to do it and the first Harriet and I knew the notice was up. We were stunned, but there was no persuading him otherwise. He was adamant. His broken ankle was a big factor; he's never had an injury nor a serious illness which affected him so badly. We all felt so sorry for him but, privately, Harriet and I felt he'd made a bad decision. Nothing would get him to change his mind, however. The damage to the Store was the last straw.'

'But what about this chap who stalked Beth? Caroline said everyone thought he was to blame, besides apparently murdering his wife.'

'Well, that was a big factor. It appears he started this feud against Jimbo because of something which happened when their paths crossed years ago at Cambridge. He wasn't called Andy Moorhouse then, so at first Jimbo couldn't understand what had caused the feud. Then he recalled his old name, but won't tell neither Harriet nor me what it was, nor what the feud was about. What really hurt was him badmouthing Jimbo to all the village.'

'I see. Nasty. Will Jimbo be back shortly, do you think?'

'Oh, yes. Just gone into Culworth with Harriet for some shopping. You see, closing the Store has given him so much more time, which he was seriously in need of.'

Peter stood up, 'You're staying here permanently?'

'No, no. I'm moving back to my dear little cottage when they get back. I only really came here when Jimbo broke his ankle because they needed help, but now they don't and I thought Anna and I would spend the next week or so together in my dear little cottage. Heal the breach, don't you know? I'm all packed now, and glad to be going home. We're having a welcome home meal together tonight, thoughtfully cooked by Anna.'

'So it didn't work out, then? When I went back to Africa?'

Grandmama smiled. 'A few days would have been all right, but a few months, certainly not.' She ruefully shook her head. 'You see, we're both strong-minded, self-opinionated women and that never works, does it? She's done extremely well with the parish and worked hard, but two strong-minded women in the same small kitchen . . .'

Peter had to smile.

He left, leaving behind a worried Grandmama Charter-Plackett. He'd aged. Gone was that wonderful appealing charisma she'd always loved about him. Poor chap.

An hour after he arrived home Jimbo was at the door. Peter noticed him heading his way and was already opening the door for him.

'Jimbo!'

'Peter! Mother said you'd called. I've got her cheerfully unpacking in her own cottage, so having settled her I've come to see you.' The pair of them headed straight for Peter's study. When Jimbo had made himself comfortable in the easy chair he said, 'Well now, Peter. It looks as though you've lost a lot of weight.'

'Not much food about, that was the trouble.'

'I see. And the children, have you managed to sort out their problems? They've found life almost intolerable.'

Peter needed to tell someone but Jimbo wasn't the one. 'Yes, things will be getting better from now on. Thank you. But what about you? When I learned you'd closed the Store I found it unbelievable.'

'Yes, well.' Jimbo smoothed his hand over his bald head

and grinned apologetically. 'I had an accident and broke my ankle – I have never known such pain in all my life. It absolutely rocked me to my foundations. How women carry on having babies like they do, knowing what pain they will have to face, I do not know. I had to have it broken again because it wasn't setting right and hell, did I get upset.'

'And of course, your poison pen letters didn't help.'

Jimbo looked slightly furtive and waited almost a minute before he answered. 'I've dropped any charges with respect of the windows and the paint and the letters. Better that than it all come out in court.'

'Should you perhaps need to talk about it?'

'Knowing as I do how much you've had to face since you came back, maybe now isn't the right time.'

'Is there ever a right time? Does Harriet know the connection?'

Jimbo went on red alert and said firmly, 'No, she does not, and I don't want her to know. So if I decide to tell you—'

'I shall not disclose anything to anyone, as you well know.'

'Of course, I know that. Well, then, I'll tell you but in strictest confidence. When I went up to Cambridge, Father always saw that I had money, on the principle that I would only be up at Cambridge once in my life and I might as well enjoy it. I had a secret hiding place for my ready cash so I wouldn't have it on me and be seen flashing it around. Well, there was this chap, Victor Martin, a college servant who seemed to fill in wherever he was required. One minute he'd be serving in the dining room, another cleaning the rooms, or serving in the bar. Useful all-rounder, I suppose, in an emergency. Then one day he was on my landing and doing my room. He'd been doing the cleaning for, I suppose, three or four weeks when I went to my secret cache and found I had ninety pounds less than I thought. It worried me all day, trying to think where on earth I'd spent ninety pounds. I even got out a piece of paper and worked it all out. Yes, I definitely had lost ninety pounds. My first thought was that the slimy so-and-so Victor Martin had taken it. He did a great job of dusting and cleaning in absolutely every single possible corner – couldn't fault him on the cleaning side at all – so it appeared very likely it was him.

'Well, of course, I reported the incident. Got it in the neck for keeping such a large sum of money in my room, but the staff were all questioned about it. And, of course, especially Victor Martin. He flatly denied it, and as they couldn't find any evidence, it would have been unfair to dismiss him. But mud sticks and he stayed under suspicion, but was taken off room cleaning.'

'So what happened then?'

'Well . . . sorry it's taking a long time but . . . anyway, one evening, a girl I'd been attracted to came up to me in the bar. Charlotte, her name was. Full of life, lots of get up and go, and we hit it off immediately.

'You see, so as far as women were concerned I thought I was a real catch and so it seemed. I had the pick of the girls. Oh, yes, very popular was Jimbo. However, I'd seen this Charlotte around here and there, and though she wasn't doing my subject our paths seemed to cross frequently. I remember thinking she seemed up for it with anyone who took her eye. You know, free and easy morals. God, I sound like an old man. Maybe I am. But the upshot was I invited her to my room for coffee. Coffee! I ask you.' Jimbo grinned apologetically.

'She couldn't get there fast enough. Things hotted up and we . . . you know . . . we had sex. Next news she was screaming, "Rape!" at the top of her voice. I was completely devastated. I put my hand over her mouth and tried to reason with her but she struggled free and headed for the door, still behaving hysterically, but the door burst open and there stood Victor Martin, master key in hand, witnessing her distress. She went straight to him and he tried soothing her down, but she'd have none of it and he said, "This will have to be reported, Mr Charter-Plackett. I've no alternative." '

'What was he doing with a master key?'

'Exactly. He must have made a copy when he was cleaning. However, that didn't occur to me. All I thought about was being sent down.'

'But you weren't.'

'Well, no. Mother dragged my father up to college and in a trice he'd persuaded the girl to rescind her accusation by paying her a large sum. In retrospect I believe that dear old Victor had put her up to it and also got a big payout from her for his cooperation. He was dismissed shortly afterwards for insolence and various other minor matters which the college managed to make stick.'

'So how does this connect with Andy Moorhouse?'

'He *is* Victor Martin. I didn't recognize him at first – thirty years having gone by, busy life, lots happened in the interim – and he'd changed his name, and though I felt I knew him I just couldn't place him. However, having escaped being sent down by the skin of my teeth, I kept myself hard at work after that and dropped any pretence of being the best chap on the block, got my degree and went to work in the City. About a year after that I met Harriet at a party and it's been roses, roses all the way ever since.'

'When did you realize who he was?'

'Can't remember when it was. I certainly had my ankle in plaster when I made the connection. I was stunned, believe me.'

'So is this the reason you've dropped the charges?'

'Yes. I don't want all my dirty washing airing in public. My mother would die of shame, but worst of all I should have told Harriet before we married but I damn well daren't.'

'I can understand that. A stain on your character, kind of, which wasn't your fault.'

'I couldn't bear for her to think badly of me. And I most certainly do not want the village to know about it. That's another reason I've dropped the charges against him.'

'But you didn't do anything wrong.'

'I know I didn't, but that kind of thing sticks in a very nasty way, and we've always been honourable to each other, Harriet and I, and that's how I want it to stay. OK?'

'Of course. Now the other thing.'

'Yes?'

'The Store. I had a deputation the other day, asking me to speak to you about re-opening it.'

'Ah, well. Yes.'

'It's so wonderful for everyone to have the Store in the village, and a real hardship for people without cars. Also, it was such a centre for companionship, wasn't it, to say nothing of the gossip. How about it? Think of all those put out of work because of your decision.' Peter smiled encouragingly and waited for a reply.

'Think of all those with more work to do because my internet site has pulled in so much more business already,' Jimbo replied, 'I'm even thinking of moving on to cakes and puddings it's doing so well. So I shall need the whole of the property to cope with that.'

'I'm glad the website is turning out well, but methinks he doth protest too much . . .'

Peter waited for Jimbo to fill the silence.

Eventually Jimbo said, 'Running a Store is a tremendous undertaking if it's to be done properly.'

'Get the right manager to do the nitty-gritty and all you do is keep an eye.'

'Six days a week?'

'I have a suggestion.'

'So has Harriet. So has my mother. If your suggestion is the same as theirs I might, just might, listen.'

'I went into Culworth main Post Office and saw Tom behind the counter. He's like a fish out of water there, all faceless people and he's a people person at heart. He'd be the one, he'd be back tomorrow if you asked him.'

'How do you know that?'

'He told me so.'

'Any minute now I shan't have a mind of my own,' Jimbo growled. But he smiled as he said it and added, 'You've a very persuasive tongue, Peter. Can I say I will give it my most serious consideration.'

Peter decided to push the matter on, seeing as he appeared to have made a chink in Jimbo's armour. 'After all, Tom is no fool and he knows all about your strict standards. I'll leave it with you. Think how much you enjoyed the cut and thrust of the busy days, to say nothing of the gossip. What you've told me about this Andy Moorhouse, or whatever his name is, will be in the strictest confidence. But think hard about the Store.'

'All right, all right.' Jimbo got up to go. 'Caroline in? I'll go have a word.'

Peter couldn't resist saying, 'Just think, you might get Linda back for half days for the Post Office to relieve Tom.'

'Over my dead body.'

They both laughed.

Jimbo found Caroline reading the morning paper in the kitchen. 'Thought I'd pop in for a chat. Long time no see.' When Caroline looked up, Jimbo got the immediate impression that something in her life was hurting very badly. 'My dear Caroline, what is the matter?'

'Oh, Jimbo. Close the door. I've no right to be miserable, I should be on top of the world, because the children have told Peter all about when they were missing and they are feeling so much better. They've gone down to see Dottie without any anxiety and that's a definite plus.'

'It is, that's wonderful. I'm delighted. But why aren't you pleased? Frankly you look dreadful.'

'Thanks.'

'I thought Peter back home would solve everything. That's why I've come to get cheered up.'

'Why do you need cheering up?'

'Because my nearest and dearest, which includes Peter, want me to open the Store again with Tom as manager, Evie doing the window-dressing and displays, and me, well, me back in harness once more.'

'Whoops! I can see you're under pressure. Well, to be honest, I'm on their side not yours.'

'See! There we are again. Everyone knowing better than me what I should do. But I must admit I miss the gossip and the adrenalin flowing when a customer has a row with someone and I have to wade in. The free time is wonderful, though. But don't bother about me – I shut the door at your request and I still haven't heard a word about what is upsetting my favourite girl.'

'Favourite girl indeed. You flirt. I'll tell you what has upset me – the fact that the children have told Peter what all their anxieties have been about but he hasn't told me and neither have the children. I'm shut out, Jimbo, completely shut out, and it isn't fair.' Caroline looked at him sitting across the kitchen table from her, and tears brimmed in her eyes. 'Not a word. I am their mother – well, to all intents and purposes their mother – and it hurts.'

Jimbo reached across the table and took hold of her hand. 'See here, has it ever occurred to you that what happened doesn't bear telling to you? Maybe the children have been shielding you from the truth because they didn't want to cause you pain and maybe Peter's doing exactly the same thing.'

Caroline almost shrivelled in front of his eyes. 'Too terrible? Too terrible? My God, what on earth happened, then? Peter's gone completely distant from me, he's not like my husband at all, and I know he's hurting, quite desperately. That's the trouble of being Rector, one has to absorb everyone's troubles and carry on regardless. He's so distressed.'

'Be patient. He'll tell you when he's ready. He's being his usual generous self and absorbing the angst to save you. Look on the bright side; the children are much better, aren't they, since they told him?'

Caroline's face cleared for a moment, 'Yes, they are. Jimbo, you don't happen to know who owns Dottie's cottage, do you?'

'As a matter of fact I do. It's Arthur Prior.'

'Arthur Prior?'

'Yes, it used to be a tied cottage for their farm. Why?'

'Beth tells me it's almost falling down. The ground floor slopes away from the fireplace and she swears the living-room window is on the slide, too, and won't shut properly. The thatch is leaking, and there are no mod cons to speak of. In fact, it's a mess.'

'Go see him. Ask him what he's playing at.'

'Dottie's been so good for Beth, forthright, you know, and down to earth. Better than me, sad to say.'

Jimbo got to his feet. 'Well, get your teeth into that, then, instead of sitting here feeling sorry for yourself. There's Peter and Alex and Beth all doing their best to keep you from harm. The least you can do is to get Arthur Prior galvanized into doing something for Dottie, seeing as she's helped Beth so much.'

Caroline looked at him and he saw from the change in her face that she was willing to take on his challenge. 'Of course, you're absolutely right. I must do something practical. And here I am feeling sorry for myself when in reality the ones I love most are trying hard to make my life bearable. Yes, you're right. I will.' She stood up walked round the table and, putting her arms round Jimbo, kissed his cheek. 'Thank you, you're a dear friend.'

He kissed her back. 'So are you. Take care, Caroline.' As he went out of the kitchen he looked back to say, 'You've been so very brave in the past taking on Peter's children as you did, no one braver, believe me, so just remember that.'

So Caroline did just as Jimbo had said. She talked to Dottie, wrote down all her problems and decided to walk to Wallop Down Farm.

It was a pleasure to walk into the yard, with its well-painted stable doors and tubs of flowers dancing in the warm summer breeze. The yard was so well cared for, it was almost as if there were no cows or animals of any kind on the farm. But at the same time it irritated her that Dottie was allowed to live in such awful circumstances; Arthur's cows had a better home than Dottie.

She knocked on the front door of the house and got no reply. So she tried wandering around the stables and discovered Arthur sitting in one of them on an upturned wooden crate drinking beer.

He leapt to his feet as quickly as his arthritis would allow, took off his tweed cap and said, 'What a lovely surprise, I'm in here keeping out of the way. School holidays, you see, and five grandchildren at home all day is more than a grandfather should be asked to cope with. Now, Doctor Harris, what can I do for you?'

Caroline had just opened her mouth to explain her errand when Arthur Prior said, 'See here, there's another crate you can sit on, that's if you don't mind.'

'That would be very welcome. I walked here thinking the exercise would do me good. Freshens the mind, doesn't it?' She settled herself on the upturned crate and wondered how to begin, but she didn't get a chance to start because Arthur said, 'A rough time you've been having with your Alex and Beth. I've felt really sorry for you. How are things?'

'Much improved since Peter came home, thank you. They're beginning to get back to normal.'

'What was it, then?'

'I've no idea. They won't tell me. Peter knows and he seems to have sorted things out for them, but as for me . . .'

Arthur leaned across and patted her hand. 'See here, I reckon Peter will tell you all in good time. He's a very wise man, is your husband. Remember that. Now what is it you've come to see me about?'

'You know Dottie Foskett has helped enormously, she cleans for me now and Beth has been able to speak to her about her troubles more easily than to me. I've talked to Dottie and I understand her house is reaching the point where it will need massive renovation. It is listing quite badly and the thatch is leaking. It has no modern conveniences and needs the owner to do something serious about it. Obviously Dottie can't afford to do it herself you see so I wondered . . .'

Arthur wagged a finger at her. 'That cottage has been the bane of my life for years. I sacked the worker who lived in there because he was idle in the extreme, but he refused to leave the cottage. Short of putting him and his parcel of kids out in the lane and giving myself a bad reputation there was nothing I could do. A year after I sacked him he got a job working on the by-pass and was earning more money each week than I was with my farm, and still he wouldn't move out. That riled me.'

'I'm sure it must have.'

'I vowed I wouldn't have a tied cottage again so eventually he left with enough money to buy a house for himself. I rented it to Dottie at a ridiculously low rent and she turned it into nothing short of a brothel. Believe me, I've had it up to here,' he touched the top of his head to illustrate his frustration, 'and I don't even want to think about it, never mind rebuild it.'

Arthur emptied his glass of beer and then remembered his manners. 'I'm sorry, do you drink beer? You can have a glass if you like.'

Caroline shook her head. 'Well, you can rest assured she is no longer a prostitute. So, think of how much money you could get for that cottage were it up to scratch. It has a wonderful position overlooking the fields, second to none in fact, a far better outlook than any of the houses in the centre of the village, a glorious garden, the little orchard at the end with the stream running by. Three hundred thousand at today's prices, I've no doubt. Even better, the end of the garden has good access to the Little Derehams road; you could possibly shorten Dottie's garden and sell the land off for another house. I'm sure Dottie wouldn't mind; she's not much of a gardener but she does know how to clean. None better. Once done up she'd keep it beautifully.' Warming to her task, Caroline had another inspiration. 'There's that funny outbuilding adjoining the cottage which she never uses because the roof is giving way. With a bit of attention that could be made into a garage, or even an extension to the cottage. How about it?' Her eyes sparkling with enthusiasm, she looked hopefully towards receiving the answer she wanted. But the answer wasn't yes.

Arthur looked her straight in the eye and said, 'If I did do any such thing, and I'm not of a mind to at all, I'd have to consult my son, Jake. He's the next owner of this farm. He might not think it worth the money. Bit tight-fisted is our Jake. Cheaper to pull it down.'

'Oh! I do hope not. I've given my plan a lot of thought and it . . .' Caroline didn't think he'd want to know how much she needed him to take her plans on board, if only for the sake of a comforting balm to ease her own desperation

Arthur recognized her longing and he almost said yes, if only for the sake of her husband, whom he regarded highly. He did want to please her, she'd been through such a lot lately. 'I'll think about it. That's all I can say at the moment.' He struggled to his feet again and Caroline took the hint.

'It's an eyesore, you know. Spoils things. Please think about it.'

Somewhat sharply Arthur said, 'I've already said that's what I'll do; I'll think about it. Thank you for calling and my very best wishes to the Rector. I hold him in great esteem.'

Caroline glowed with pleasure. 'So do I.'

They shook hands and parted friends, though Caroline wasn't too sure about the successful outcome of her plea. She'd felt positively inspired by her plans for the cottage, and considered they made such absolute sense, he couldn't possibly do anything other than agree. But she decided not to mention the conversation to Dottie in case nothing came of it. She'd even let Dottie have their attic bedroom while the house was put right and then help her out with some bits of furniture.

Her high spirits were destroyed by Peter saying to her when she got back home that he was going to see Andy Moorhouse in prison that afternoon.

'Going to see Andy Moorhouse? Whatever for? Have you gone mad?'

She'd never queried his decisions concerning his calling, just as she hadn't when he'd decided to go to Africa, and he felt alarmed by her response.

'I've rung the prison and I can go this very afternoon.'

'But what for? He murdered his wife, we understand, almost destroyed our daughter, and would have done given half a chance, and you want to *visit* him?'

'Yes. I must. If anyone needs help it's Andy Moorhouse.'

'What about me? Don't I need help? Do I get any? No, I don't. Everyone else but me. It's so unfair.' Caroline turned away and refused to look at him.

'Caroline. Caroline, please look at me.'

'I don't want to. Arthur Prior told me he holds you in esteem and I said I did too, but I do wonder now if I do.'

'Don't you know why I can't tell you what the children told me?'

'You claim I'm their mother, but I'm shut out so cruelly.' Caroline banged her fist on the table to emphasize how grieved she felt.

Peter turned her around and held up his hands. 'Guilty as charged.'

'Then?'

'What they told me shocked me to the core, and I dread telling you what happened. The whole matter is so ghastly. The children don't want you to know, but obviously you must be told and I don't know how I shall find the words to tell you. Give me a little more time and perhaps the words will come. What I can say is this: I've told them I am to blame, not them, and one day when I can no longer keep it to myself I shall have to tell you. Then perhaps we shall all be healed. Until then I am going to the prison this afternoon. I *know* I must.'

Caroline shrugged and turned away from him again, unintentionally breaking his heart.

The father in him wanted to punch Andy Moorhouse till there was nothing left of him. Just punch and punch and punch. But the priest in him knew the man needed help.

The prison officer was undecided about leaving Peter

alone with Andy. 'He's very truculent sometimes, padre, I wouldn't want him to turn awkward.'

'I'm big enough to cope. I've not come here to upset him, only to talk, and he won't if someone else is listening.'

'Sometimes they talk more, you know, liking the audience, wanting to impress. I wouldn't say a word, I promise.'

'No. Thank you.'

'I'll have to tell the governor's office, give them a call. Clear it, you know.'

Peter nodded. 'Very well, then.'

They brought Andy in to the visiting room. He sat down in the chair and looked belligerently at Peter, who shuddered inside at Andy's dead eyes. When Peter had finally made up his mind that he'd have to be the first to speak, Andy said, 'If you think coming here and talking to me is going to do any good, you're wrong. The Church has nothing to say to me, and I've no intention of even giving you the chance to say what you've come to say. It'll only be pious tommyrot, anyway.' Andy folded his arms and glared at Peter.

'So why did you agree to see me?'

'The chance to get out for a few minutes and the possibility of a cup of tea.'

'In that case I'd better ask for one right now because if you're not staying long you might miss out. Excuse me.' Peter opened the door to the visiting room and asked the warder sitting outside for two teas, if possible.

'For you, yes, sir, the kettle's just boiled. Milk and sugar?'

Peter asked Andy if he wanted milk and sugar.

'Both, please,' Andy answered without looking up.

'One with milk, one with milk and sugar.'

The warder jerked his thumb towards Andy. 'Makes a change him saying please.'

While they waited for the tea they were both silent, Peter on purpose, Andy because he was willing himself not to speak and more so willing himself not to look into Peter's eyes, because he had the feeling that Peter would see into his very soul . . . if he still possessed one, which Andy very much doubted.

The tea was hot and bitter-tasting and not at all palatable, and Peter said, 'My word, if this is prison tea then I'm glad I'm not in here permanently.'

'I am, or will be after my trial comes up.'

'I think water would be preferable.'

Andy remembered he wasn't supposed to be talking, but the temptation to speak to this man, his one and only visitor, whose daughter he'd seriously intended to defile, was too much. 'Have you come as a padre or a father?'

'To be honest, I'm not quite sure which. As a father my instinct would be to knock you senseless for the grievous upset you've caused my Beth. She was beginning to come to terms with what happened to her when we were in Africa, and your actions brought it all back. As a priest I've come to see if I can help, in any way at all. Have I come to see Andy Moorhouse who allegedly killed his wife, or some other person? I don't know. I just knew I had to come. After all, you're under my care when I'm your Rector.'

'No, I am *not*. I simply bought a house in the village where you happen to be Rector. Other than that you've no need to care for me. It's so long since I used my real name I've almost forgotten what it was.'

'Then I'll call you Andy Moorhouse. Someone has to care about you.'

Andy stayed silent for a while, sipping his tea. 'She did. Jenny.'

'She did what?'

'Cared for me. To begin with. Then I tricked myself into a job with the Social Services with forged references and qualifications, thinking they were a soft touch. Then I panicked about it and things went terribly wrong. I admit I just wasn't quite clever enough to pull it off. Over-stretched myself, you could say. Then I grew to loathe Jenny, she reminded me so much of my mother – that is, on the rare occasion my mother paid me any attention. I expect you had a wonderful childhood; nurtured, loved, cared for, well fed.' Andy sneered at Peter, an angry sneer that no amount of consideration on Peter's part would allay, so he decided to be absolutely frank.

'I did.'

'Only child?'

'Yes, my mother almost died having me so there couldn't be any more children, and she longed for a big family.'

'Lucky you. No one wanted me.'

'Surely you're not going to blame everything that has happened on a ghastly childhood, like so many people do? There comes a time when one has to stand tall and take responsibility for one's actions despite what has happened in one's past.'

Andy carefully placed his paper cup on the table and snarled, 'Is that so? Very easy to say, damned hard to do.'

'Yes. You didn't murder Jenny because of a difficult childhood. You murdered her because you wanted to.

262

You hankered after my daughter because you wanted to. A *child*. Only thirteen.'

Andy's hands tensed, and he glared at the table. Sarcastically he answered, 'She's a woman or hadn't you noticed? Then I don't suppose you do, her being yours, but I did. Such thoughts wouldn't enter your head, I expect.' He paused to think about Beth and what a splendid life she had in front of her. Full of promise and plenty of choices, and was glad for her. 'All my life I have never had the chance to decide for myself about anything. No choices, you know. Never got a qualification because I never stayed at any school long enough, therefore no chance of a good career, which meant pathetic lowlife jobs. Never got enough money, never got the right girl, now my life is on hold while I'm in prison with even fewer choices . . .'

'Just a minute. Who did all the things you did? Only you. No one *made* you do what you did.'

'My sins go a long way back. I married Jenny when I already had a wife. I killed Jenny and hid her body. I fancied your daughter so much I ached with the feelings I had for her. But I couldn't help any of that. I'd no power over it and you can't say I had. If only I'd had—'

'Be honest with yourself, face what's there, not what might have been *if only I—*'

'It's hard when the cards are all stacked against you and you get tempted.'

'I'm sure it is. I know all about temptation and how hard it can be to resist.'

Andy scornfully dismissed the idea of Peter knowing anything about temptation. 'You? Temptation? You in your ivory tower? Huh!'

'Yes. Me in my ivory tower. However, it's not me

we're meant to be talking about. It's you. I've come to ask if there's anything you need.'

Andy pondered for a minute. 'There's absolutely *nothing* that you in your dog collar and your cassock, and that thumping great cross you wear, can do for me or for anyone for that matter. Perhaps one day you'll wake up to the fact that it's all a fairy story. Then where will you be?' Andy's face and tone of voice were venomous.

'Coming here to visit you if you ask me to.'

Peter's reply silenced Andy for a moment, and when he broke the silence Peter was surprised.

'Is it all too late to change things?'

'It's *never* too late to change. You can be full of remorse on your *deathbed* and your plea will be heard.'

'You honestly believe that?'

Andy couldn't doubt Peter's confidence when he answered, 'Absolutely.'

'So there's a chance even for *me*, then?'

Peter nodded. 'Yes.'

'I'm not really a bad man, you know. I spiralled down into madness, frighteningly crazy madness for a while.' He glanced round the interview room and at his paper cup still half-full of that revolting tea. 'Look where having no choices got me.'

Andy gave Peter a sad smile, got to his feet, opened the door and requested to be taken back to his cell.

Peter asked to shake his hand before he left. 'I'll come again if you wish. Believe me, I would certainly find the time.'

'Will you? Well, only if I ask for you. Don't go much for this religion lark, and I can't understand why you're so interested in me after what happened with your daughter.'

'Compassion, that's what. It's a deal. I'll come if you invite me.'

They shook hands. Peter smiled down at him and thought for a moment he could see a very small flicker of life in those dead eyes.

As he put the key in the ignition he noticed there was one of Caroline's scarves, the one she thought she'd lost, peeping out from below his seat. He reached down and picked it up, intending to put it on the front passenger seat. Instead he held it close to his cheek, enjoying her perfume lingering in the folds of the scarf, and he sat thinking about her for a while. What was it he'd once said to her? That she was 'the beat of his heart'. Yes, that was it. She was. He couldn't bear her rejection when she'd turned away from him earlier. Of course she felt ignored. Here he was keeping from her the deepest, darkest confessions of their children, and imagining it was for the best. Caroline was no fool. It would break her heart but she needed to know. A rift between them when the children needed them both so much would only spell serious trouble, and he needed her right now. Peter felt his longing for her consume him; he couldn't leave it another moment to heal the breach between them.

He put the car in gear and drove home, absolutely intent on settling things between them.

'Caroline? Caroline! Where are you?'

A voice floated down from the attic. 'I'm up here.'

He put her scarf on the hall table, raced up the stairs, ducked his head as he went through the low door leading to the small attic and blurted out, 'Darling! Forgive me.

Can I tell you about the children? Right now. This minute. Where are they?'

Caroline was looking through Alex's and Beth's precious baby clothes, hugging them to herself, treasuring the memories. She put a baby shawl she'd been hugging down on her knee, and looked up at him, her heart full of apprehension but also of joy that he felt able to tell her. 'In Culworth at the cinema. Pull that box closer – look, there – and sit on it. Tell me right away, up here, where my memories are kept.'

She took hold of his hand in a firm grip and waited for him to begin.

Caroline listened right through to the end of the story without flinching, except for some agonizing, horrified groans which she couldn't hold back. Her hands, clasped in his, trembled from start to finish. He was right, it was ghastly, and they'd never be able to talk about it to anyone except each other.

'So there you have it. Now you know it all.' Peter looked steadily at her, waiting for her response. 'Now you know why they are so afraid and why I shrank from telling you.'

She released her grip on his hand and reached out to stroke his cheek with tender, loving fingers. 'No wonder you couldn't find the words. No wonder at all. I can hardly take it in. I even began to get angry with Beth when she wouldn't confide in me. Now I know why she wouldn't. How can a child tell her mother she's helped to murder someone? I'm ashamed of myself. Poor Beth. Dear precious Alex, bless his heart.'

'They were so afraid of some terrible punishment coming down on them.'

'Is that how they see it? How did they come through it

all? How did they bear it? You see, Alex is just like you, strong and protective, willing to take responsibility to save others from anguish.'

'He's worried about Beth, he says.'

'I'm sure he is. So am I. I can see why she was driven to carrying that knife with her. That Andy Moorhouse has a lot to answer for. Does he show any remorse?'

'Almost. He's thinking about things, at least.'

'Do you think that gradually they'll get over it? That it won't colour everything they do for ever?'

'That's something we won't have an answer to for a long while, if ever.'

Caroline trembled. 'I'm glad you've told me, if only for your own sake. It's too much to carry alone. Don't blame yourself for it, my darling. After all, I agreed to go and I could have said no and not gone and kept the children here, and you would have agreed.'

'Darling.' Peter put his arm around her shoulders. 'I wanted to spare you this. It's been very hard for me to tell you, especially as the children didn't want you to know. But I, as an adult, knew you *had* to be told.'

'I shall tell them I know. Somehow. Sometime. Then we're all together in this.'

'Yes, you're right. All together.' He leaned forward to kiss her lips, a kiss that began as a tender salute to her bravery and turned into a kiss full of rugged desire and which drew an eager, clamouring response from her.

The telephone rang and Peter said, 'Dammit, they'll have to leave a message.' So they went down the stairs to their bedroom to the sound of Sheila Bissett's voice asking when she could come to see him about some new ideas she had for the Harvest Festival.

Expecting Peter would relent and pick up the receiver,

Caroline began to protest, because above all, *at this moment*, she wanted the two of them to make love to celebrate the understanding they'd finally reached and above all to express their passionate love of each other, but he silenced her protest by kissing her again and beginning to undress her.

Chapter 19

Sheila came round the following afternoon to tell Peter her ideas. 'I know you'll like what I have to tell you. It'll put a new slant on the whole festival, and we've never done it before.'

'Come into the study.'

Ah, thought Sheila, the study, the place in her mind she called the confessional. It was so comfortable in there, secret and kind of womb-like and reassuring.

'You sit down and tell me all.'

Sheila settled herself, put her handbag beside her and began. 'For the Harvest Festival we always have the Morning Service, put our offerings of fruit and veg round the altar table, then go back and sit down, and that's it over with for everyone, apart from the people who volunteer to take the stuff into Culworth and deliver it to the residential homes and the Women's Refuge and such. So my new idea would involve people more. Well, I've heard it said that sometimes they get so much stuff from so many churches, all round about the same weekend, that sometimes they are guilty of having to throw it away because they can't eat it fast enough. So . . .' she took in a deep breath, 'I thought maybe after the Service we could all go and have lunch, like a Ploughman's or some such – easy you know, three pounds fifty a head – in the big hall and then have an auction to sell all the produce. The money could then go to *buying* something for the Refuge or the residential homes that they really need instead. There, what do you think?'

'Mmm.'

'I know other churches that do this, except we've never done it.' She cocked her head speculatively at him and waited for his reply.

'Should we sound people out about this? Have you discussed it with anyone else?'

'Of course not, I've come to you first.' She relaxed enough to say gushingly, 'You know, we're so glad you're back. All of us are. It's lovely sitting in here and talking like we used to. I always feel so free to talk to you.' Whoops! thought Sheila, I'd better be careful, those eyes of his . . .

Peter's answer alarmed her. 'I was sorry to hear about Louise's tragedy. It must have been a terrible blow to you all, losing a baby like that, I can't think of anything worse.'

Sheila went quite wobbly inside that he'd so astutely picked up on her thoughts. The sincerity of what he'd said couldn't be denied, but she'd never intended mentioning it. 'Yes, I mean, no. He was very premature, you know, and not just that he was badly . . . well . . . let's call a spade a spade, deformed is all you could call it. The hole in his heart, his hare lip, his cleft palate, his twisted feet and legs, possibly blind too, they thought. He'd have needed years in hospital to put everything right, if they ever could, which I doubt . . . it was heartbreaking to see him. Gilbert, I've never seen him so distressed, but he was willing him to pull through. Poor, dear little Roderick, so tiny. It broke my heart.'

'I'm so sorry, Sheila. I just wish I could have been here, perhaps I would have been able to help in some way.'

'You would've, though Anna was excellent. They both found it hard when he died, so very hard, but, you know, it was for the best. When you think what happy lives their other children lead, little Roderick would have had nothing but pain in his young life. I think eventually even Gilbert saw it the same way as me.'

She got out her handkerchief and blew her nose.

Peter said, 'You felt it for the best when he died?'

'Of course, what else could a grandmother think? It sounds hard, but it was hard facts that had to be faced. I . . . felt nothing but relief, and I just couldn't grieve for him, but I did for Gilbert and Louise, they took his death very badly.'

'I'm so sorry.'

Sheila pulled herself together, stuffed her handkerchief in her bag and said, 'Well, now, I'll leave it to you to ring me when you've decided. The WI will make the Harvest lunch and serve it, I'm sure. The other thing I've thought of is we could sell the flower arrangements, too. That would bring in quite a bit, wouldn't it?' She heaved herself out of the comfy sofa and before she made her way to the study door she said, 'Thanks for listening, I feel better now.'

Peter said, 'Well, perhaps telling me has healed things a little for you. You were in a very difficult situation, weren't you?'

Sheila looked up into his eyes and her gaze faltered as she saw the intense, penetrating look in them. She said very emphatically, 'Don't discuss anything with Ron, he knows all he needs to know. And certainly not with

Louise, they're trying so hard to put it all behind them. They're striving to be normal, you see.'

'Of course, of course.' Peter wasn't entirely sure that he and Sheila had been talking about the same thing. Had she or hadn't she hastened Roderick on his way? Nothing she'd actually said implied that, but nothing he'd said did either. 'Bye, Sheila, I'll be in touch as soon as I can. I think it's a very good idea; it will make much more of a celebration of the Harvest, won't it?'

The telephone rang then, and he had to switch his mind to other things.

Beth and Alex, unaware that their father had explained to their mother what had happened in the bush, were improving by the day. They sometimes went down to Dottie's and on two occasions had gone into Culworth on the bus and enjoyed shopping, walking round the market and meandering along beside the river.

Caroline was thrilled at their progress and, when Beth began talking about getting back to school after the summer holiday, and really sounding as though she meant it, she was ecstatic.

'We're having a week's holiday before then, just going somewhere in England. It'll do us all good.'

Alex agreed. 'Yes, it will. Shall you be taking your bucket and spade, Beth?' He dodged hastily out of the way when Beth threatened to hit him with the book she was reading.

'Cheek! I remember you did more digging with my bucket and spade than I did the last time we went to the sea.'

'I did not.'

'You did.'

'All right, then, but you were hopeless at digging that moat round your castle.'

'I wasn't.'

'You were.'

'I'm not taking it anyway, I'm much too old now. I shall sit in a deckchair and read when we're on the beach. But you can borrow it for the whole holiday, if you like.' She rushed swiftly up the stairs as Alex picked up a wooden spoon and looked as though he was going to threaten her with it.

Caroline relished their tormenting of each other; it had seemed an age since they'd played the fool. Perhaps it would soon be time for her to pick up the threads of general practice. Give Beth a few weeks at school; see how she settled first, though.

The next day Peter received a call from the prison asking him to visit Andy Moorhouse again. 'Has he specifically asked for me?'

'Oh, yes. He's asked for you. This afternoon, we thought. Is that OK, padre?'

'Yes. It might be about four o'clock; is that convenient?'

'Absolutely. We'll have the kettle on, sir.'

'Thank you.'

He hesitated to tell Caroline that he was going to the prison, but it was his duty to go and go he must.

'Caroline?'

'In the sitting room.'

'This afternoon . . .'

'Yes?'

'I'm going to the prison again.'

'OK, darling.' She turned back to playing 'Beat Your Neighbour' with Alex and looked perfectly happy with the idea. 'I've a huge bar of Dairy Milk in the cupboard. Do you think he'd like it? Are they allowed?'

'I don't know, but the warder has taken a shine to me, so maybe it'll be in order.'

'Who doesn't take a shine to you? Everyone does.' She turned round to smile at him while Alex made up his mind what he was doing next. Peter bent down and kissed her, whispering, 'Thank you.'

'Love you.'

'And me, you.'

Considering it was still summer the afternoon was cold, with grey skies and a blustery wind which had blown up from nowhere. It did the prison no favours, for it made it even more bleak and unwelcoming as Peter approached it over the Culworth Bridge. The river lashed along, slapping at the concrete sides of the embankment. Somehow it made him shudder, and the clang of the gates and the chill of the air when he got inside only served to make him more depressed. He showed the warder the bar of chocolate.

'That's fine, padre. You go in and we'll bring him round to you. Tea's almost brewed. He's not too good these last few days, by the way, very quiet. When we ask him if he needs help he shrugs us off and says . . . well, anyway, he intimates he doesn't need any help from the likes of us.'

When Andy was brought in he noticed the teapot and some biscuits on the tray. 'My word, you must have some influence round here. Teapot and a sugar bowl and *biscuits* would you believe. You can come anytime, sir.'

Peter laughed as he poured the tea. 'Here you are,

Andy. I do believe it looks much more appetizing than the last cup we had together. Here's the sugar.'

'And proper cups!'

The two of them took a sip of the tea and Peter said, 'It is better than the last time. Now, Andy, you asked me to come, so here I am. Fire away.'

Andy tipped another spoonful of sugar into his cup, stirred it round with the plastic spoon and quietly said, 'Thanks for coming.'

'That's fine, all part of my job.'

'There's not many would come to see a fella who'd had designs on his daughter.'

'Well, I have.'

'I took note what you said last time.'

'Yes.'

'Never had no need to worry about my conscience before – well, to be honest, I never had one so there was nothing to worry about. But in here, with so much time to spare for thinking, I've suddenly developed one, albeit a small one.'

'Right. That's what any completely whole person has.'

'I expect so. That daughter of yours, I'm so very sorry about frightening her. Given the chance I would have . . . you know, I must have been mad. She's going to be a beautiful young woman, you'll have to watch out for her.'

Andy stared into space for a moment, took a deep breath and said, 'When I look back on my life it's been a complete and utter mess from day one. My mother was fifteen when I was born, a right tart. She wanted to have me adopted but her mother persuaded her differently: "can't part with your own child to strangers, our Netta, wouldn't be right." So she kept me. Perhaps if I'd been adopted then I might have had a better chance. At least they would have wanted me.'

Andy paused to think. He sipped his tea, took a bite of his custard cream, looked into the distance and obviously made a decision.

'I used to dream about being adopted and what it would have meant, what a difference it could have made to me: nice manners, doing well at school, baths, clean clothes and, above all, a welcome when I came home from school. I don't think parents realize how important that is, someone there when you get home, instead of digging down your shirt-neck for the key on its scratchy string. Damn and blast.' Tears almost brimmed in his eyes and he brushed them away, looking anywhere but at Peter.

'Anyway, sir, you don't want to hear about a no-good fella heading for a certain life sentence. My God, you must hear some tales and not half in your job.'

'I do, but they go no further than me. Believe me.'

'Well, one day I might tell you the rest. I've begun using the prison library, and that's a first. Flipping funny collection of books they've got. Not my sort at all, but then I never did read books, so maybe I'm no judge.'

'Read to enjoy, that's my motto. That's what counts.'

'Some I start and I can't get into 'em at all; others I can't put 'em down. Funny that.'

'There you are, then, the ones you can't put down are the ones for you.'

'At least it helps me to leave these damned walls for a while.'

'Exactly. Was there something in particular you wanted to see me about?'

A wry smile touched Andy's mouth and he said,

Nothing really, just needed a conversation with someone from outside.'

'I get the feeling there's something deep down serious you need to talk about?'

Andy hesitated, opened his mouth to begin speaking and then changed his mind. 'No, not really, but—'

'I'm a good listener. Perhaps you'll tell me next time I come when you've had more time to think it over.'

Andy raised his hand in protest but Peter interrupted him, 'Yes, I know, only if you ask for me. No pressure.'

'That's right. Thanks. I'll go now.' He popped the bar of chocolate into his pocket. 'Thanks. You're very kind.' It was Andy this time who offered to shake hands.

'Perhaps I'll see you again. Like I said, I'll visit anytime. Good afternoon, Andy.'

'Good afternoon, sir.' He paused with his hand on the door knob as if intending to turn back to say something more, but then seemed to change his mind, and left.

Chapter 20

Anna stayed on with Grandmama in her cottage for an extra two weeks. They'd agreed to stay friends and be tolerant of each other after a full-scale discussion of the problems they'd faced before and a generous agreement on the part of each of them that they'd behaved badly to each other the first few weeks after Peter went back to Africa.

'I can't think what got into me, Katherine. I think I felt very much out of my depth. Peter is a very deeply committed priest, on a higher plane than most of us, and beside him and his learning I felt totally inadequate.'

'I was pig-headed and very intolerant. Comes of living on my own for something like thirty years. But . . . I have learned my lesson and you've made me decide to be much less aggressive in my dealings with people and make myself more tolerant of their shortcomings.' She hastily added, 'Not that you have any shortcomings, my dear. Just the opposite.'

'Thank you, you're more than generous.' Anna leaned across and kissed Katherine's cheek.

'Friends, then?'

'Friends. I'm glad Peter's decided to take some time off because it's given you and me the opportunity to put our new resolutions into practice.'

Grandmama drew a deep breath and replied, 'Exactly.'

Originally Peter and Caroline had decided to go away for a whole week's holiday but Alex had disliked the whole idea and Beth wouldn't even discuss it.

Alex, usually so self-contained, burst out abruptly with his protest. 'I'm *not* going for a whole week, Dad, it's too long and I don't want to go. I'm staying here.'

'Beth, how do you feel?'

She looked at Peter with a measure of fear in her eyes. 'I don't want to go for a whole week, either. I'll stay here with Alex, and Sylvia can come again.'

'Oh! Right. Days out, then?'

Beth, relieved, hugged Peter. 'I'll agree to that. I want to come home to sleep where . . . everything's safe. Where we're safe.'

'Right then, we could see films, go out to a stately home one day, visit the coast? Go walking? Or cycling, perhaps?' Caroline would have loved a week away but it was obvious the children didn't feel confident enough for that.

So Peter handed his study back to Anna and the four of them had a glorious week visiting places they'd promised themselves for ages they would but never got round to, relaxing on beaches, swimming in the sea, walking, cycling, going to the cinema, and sometimes just doing nothing but enjoying each other's company. Caroline thought she might find an opportunity to let the children know that Peter had told her precisely what had happened to them when they were missing but the moment never arose. So she decided to leave things as they were, especially as they were just beginning to leave the horror behind them.

They'd agreed they wouldn't open any post, check up on e-mails or read any newspapers that week, thus making it a more complete holiday, so it wasn't until the second Saturday of their holiday that Caroline took in a cup of tea to Peter in his study and asked if there was anything for her. 'Might be some voicemails; haven't got round to listening to them yet. Thanks for the tea.'

There was, however, an envelope from the prison. When he opened it up there was another envelope inside addressed to the Padre. The first was from the Governor's office and inside the second envelope was a letter to Peter from Andy Moorhouse. Peter was appalled to find out that Andy had died.

Dear Padre,

I am writing to thank you for coming to see me. It meant a great deal to me that someone actually cared, which you obviously did. I found I hated myself for what I'd done, hated the way I'd turned into a monster. Don't say I'm not a monster because I am.

A monster first to Alison Dunne, my only wife. I told her I was going out to get the morning paper and just never went back.

Next to Jenny, who loved me to bits and believed she was my wife, and I turned all her love to ashes and finally to her death. Poor Jenny, she didn't deserve that ugly death.

Then fancying your Beth. Tell her all the blame is mine. I was despicable for having designs on such a lovely, unspoilt girl. Treasure her.

I picked up a Bible in the library and saw the Gospel written by John so I read it, because John was my granddad's name. It took all night by the light of a torch I pinched from one of the warders. By morning I knew without doubt I couldn't face trying to pull myself up by

*my shoelaces from the deep black mud I'd fallen into.
Don't take any of the blame yourself, the decision is
entirely mine. Though I remembered what you said about
remorse and I'm full to the brim with it. If God is still of
the same mind and full of forgiveness for sinners even at
the last hour, then here I come.*

   Sincerely,

   *Leslie Dunne (Andy Moorhouse, Aidan Thomas, Ben
Dunne, and Ah! yes, Johnny Dunne).*

When Peter read the Governor's letter he was shaken to
the core. Apparently, during the night following his
writing of the letter to Peter, Andy had managed to get up
into the roof space and then onto the roof of the prison.
He'd thrown himself off the top. He was still alive when
they found him, but never regained consciousness, and he
died twelve hours later.

Caroline went to tell Peter their meal was ready and
found him deep in thought. 'I'm just about to serve. What
is it, darling?'

'Andy Moorhouse has died. Committed suicide.'

'Oh! I'm so sorry. Am I? I don't know. Are you?'

'I cannot possibly condone suicide under any circumstances.'

'But darling, he had no one, no one at all to support
him. What's worse, no one to love him. No hope. He
must have felt desperate.'

Peter studied over what she had said and then replied
cautiously, 'Maybe. Having no one who loves you must
be dreadful.' He took hold of Caroline's hand and kissed
it. 'Maybe he's done what was best for him. At least he
was full of remorse.'

'Well, then.' They were silent for a moment and then

Caroline added, 'For the best I expect in the end. Poor chap.'

'Possibly.'

The following Monday morning Dottie came in to clean, glad to see them back again and eager to tell them her news.

'They're starting on my house in two weeks' time. It's going to be a massive job. Foundations to begin with, 'cos it's sinking as we all know, then the damp, which will mean a complete re-thatch, and then it's going to be all mod cons for Dottie. A big kitchen made out of the outbuilding stuck onto the house that I've never used because the roof leaked something chronic, all new cupboards and everything, and then a bathroom out of that boxroom that isn't big enough even for a bed.'

'Then how will they get a bath in there, Dottie?' asked Beth.

'Making it bigger by taking a bit off the landing. I'm thrilled to bits. Mr Prior came down with the builder while you were holidaying, such a nice man.'

'You can stay here, then, Dottie, like I promised.' Caroline smiled and noticed Dottie looked a mite uncomfortable.

'Well, Doctor Harris, much as I would like to live here – which I would, there's no doubt about that – my cousin in Little Derehams, our Lucy, she's already cleared out her second bedroom and she's a new bed coming next week and she wants me to stay with her. Thank you all the same, but she's dead set on it and I can't refuse, she'd be that hurt.'

'I don't know Lucy,' Peter said. 'Which cottage does she live in?'

'Doesn't go to Church, doesn't our Lucy, so you probably've never met her. The Old Forge, bottom of the hill by that medieval prison Mr Fitch restored.'

'Oh, yes. You'll be able to get the bus from there, won't you?'

'Stops just up where the old pub used to be. It's very convenient for most things. You don't mind, Doctor Harris? Bit difficult with it being family.'

'Of course I don't mind. You do what's best. Ironing this morning, Dottie, and we said we'd clear out the linen cupboard on the landing this week.'

'No sooner said than done. Harvest next Sunday, Rector. All ready? Going to be a big do.' Dottie clapped her hand to her mouth. 'Oops, sorry, a big do for the Reverend Anna, you know, the farewell do, combined with the Harvest Lunch. Best get on. She was very good in her way and was mighty kind and thoughtful to lots of people but, let's face it, she wasn't you, sir, now was she?' Dottie gave him an enormous, very daring wink and then scurried off to spring the ironing board into action before she said too much.

Sheila Bissett's new idea for the Harvest Festival had delighted every person who heard about it and it had gone from being a light in Sheila's eye to a welcome home for all the Harrises, a warm celebration of Anna Sanderson leaving them all, a big lunch (tickets available from all regular churchgoers), and a big auction afterwards, which included any items other than Harvest Festival things people thought fit to give. Sheila had grumbled that some of the extra items people had given were not even fit for a jumble sale, but nevertheless she'd arranged for them to be available for sale on a separate table during the auction, (any offer accepted).

Sheila had worked so hard for this new idea that she had one of her panic moments the night before.

'Look, Ron, it's no good, I shall be awake all night and like a wrung-out dishcloth all day tomorrow. I think I'll retire to bed and not bother getting up tomorrow.'

'Look! You were like this over the skinny-dipping and what happened? One of the best nights we've ever had in Turnham Malpas. So you can take one of your herbal tablet thingies and calm yourself down. Are you listening?'

'Have we got enough food organized? You know how the WI hate to get anything wrong. God, Ron, I feel terrible.'

'Now come on, old girl, just cheer up.'

Sheila sat bolt up right. 'I've told you before, I am *not* your old girl.'

'Sorry, just a term of affection.'

'Well, it doesn't feel like it to me. The church is looking gorgeous. They all worked so hard today, setting it all up.'

'There you are, you see, it is going to be successful. Our Louise inherited *your* organizational talents. There's no one better than you.'

'She's looking better, isn't she? I mean, after . . . the . . . baby, don't you think?'

'Yes, much better.'

'I just hope they don't try again. I couldn't bear it.'

'That's their choice.'

'I wonder if Peter realizes the big do we've made of it.'

'He'll soon find out.'

'I've to be up at six-thirty in the morning. Set the alarm.'

The heady scent of the flowers and the fruit hit Peter's nostrils the moment he turned the key in the main door when he went into the church for his daily prayers. The whole place felt to be alive. The trailing wreaths around the stone pillars, the exuberant arrangements on every window-sill, the fruits arranged around the font, the density of the foliage along the high stained-glass window-sill above the altar, the vines wrapped skilfully around the carved woodwork of the pulpit, and the careful threading of sprays of green leaves amongst the carving of the screen shielding the memorial chapel.

Peter's heart almost burst with joy. What a sight! What a wonder! What faithful people his congregation were. So loyal. When he returned in time for the 8 a.m. service he found Sheila busy checking the flower vases and putting to rights flowers which had drooped during the night.

'Good morning, Rector. What do you think?'

'Absolutely wonderful. You're a miracle-worker, Sheila.'

'Well, it's not just me. All my flower ladies have made a big effort.'

'All swept along by your enthusiasm.'

'To be honest, Peter, I've no talents at all except this. Absolutely none. I couldn't give a sermon, say, to save my life.'

'I wouldn't worry too much about that. This one talent more than makes up.'

Sheila blushed. 'That's kind saying that. Thank you.'

The congregation at the early service was as nothing compared to the one at ten o'clock. Every single seat in the pews was taken, even the front row, and Zack the verger had brought in extra chairs from the hall, only to find he also needed the bench from outside the boiler house, with all the bird mess cleaned off and a chenille tablecloth, that his wife had brought from home to spread over it. It looked quite inviting there, in front of the font, for the latecomers.

The altar looked magnificent with all the ancient church silver splendidly displayed, it being a special day. The tall floor-standing silver candlestick holder caught the gleam of the sun as it came in through the stained glass and made it look almost celestial. The silver collection plates standing on the altar along with the chalice reflected the colours of the fruit and flowers so tastefully arranged around them; an artistic triumph, thought the congregation. Good old Sheila. She might get their goat a lot of the time, but she'd certainly come up trumps today.

The lunch proved to be not a simple ploughman's at all, but a feast, of which the WI was rightly proud. After the lunch came the auction, which raised almost £400 for their charities.

When the announcement was made of their triumphant total Sheila wanted Anna to make a speech, and prompted her into doing so by stamping her feet and calling out, 'We want Anna, we want Anna.'

Anna gracefully agreed and got to her feet. 'I'm quite sure that this event is really for welcoming your very dear Rector and his family back home where they belong. I've tried my best to fill his place in your hearts, but I think I've only been partially successful.' This brought a howl of protest from everyone and Anna blushed with embarrassment. 'Well, maybe more than partially. I've loved it here. You all made me so welcome I couldn't fail to be warmed by your approval. But I'm off back to that den of iniquity, the Abbey. I hope that sometimes I will be able to come back and see you all. God bless!'

Jimbo stood up and shouted for three cheers for Anna and they all joined in. After all, she hadn't been that bad, had she?

But then the call was for Peter to speak. So he stood up and looked around at them all, smiling with such delight that more than one had a sob caught in their throat. His heart was filled with such joy and he thanked everyone he could think of for all their efforts:

'"A ploughman's lunch", I was told. Well, if ploughmen ate as well we've done today, I'd be a ploughman any day! We're all four of us so glad to be back in Turnham Malpas. While our tour of duty in Africa had a frightening end I cannot say we wished we hadn't gone, because we met some wonderful people struggling desperately to be Christians in a very alien place; not for them the coming together with total freedom as we have done today, but facing murder and fear and hunger, yet still remembering to be grateful for life's mercies.

'Especially I would like to thank Anna for taking care of my particular patch so magnificently. Everything in my study is in apple pie order, and so is my congregation. Thank you, Anna.'

Peter walked across to her and kissed her cheek. She flung her arms around him and kissed him back, and more than one eyebrow was raised amongst the onlookers. But they all gave three more cheers for Peter, then the time came to collect their purchases and wend their way home.

The Charter-Placketts, having done their bit towards the clearing-up and staggering under the weight of the fruit and flower arrangements they'd bought, went home. Harriet went to put the kettle on to make a cup of tea, but Jimbo said, 'No. I've got champagne in the fridge.'

'Champagne? Whatever for?'

'All will be revealed. I've got the tray. You get the glasses. Don't forget Mother, she won't be a moment.'

'Jimbo! What's this all about?'

'Wait and see, you impatient woman, you. Fran is having a glass, too.' Jimbo walked into the sitting room carrying the champagne.

Finlay said, 'I thought we were having tea. What's the champagne about?'

Flick and Fran said nothing, because their Grandmama said it for them. 'So, Jimbo, dear, what's this all about? Some new venture?'

'Not exactly new, no. Everyone got a glass?'

Fran counted the glasses. 'Am I having champagne, too?'

Jimbo nodded. 'Oh, yes, most definitely you are.'

'Dad, Mum's not having another baby, is she?' Finlay winked at his father.

Harriet said loudly and firmly. 'Very flattering but absolutely not.'

Grandmama snapped at Finlay, 'That, young man, was very vulgar of you, and what is more, thoroughly impolite to your mother.'

Flick laughed and raised an eyebrow at Finlay.

Jimbo called for silence. 'Now, listen hard. I've been in consultation with Tom and Evie and, after a lot of thought and due to the pressure brought to bear on me by my wife and my mother, to say nothing of Peter Harris and all the rest of Turnham Malpas, Little Derehams and Penny Fawcett, I have decided . . . .'

Harriet interrupted, 'You're not . . . are you . . . you are!'

'Hush!' He paused significantly. 'After due consideration, I am re-opening the Store at the end of next month,
which gives me eight weeks to rev things up.' A loud gasp
of surprise interrupted him. 'I ask you all to raise your
glasses. A toast to the re-opening of the Turnham Malpas
Village Store.'

They all gulped their champagne, hugged and kissed
each other, asked questions, kissed Jimbo several times and
roared with laughter. Everything restored to normal.
Thank goodness. What a spectacular ending to a wonderful day.